Love Finds You™

at Home
for Christmas

Love Finds You™

at Home for Christmas

BY ANNALISA DAUGHETY

AND GWEN FORD FAULKENBERRY

summerside
PRESS™

Summerside Press, Inc.
Minneapolis 55378
SummersidePress.com

ISBN 978-1-60936-687-2

Cover Design by Koechel Peterson & Associates | www.kpadesign.com

Interior design by Müllerhaus Publishing Group | www.mullerhaus.net

*Summerside Press™ is an inspirational publisher offering fresh,
irresistible books to uplift the heart and engage the mind.*

Printed in USA.

Sweet Southern Christmas

ANNALISA DAUGHETY

This book is dedicated with love to my grandmother, Ermyl McFadden Pearle and in memory of my grandfather, H.B. "Pudge" Pearle. Not a day goes by that I don't thank God for giving me such wonderful grandparents. Grandma, you are an inspiration and a role model. I love you very much.

Acknowledgments
....

Vicky Daughety and Jan Reynolds—thanks for reading along and offering valuable insight. I appreciate you so much! Ermyl Pearle—thank you for sharing your story with me and for answering my endless questions about your life as a WOW. Gwen Ford Faulkenberry—thanks for being a part of this with me! I had so much fun working with you! Rachel Meisel— thank you for your help and for your amazing editing skills. You helped make this story as good as it could be, and I am so thankful for the chance to write it! Thanks to my wonderful agent, Sandra Bishop, for the prayers and guidance! Kelly Shifflet, Kristy Coleman, Vickie Fry, and Megan Reynolds— thanks for the encouragement and prayers. It truly takes a village.

Chapter One

....

June 1943

Ruby McFadden aspired to be a lot of things, but a pig farmer wasn't one of them.

"I'm not going." She heaved her suitcase out of the back end of her brother's 1939 Ford De Luxe and set it on the ground with a thud. She and Wade had been arguing outside of her dorm at Harding College for the past fifteen minutes, and as far as she could tell, it was a draw.

Wade sighed. "Come on, R.J., don't be like this. You know Papa only wants what's best for you."

His use of her despised childhood nickname did little to improve her mood, nor did the mention of their papa, whose master plan for Ruby's summer included raising pigs.

"In three months I'll start my last year of college. Everyone in the world seems to realize that I'm an adult—except for my family," Ruby said. "Y'all act like I'm still a little girl."

Wade leaned against the De Luxe and crossed his arms. "It isn't like that. We're just worried about you and want you home with us for the summer."

"Girls my age are married with babies of their own. Look at cousin Lucille. And I don't even have to tell you how many boys from my class are overseas right now." With the country at war, Ruby sometimes felt like she attended an all-girls college.

"But the ordnance plant is no place for a girl like you. It will be hard work—dangerous even. I know a fellow from Beedeville who worked at one of the plants down South, and he said the hours were long and the work was tedious." Wade frowned. "Why would you want to put yourself through that when you could just come home?"

The Arkansas Ordnance Plant in Jacksonville wasn't too far from the Christian college Ruby attended in Searcy. "I can't fight," she countered back, "but this is something I can do. After everything that's happened over the past year, I have to do something besides just ration my sugar and nylons."

"Plant a victory garden?" Wade asked hopefully.

She shook her head. "That isn't enough."

"Are you sure this is really what you want? Have you thought it through?" With his chiseled jaw and blue eyes, Wade looked more and more like their father every day. The oldest of the McFadden siblings, he'd always been able to reason with Ruby, the strong-willed baby of the family. At least until today.

Ruby nodded. A few weeks before, she'd seen a poster in the student center depicting a young woman in work clothes. Emblazoned underneath were the words: "THE GIRL HE LEFT BEHIND" IS STILL BEHIND HIM. SHE'S A WOW. From that day forward, Ruby had been determined to do her part to serve her country. "I want to be a Woman Ordnance Worker. It's the least I can do. Think of all those boys giving their lives for our country. Think about Raymond and Jack. They're doing their part. I want to do mine too."

At the mention of their brothers, Wade's face softened. "But where will you live? And are you certain you're qualified?" He sighed. "I don't like the thought of you being on your own so far from home."

Despite her irritation, Ruby was touched by his concern. "There's a women's dorm on-site, and Hazel says more women than men work there—if *they're* qualified, I'm sure I am too. I'm a quick learner. Besides, Hazel lives near the plant with her parents, and they'll be around if I need anything." Her friend and former suitemate, Hazel Collins, made the work sound so exciting. "The pay is good too." Ruby softened her voice. "Jacksonville isn't too far from here by bus. I won't be much farther from home than I am during the school year."

Wade raised an eyebrow. "But won't you miss Lucille? And Mama has been so looking forward to having you home between semesters."

For a moment, Ruby faltered. She missed her mama something fierce; that was for sure. And Lucille was her favorite cousin. They were three months apart and had been the best of friends since they were just babies. But Ruby couldn't help but feel that Lucille, who had a husband off at war and a baby to raise, lived in a different world.

"I know how busy Mama is during the summertime with the garden and all. And little Annie Sue is probably keeping Lucille busy from dusk till dawn." She managed a smile. "Tell them I love them, and I'll write as soon as I get settled."

"You sure are stubborn." Wade shook his head. "Maybe President Roosevelt should send you in to negotiate the end of the war and bring the boys home. You don't back down easy." He grinned and reached for her suitcase. "But I guess I know when I'm beat. Now where should I put this? Back inside?"

She returned his smile. "Just put it down. Hazel and her cousin are coming to pick me up. They'll be here any minute."

Wade scooped her up in a hug. "Don't you forget where you come from, Ruby Jean," he whispered against her hair. "Not everyone has the same values as you." He pulled back and looked her in the eye. "Promise me you'll call me if you need me, okay?"

Tears stung her eyes. She might complain about her brothers being overprotective, but they always wanted what was best for her. "Don't worry about me. I'll be fine. This is what I want."

Wade nodded. He gave her a quick kiss on the cheek. "I have something for you." He grinned and pulled a burlap sack from the front seat. "I guess out of all of us, Mama knows you best. She was so sure you'd go through with your new summer job, she sent you a care package to take with you."

Ruby eagerly grabbed the sack from his hands. "Pecans and sorghum molasses!" She rifled through the bag, already imagining a batch of her famous chewy molasses cookies, which she'd whip up once she had access to a stove. "And letters from Mama and Lucille!" She knew Mama would be disappointed she wasn't coming home this summer, but this was her way of letting Ruby know it was okay. "Thanks for bringing this." She hugged Wade one more time then watched him get in the car.

"Bye, R.J. See you soon." He pulled the car away from the dorm. "And be careful," he called with a wave out the open window.

Ruby stood on the sidewalk and watched until she could no longer see the taillights. Despite the butterflies in her stomach, she felt proud of herself for sticking to her guns and taking a job in the city. She'd come to college without knowing anyone, and that had turned out okay. And starting her new job at the plant would be even easier, because she already knew Hazel, and they were going to try to get on the same shift.

She glanced down at her stuffed suitcase, thankful she'd had enough room inside to include her prized possession. She'd saved up all last year to buy her own radio. The other girls in her suite used to come to Ruby's room to hang out just so they could hear Frank Sinatra croon one of his hits.

An older model sedan pulled up alongside her.

"Excuse me, miss." The driver stuck his head out the window, and Ruby found herself staring into the crystal-blue eyes of the most handsome man she'd ever seen in real life.

"Yes?" she asked, smoothing the skirt of her dress. At least she'd put on some lipstick before she left the dorm.

"Can you tell me where the women's dorm is? I've never been to campus before." He grinned.

Ruby chuckled. "Well, you did a pretty good job for someone who's never been here. You're right in front of it." She gestured at the large brick building behind her.

The man put the car in park and climbed out. He had an athletic build, and his blond hair had a slight wave to it. Not curly, just wavy. She thought she saw the slightest hint of a dimple in his chin. He caught Ruby's gaze, and his blue eyes twinkled. "Is everything okay?"

She realized she must've been gawking and felt the heat rise up her face. "I'm fine. Just waiting on my friend and her cousin. They're giving me a ride to Jacksonville. I'm starting a new job there." She didn't know why she felt the need to offer an explanation.

His grin grew wider. "You must be Ruby McFadden. Hazel told me all about you." He stuck out a hand. "I'm her cousin, Cliff Hamilton."

Ruby took the hand he offered. "Where's Hazel?" She noticed he had strong hands. They were calloused from working, just like Papa's. Papa had always said you could tell a lot about a man by his hands.

Cliff reached into his shirt pocket and pulled out a folded piece of paper. "Here you go. This should explain."

"Ruby!" Betty Jo Simmons called from the dorm entrance. "Can you come here for just a second?"

Ruby flashed a smile at Cliff. "Excuse me for a minute. That sounds important." She hurried toward the dorm, resisting the urge to look over her shoulder to make sure Cliff wasn't some kind of mirage. A very handsome mirage.

Betty Jo grabbed Ruby by the arm and pulled her through the door. "Who *is* that?" she asked, her round face glowing.

Ruby giggled. Of all of her friends, Betty Jo was the most boy crazy. Of course she'd want the details of the handsome man outside.

Ruby quickly unfolded the note he'd handed her and skimmed Hazel's neat script. "Apparently he's Hazel's cousin. Hazel says she couldn't make it, that she has big news and will see me in Jacksonville."

Ruby furrowed her brow and looked back up at Betty Jo. "But I can't ride with him all the way to Jacksonville. He's a stranger."

Betty Jo gripped Ruby's arm tighter as she looked out the dorm window. "A stranger who is putting your suitcase in his car," she squealed. "Of course you can go with him. He's Hazel's cousin. It's only a couple of hours. Besides, he's absolutely drooly!"

"I'll ask him to take me to the bus station. I'm sure he has better things to do than play chauffeur to his cousin's friend."

"I don't think so." Betty Jo grinned, her brown eyes gleaming with mischief. "Any guy would love to play chauffeur to a pretty girl like you. Has anyone ever told you pink is one of your best colors?"

Ruby glanced down at her red-and-white gingham dress. "I'm not wearing pink."

"I'm talking about that blush on your cheeks." Betty Jo giggled. "Admit it, you think he's dreamy."

Ruby crossed her arms. "I don't know him. And you know good and well that I don't date anymore." It was a long-standing argument between them. Betty Jo just couldn't understand Ruby's resolve to stay single.

Betty Jo made a face. "But it's so romantic. He's come to pick you up and will probably fall in love with you on the way to the ordnance plant." She clasped her hands under her chin and batted her eyelashes. "It's just like in the movies."

"This movie is going to end at the bus station." Ruby shook her head. "Now I'd better go." She patted her friend on the arm. "See you in the fall. Try and stay out of trouble this summer."

Betty Jo frowned. "I'll be stuck here in classes and you'll be off in the city, falling in love with a man who looks just like that picture of John Wayne hanging on my bulletin board." She'd torn the cover off of an issue of *Look* magazine last year and had been mooning over it ever since. Betty Jo sighed dramatically. "Some girls have all the luck."

Ruby giggled and looked out the window. He *was* ruggedly

handsome; even she could admit that much. But since she wasn't in the market for a beau, it didn't matter.

Not even a little bit.

* * * * *

Cliff Hamilton paced the sidewalk in front of the girls' dorm. It had been a few years since he'd been on a college campus—not since he was the star football player at Arkansas A&M. Just the memory of the time he'd spent there was enough to make him long for the past.

Thinking of football made him think of high school, when he and his little brother, Charlie, had been the big guys on campus. The quarterback and running back for the Ozark High School Hillbillies, they'd been inseparable.

When Charlie had been drafted, Cliff had left college and joined up immediately. No way was his baby brother going off to fight in a war without him.

Cliff stopped pacing and put the memory of Charlie's freckled face out of his mind. This was not the time for a trip down memory lane.

"Cliff?" Ruby asked softly. "You look like you're a million miles away."

She wasn't far from the truth. He forced a smile. "Ready?" He jerked his head toward the car. "I've already put your suitcase in the car." He chuckled. "Your *heavy* suitcase. What do you have in there? A boulder?"

Instead of laughing like he'd expected, she frowned. "I'm sorry. I didn't mean for you to pick it up at all. I could've gotten it myself."

He opened the passenger door and motioned for her to get in. "I was only kidding about the boulder." He grinned. "Maybe just a rock collection?"

Finally a grin. "It's my radio. I couldn't bear to leave it behind." She absently raked a hand through coal-black curls. "I know there's a possibility the roommate I'm assigned to will have one, but I don't want to take the chance. I sure don't want to be without music all summer."

"A girl after my own heart. I'm partial to Glenn Miller myself. How about you?"

She nodded. "He's one of my favorites too."

Cliff motioned toward the car again. "Are you going to get in? We won't get very far standing out here on the sidewalk."

Ruby leveled her green eyes on him. "I suppose you're right. But don't worry about taking me all the way to Jacksonville. You can just drop me off at the bus station." She primly climbed in the car and looked up at him. "If you don't mind, that is."

Cliff closed the door and walked around to the driver's side. Leave it to Hazel to send him on a wild goose chase after some girl who didn't want his help in the first place. He started the car and looked over at Ruby. "I do mind."

She turned to face him, her eyes wide. "You do?"

He nodded. "I told Hazel I'd give you a ride to Jacksonville, and that's what I'm gonna do."

"I'd prefer to take the bus." She lifted her chin, a defiant expression on her pretty face.

Cliff shook his head and turned the car toward the main road. "Have you taken the bus to Jacksonville by yourself before?"

She cleared her throat. "Well…no. But that doesn't mean I can't."

"Can't and shouldn't are two different things. Besides, you won't know where to go once you get to Jacksonville."

"I could figure it out, I'll bet."

He couldn't help but grin at her independent streak. "I'm sure you could, but there's no need. See, I'm headed that way myself. And I know we just met and you'll have to form your own opinion about this, but I'm a gentleman. And a gentleman doesn't leave a lady with a suitcase as heavy as yours on the side of the road so she can take a bus to a strange place." He didn't have to look at her to know she was sending a dirty look in his direction. "Besides, what would your daddy say if I dropped you off to fend for yourself like that?"

"He'd probably say that I'm a smart girl. And if I'm able enough to go to college and get a job at the ordnance plant, then I'm able to find my own way."

Cliff laughed. "How about we agree to disagree? You just settle back and enjoy the ride. I'll take care of the rest." He flipped on the radio. "And if we're lucky maybe we can hear some Glenn Miller." He looked over and gave her a wink. "I might just sing along."

Ruby rolled her eyes but didn't fuss when they passed the bus station.

Cliff fought to keep his eyes on the road ahead and not let them stray to the girl in the passenger seat. Her simple red-and-white checked dress showed off a dynamite figure, and her heart-shaped face reminded him of Vivian Leigh. She was definitely a looker, and boy did she have spunk.

His daddy had always said that the good Lord sent people into your life at the moment you needed them.

And he had to wonder if Ruby wasn't just what he needed.

Chapter Two

. . . .

The nerves hit Ruby once they arrived at the gatehouse outside the ordnance plant. Even though she had looked forward to having an adventure and doing her part for the war effort, she couldn't help but wonder what she'd gotten herself into.

"You okay?" Cliff asked once he'd shown the guard his credentials and they'd been granted clearance to move on.

She frowned. "I'm fine." She didn't want Cliff, of all people, to know how nervous she felt. For some reason his "in charge" attitude annoyed her. She'd spent her whole life trying to prove to her brothers that she was just as capable as they were. But Cliff didn't seem to think she could find her way out of a paper bag.

He pointed toward a large multi-story building. "That's the administration building. That'll probably need to be your first stop. I think you'll need to fill out some paperwork and get your photo badge and all." He reached into his shirt pocket and pulled out a round badge with his photo on it that was emblazoned with his name and FORD, BACON, AND DAVIS, INC., ARKANSAS ORDNANCE PLANT in bold letters. "You'll have a badge similar to this that will give you access at the gates and buildings." He peered at her. "Do you know what your job will be? Powder weigher? Detonator girl?" He grinned. "Or maybe some kind of secretary?"

She hadn't given much thought to what her job would be. Hazel had told her the money was good, and it would definitely pay better than pig farming. "I'm not sure," she murmured. "But whatever it is,

I'll do my best." She raised an eyebrow, hoping it made her look like Scarlett O'Hara from *Gone with the Wind.* "And maybe I'll end up being a line inspector or supervisor. Hazel says sometimes girls with a few years of college get promoted quickly."

Cliff nodded silently, as if sizing her up. "You know what? I wouldn't put it past you. Just as long as you don't end up supervising me." He laughed. "I'm an electrician."

Ruby grinned. "I'm not planning on working in that department, so I don't think you have to worry about it." She sighed. "Thanks for the ride."

"Oh, I'm not just dumping you out here. You'll have a hard time with that suitcase. I'll wait right here until you're through so I can help you to your dorm."

She paused with her hand on the door handle. "You don't have to."

Cliff chuckled. "I told you I was a gentleman. Besides, I don't have anywhere else I'd rather be." He nodded toward the administration building. "I would offer to show you where to go, but I suspect you'd shoot me down." His blue eyes twinkled.

She smiled. "Thanks." She clutched her handbag and strode toward the entrance, hoping it looked like she knew where she was going.

She and Cliff had barely spoken all the way to Jacksonville, but she hadn't found the silence uncomfortable. Every now and then, he pointed out a landmark or gave a bit of commentary, but mostly he'd just driven, singing softly to the music on the radio.

It was kind of nice. Sometimes Ruby felt as if she had to carry conversations to put others at ease, but she sensed Cliff was at ease no matter what. He intrigued her. She wondered why he wasn't enlisted and tried to remember if Hazel had ever mentioned him.

Not that she was interested in being more than friends, with Cliff or anyone else. She'd learned the hard way that future plans meant nothing during war time. And now that she was on the cusp of independence and adventure, she wasn't going to throw it away for the first handsome man she met.

It struck her as almost funny. Here she was, ready to take on the world and prove to her family and friends that she could make it on her own—without a man to support her—and the first person she met on the journey was an incredibly handsome, charming man.

Maybe it was some kind of cosmic test.

And if so, she was determined to pass with flying colors.

* * * * *

Cliff hadn't the heart to fill Ruby in on Hazel's big news. Partly because he was afraid that if she'd known the truth, she wouldn't have come at all. It was funny if he thought about it. Seventy-five percent of the workers at the AOP were female, and at least half of those were single women clamoring for his attention. But he barely looked twice at any of them. But Ruby, with her black hair, fair complexion, and green eyes, was already under his skin.

He'd barely said a word all the way to Jacksonville. And finding himself tongue-tied around a woman was new territory. Nothing ever made Cliff nervous. He'd led his football team back from sure loss time and again. He'd marched into battle with as much strength and bravery as he could muster. But put him in the car with a woman like Ruby McFadden and he could barely string together two sentences. His buddies would have a field day if they found out. Cliff was known for being a great orator. He could give speeches and pep talks without any preparation. Yet he'd barely been able to form a sentence around Ruby.

He couldn't help but think of how Charlie would've enjoyed seeing him finally meet his match. His little brother would've laughed and poked fun at the sight of Cliff at a loss for words. He could almost hear the words Charlie would've said. Probably something like, "There's a first time for everything."

Someone rapped on the window and Cliff jerked upright. He looked up to see Hazel, a broad smile on her face.

She motioned for him to roll the window down. "What's buzzin', cousin?" she asked with a grin.

"Just waiting for Ruby to finish in the admin building."

Hazel leaned against the car "Thanks for driving her." She raised her eyebrows. "Did y'all get along okay?"

Cliff nodded. "We did. Even though I refused to drop her off at the bus stop so she could make her way here by herself."

Hazel burst out laughing. "I should've warned you that Ruby has an independent streak." She leaned into the car. "Did you tell her my news?"

Cliff made a key-turning motion against his lips. "Nope." He grinned. "Your news is your news. Besides, I've worked here long enough to know that loose lips sink ships." Signs in nearly every building reminded all of the AOP workers to keep quiet about what they heard and saw.

She beamed. "Thanks. I hope she's not too disappointed. She might decide to turn around and go back home. Although I think the alternative for the summer had something to do with raising pigs, so maybe not."

Cliff chuckled. He couldn't imagine prim and proper Ruby slopping pigs for the summer. "Something tells me she'll be determined to stick it out here, just so she can say she did."

Hazel nodded. "Probably so." She sighed. "I just hope she isn't mad. Will you promise to look out for her here? She's going to need a friend." She leveled her gaze on Cliff. "She might appear independent and act tough, like she doesn't need anyone, but she's really a big softie." She grinned. "Besides, I suspect she might do you some good."

Cliff furrowed his brow. "I'll try to be her friend, and I'll do my best to look out for her, but something tells me that might be tough."

"She's worth it, trust me. You'll never meet a more loyal friend.

And she's so kind-hearted." Hazel grinned. "It's part of the reason she'd be a terrible pig farmer. She'd name all of them and they'd turn into family pets."

Cliff watched as Ruby exited the building and hurried down the sidewalk toward Hazel. He'd be fooling himself if he pretended he wasn't attracted to her. But that really didn't matter. His life was far too complicated right now to consider getting close to someone. Better to keep her at a distance.

That way she'd never have to know how he'd failed his family—and he'd never be in danger of failing her too.

Chapter Three
....

Ruby stood, rooted to the ground. "You're getting married?" She couldn't believe it. "Your note said that you had big news, but I never dreamed this might be it." She worried her eyes might pop out of her head. "I didn't even know you had a steady fellow."

Hazel smiled the contented smile of a woman in love. "His name is Troy, and I met him just a couple of months ago. He'd just been discharged from the navy after being wounded in the Pacific." She sighed. "He's just the nicest guy. You'll love him." She chewed on her bottom lip. "Promise you aren't mad? I would've told you, but he only asked me to marry him last week. By that time I knew you were already planning on working here for the summer. And I wanted to tell you in person instead of in some old letter." She did a little twirl, her full skirt following her.

Ruby had to smile at her friend's happiness. "Of course I'm happy for you. Don't worry about me." She fought another wave of nerves. She and Hazel had planned to learn the ropes at work together and pal around during their free time. Now Ruby wouldn't know anyone. It would be just like starting over at college. "I'm sure I'll get to be friends with the roommate they've assigned me to. She's from Fayetteville." Ruby forced a smile. "And I'll have other friends here in no time."

Hazel pulled Ruby into a quick hug. "Of course you will. Before you know it, you'll probably be the most popular girl in the dorm." She grinned. "And if it makes you feel any better, I won't know anyone but

Troy once we get moved. We're headed to Pine Bluff. He's going to be a supervisor at the plant there." She sighed again. "The wedding is in two weeks."

Ruby tried to keep her face a mask of happiness, but she felt her bottom lip quiver.

"Please don't be upset," Hazel said, her voice soft. "You'll love working here for the summer. The pay is great, and Cliff will be here to look out for you." She grinned. "I think the two of you can be great friends."

"Thanks, Hazel, but I'll be fine on my own." Ruby narrowed her eyes, wondering if her friend was trying to set her up with Cliff. "I won't be needing anyone to look out for me." *Especially not someone as handsome as your cousin.* "But I'm thrilled for you, Hazel. You deserve all the happiness in the world."

Ruby chose to keep her opinion about marriage to herself. Last month when she'd declared to Betty Jo that she had no intention of ever marrying, it had sent the poor girl into a tizzy—and *she* wasn't even engaged. No need to spoil things for Hazel.

"You'll come to the wedding, won't you?" Hazel's brown eyes were pleading.

Ruby nodded. "Of course. I'd be honored. And I can't wait to meet Troy." She smiled. "I'm sure he's wonderful."

"Oh, he is." Hazel squeezed Ruby's hand. "Now let's go get you settled into the dorm. Cliff will drive us over." Hazel dragged Ruby over to Cliff's car, where he waited patiently.

"Everything okay, ladies?" Cliff asked once they'd climbed inside.

Hazel nodded. "Let's take Ruby to her dorm and help her carry her things inside."

He cranked the engine and slowly drove away from the administration building.

Ruby leaned her head against the passenger seat and listened as Hazel and Cliff chatted about people they knew. None of the names were familiar to Ruby. For what seemed like the hundredth time today, the butterflies swirled in her stomach. She wouldn't know anyone here. Hazel was about to get married, and Ruby would be left to fend for herself. So much for their fun summer together. The sigh that escaped her mouth was louder than she intended it to be.

"Nervous?" Cliff asked softly.

She looked up, surprised by the genuine concern in his blue eyes. "Just wondering what I've gotten myself into, that's all." She gave him a tiny smile.

"You'll love it," Hazel declared. "Did they tell you what your job will be?"

Ruby smoothed her skirt. "I'm going to start out measuring black powder. Hopefully after a few weeks of learning the ropes I'll become a supervisor, though."

Cliff stopped the car and grinned. "I have no doubt that you'll make it."

"I can get my suitcase," Ruby said once they'd climbed out of the vehicle.

He laughed. "I know you can, but I'd like it if you'd let me help." He pulled the suitcase out of the backseat and winced as he set it on the sidewalk.

"You okay?" Hazel asked. "Is that arm still bothering you?"

Cliff rubbed his shoulder. "It's fine. Much better."

Ruby followed them into the dorm, wondering what had happened to his arm but not wanting to pry.

"This looks a lot like the dorm at Harding, doesn't it?" Hazel asked once they made it up the stairs and into the room Ruby had been assigned.

Ruby looked around the small space and frowned. With its concrete walls and gray floor, it seemed cold—almost clinical. Would this ever feel like home? Her college dorm room had been cheerful and cozy. "I guess."

Cliff lugged her suitcase onto one of the twin beds. "You'll just need to put out a few knickknacks and maybe some pictures or something."

"Knickknacks?" Hazel giggled.

Cliff shrugged. "I'm sure she has something in this big old suitcase that reminds her of home." He shot a smile at Ruby. "Maybe that rock collection."

She managed a tiny smile. If he'd meant for his lighthearted jokes to put her at ease, he'd been successful. The fear she'd felt at the sight of this bare room started to fade. He was right. A few personal effects, and she'd be right at home. "I'll have this place looking cozy in no time."

"Oh, and there's a kitchen down the hall," Hazel said. "I'll bet when you bake a batch of your famous cookies, you'll be the hit of the dorm."

"Cookies?" Cliff raised his eyebrows. "Did someone say cookies?"

Ruby giggled at his expression. "I have a secret recipe that my mama and I came up with a few years ago."

"*Secret* being the key word," Hazel said. "But if you wanted to give your recipe to me as a wedding gift, I'd promise not to share it." She grinned.

"Or if you wanted to whip up a batch so I can give them my stamp of approval, that'd be fine too." Cliff's blue eyes twinkled.

She laughed. "Hazel, I would be honored to pass my recipe along to you." She turned to Cliff. "And I'll be sure and put you on my cookie list."

"Thanks," he said.

Cliff and Hazel said their good-byes and left her alone in the sparse room. It sure would be a quiet night. Lola, the girl she'd be sharing the room with, wouldn't be moving in until tomorrow. The woman in the administration building said she'd be arriving by bus from Fayetteville.

Ruby unpacked her things and carefully placed her radio on the wooden nightstand next to her twin bed. Maybe a little music would keep her from feeling so alone.

As the faint strains of Glenn Miller filled the tiny room, she grinned.

Cliff's favorite.

She might know what kind of music he liked, but she didn't know much else about him—like why he wasn't serving overseas alongside most of the other men his age.

Or why he'd made her heart race when, just before he'd walked out of her door, he'd winked and told her he'd see her soon.

* * * * *

Cliff dropped Hazel off at Troy's house and then drove down the dirt road that led to his aunt's and uncle's place. Between giving Ruby a ride from Searcy and then listening to Hazel chatter on about her upcoming wedding, he was thankful for a few minutes alone.

He enjoyed the quiet of the car for a long moment but knew he couldn't linger. If he sat outside for too long, Aunt Ida would come out to see what was wrong. She was always hovering, offering to cook him meals or trying to get him to talk about his parents and Charlie. She meant well, but sometimes Cliff wished he could just be left alone.

He climbed out of the car and headed toward the white frame house, shaking his head at the hound dog on the porch. Old Blue didn't even bother standing up, much less barking. He just raised his head in acknowledgment and went back to sleep.

"Worthless thing." Cliff reached down and scratched the dog's head as he passed by.

"How was your trip?" Aunt Ida met him at the door. "Did you like Hazel's friend? Is Hazel coming home for supper, or is she going out with Troy?"

Aunt Ida's gray hair was pulled back in a bun, and she wore a faded flowered apron over her dress, a clear sign she'd already started on supper. Sometimes it seemed like her main goal in life—besides trying to get Cliff to talk about his life—was to make sure he and Uncle Fred ate as much as possible.

Cliff kissed her cheek. "Ruby's a swell girl, and Hazel and Troy are going to see a movie tonight. She said she'd be home later."

Aunt Ida gave him a stern look. "Well, why didn't you invite Ruby to supper? She's a long way from home, and Hazel says she doesn't know anyone here."

Cliff shook his head. "I'm sure she wants to fend for herself. She seems like the kind of girl who doesn't like to be fussed over."

"All girls like to be fussed over." Aunt Ida smiled. "Mark my words." She looked so much like his mom when she smiled.

He didn't feel homesick very often anymore, but every now and then, Aunt Ida would cast a painfully familiar expression in his direction, and he'd long to be back in River Bend with his family. Deep down, he knew it wouldn't be the same place he remembered. He sometimes wondered if that's what kept him away.

"I'll keep that in mind." Cliff chuckled. "Now I'd better go change and see if Uncle Fred needs any help out back."

After he'd been discharged, Cliff's aunt and uncle had offered to let him stay at their place for as long as he needed. Jacksonville's housing market wasn't equipped to deal with the thousands of workers who'd descended on the town when the AOP opened. Some of the guys even slept in tents near the plant because there weren't enough houses or dorms. So Cliff had taken his relatives up on their offer, though he'd insisted on paying them as a boarder and helping out with chores.

Cliff helped Uncle Fred in the garden until Aunt Ida announced it was time for supper. After eating a delicious venison steak, he wandered into his bedroom and picked up the tattered copy of *Murder on the Orient Express* that he'd checked out of the AOP library last week. It was a good story so far, and he was anxious to see how Hercule Poirot would solve the mystery.

Cliff liked to spend his evenings with a book, but he kept losing his place tonight. Ruby's pretty face kept popping into his mind. What was she doing? Had she settled in okay?

After he'd re-read the same paragraph three times, Cliff tossed the book on his nightstand. It was no use. How had this girl he'd only just met managed to weasel her way into his thoughts? He'd met plenty of pretty girls since he'd moved to Jacksonville nine months ago but had been resolved to keep to himself. The past year had been the most difficult of his life, and he enjoyed the quiet life of solitude his work as an electrician gave him. He worked at his own pace, and after his shift was over and his chores were done, he'd go rabbit hunting in the thicket behind the house or fishing at the nearby lake. No complications. No one prying into his life, save for Aunt Ida's attempts.

Cliff had even distanced himself from his parents. He'd only been back to River Bend once in the past year. Aunt Ida kept him in the loop, reading snippets of Mom's letters or trying to get him to write a note to slip in her own weekly letter. She kept his parents posted on how he was doing, despite his protests.

He knew his parents blamed him for what had happened to Charlie. Even though they said it wasn't his fault, he knew better. He'd been there, in the foxhole next to his younger brother. He knew better than anyone who was to blame.

And just like his parents, he'd never be able to forgive himself.

Chapter Four

....

July 1, 1943

Dear Mama,

I can't believe it's already been three weeks since I started working here at the AOP. I got my first paycheck earlier in the week, and my roommate and I celebrated by taking the bus to Little Rock for some shopping. If Papa reads this (and I'm sure he's reading over your shoulder) tell him I didn't spend much, and I put the rest in the bank. It's the most money I've ever seen on a check with my name on it, but I know money isn't everything— my treasure is in heaven. Still, making my own money for the first time is neat, and I bought myself a beautiful green dress that I'm going to save for a special occasion. I'll always look at it and remember that I bought it with my very first paycheck.

I had to say good-bye to Hazel yesterday. She and her new husband are off to Pine Bluff. I'll miss her, but it's nice to see her so happy. Her cousin, Cliff, works here as an electrician. He's the one who gave me a ride from Searcy. She says he's going to look out for me while I'm here, but I haven't seen him since the day he helped carry my stuff to the dorm. Besides, I can take care of myself. I've made a couple of friends who seem nice. My roommate, Lola, is from Fayetteville. She's really sweet. Best of all, we're the same size, so it's like having twice the clothes. I think you'd like her a lot. She reminds me a lot of my friend Betty Jo Simmons from Harding.

You asked in your last letter about my schedule. Well, I work six days a week—including Sundays. That took some getting used to. But my shift ends in time for me to make it to the evening church service. I walk to the church building, and the past two weeks, a couple from the congregation offered to drive me back to my dorm after services.

The job is going well. I'm fast and accurate as I measure the powder—no doubt from years of working with you in the kitchen, measuring flour and sugar. I'm hoping to get promoted soon to line inspector. The girl who has that position now is about to have a baby, so she'll be leaving soon. You wouldn't believe all the people I've met here. Some of them are so young. I have an idea a few may have lied about their age in order to get hired, but I don't question them. I guess that's none of my business. There are older ladies too. Some of them have kids at home, so they keep house and take care of their kids during the day and then come here to work the nightshift. I don't know how they do it. They must never sleep.

But it's work that must be done, despite the long hours or the loss of sleep. We know that what we're doing is helping the boys overseas, and that's the most important thing right now. Speaking of the boys overseas, have you heard from Raymond or Jack lately? I know Wade must be lonely there without them. (Don't tell him, but I'm glad he wasn't able to go.) If you send a letter to Raymond or Jack, do tell them my news. Maybe the detonators I'm working on will eventually make their way to wherever they are! And tell them their little sister loves them and prays for them every night. I keep my ear glued to the radio when I'm in the dorm, so I can know everything that's going on.

I love you all very much and look forward to the next time we're all together. I dream of those Christmases from long ago before the war when we were all around the table, laughing and talking. Sometimes those happy memories are the only way I can face the day—and I'm sure you feel the same.

Well, Mama, I must end this if I want to get it to the post office in time to go out today.

All my love,

Ruby Jean

* * * * *

Cliff wiped the sweat from his brow. July had come to Arkansas with a vengeance. He'd been working in the shop all morning, trying to repair a lamp for one of the administration offices.

"You headed to the cafeteria for lunch, or did you bring something?" Harold White asked. Harold had been one of the first guys Cliff met when he moved to Jacksonville, Arkansas, and he'd turned out to be a good friend as well as a dependable coworker.

Cliff looked up with a grin. "I'm probably going to the cafeteria in a minute. You?"

Harold lifted a lunchbox. "Nah. I brought a sandwich today." He pulled a handkerchief out of the pocket of his overalls and wiped his forehead. "I told my sister I'd have lunch with her once her shift is over."

"Your sister? I figured you'd be meeting up with your mystery girl today." Cliff expected a reaction from Harold, but his friend kept his face neutral.

"She's busy." He grinned. "But we have someone we'd like to introduce you to. Maybe we can have a double date sometime soon and go to the movie. The theater in Little Rock is still showing *Casablanca*."

Cliff groaned. "I appreciate your interest in my love life, but I think I'll pass."

"Come on. She's a real peach. You'd like her." Harold raised his eyebrows. "Or do you have a girl back home that I don't know about?"

"There's no one waiting on me at home." That was an understatement.

In some ways, it almost seemed like he didn't even have a home any longer—at least one that bore a resemblance to the home he'd grown up in. Cliff stood up from the work bench, ready to get out of there.

"Well if you change your mind…let me know," Harold said. "But I don't know why you have to be such a fuddy-duddy all the time. A little fun might do you some good."

Cliff shrugged and stepped out of the workshop and into the bright sunshine.

Fun.

He'd denied himself most things that could be considered fun. It made him feel better somehow. Eased his conscience a bit.

But maybe Harold was right. Come to think of it, Hazel had said the same thing before she'd left for Pine Bluff.

He held the cafeteria door open for a couple of girls. They both smiled and giggled as they brushed past. There was a time when he would've made it a point to flirt right back.

He glanced down the pathway, and that's when he spotted her.

Ruby.

Cliff stood, watching for a long moment, unable to tear his eyes away.

She threw back her head and laughed at something the blond girl next to her said. It looked like she was fitting in just fine.

He waited at the door for her, eager to see how her first weeks had gone.

Ruby didn't notice him standing there as she chatted with her friend. As she stepped through the open door, she bumped against him. "Excuse me," she said.

"Well, I've been wondering if I'd ever run into you, but this isn't quite what I expected." He chuckled.

Her green eyes widened when she recognized Cliff. "Sorry about that." She grinned.

"I'll catch up with you later, Ruby." The blond flashed them a knowing smirk and hurried into the cafeteria.

"It was too bad you couldn't get off from work for Hazel's wedding," Ruby said. "I know she was disappointed you weren't there."

He nodded. "I saw them off, though, and helped load up Troy's car for their move to Pine Bluff."

"That's nice." Together they joined the crowded cafeteria line.

He cleared his throat. "So have you settled in okay? I've been meaning to stop by to check on you, but we've been a little short-handed lately." That much was true, but Cliff knew part of the reason he'd avoided her was because he'd had such a strong reaction to meeting her.

"Oh, that's okay. I understand." She smiled. "I'm doing well. Lola and I get along like we've known each other forever, and I really enjoy the work. You know, this is my first job that's not connected to my family. And doing something to contribute to the war effort is really important to me."

Cliff appreciated her attitude. "I'm glad things are going well. I hope you're finding some time for fun, though." As if he was one to talk.

She grinned. "Oh, I've gone a couple of times to the bowling alley. Some of the girls from my shift are starting a team, but I don't think I'm quite that serious about it." She giggled. "Honestly, most of my balls went in the gutter, so I think they were probably relieved when I told them I'd pass." She stood on her tiptoes to see what was being served on the line. "Looks like it's fish day." She took a tray from the bin.

He followed suit. "Do you have big plans for the weekend? More bowling maybe?"

She laughed. "No. Just laundry."

"I see." He plunged ahead despite his sudden nervousness. "Well, you know Sunday is the Fourth of July. Would you like to get together and do something after work?" Even to his own ears it sounded as if he was asking her for a date. And he sure hadn't planned to do that.

She widened her eyes. "Sunday?" She shook her head. "I work mornings, and I go to church in the evenings. I'm sorry."

He didn't quite know what to say. He hadn't been too faithful in his church attendance lately. "How do you get there?" The nearest church must be at least a mile from the plant.

"Oh, I usually walk over. But Lola says she's going to get a bicycle soon, so I'm hoping to borrow it."

He shook his head. "How about I drive you on Sunday?"

Ruby furrowed her brow. "Thanks, but it's okay. I don't mind walking."

"Why is it you're always turning down rides from me?" Cliff grinned. "I promise I won't sing this time." He hoped he wasn't coming on too strong, but now that he'd offered a ride, he suddenly wanted nothing more than for her to say yes.

A tiny smile played on the corner of her mouth. "I guess it would be nice to not have to walk in this heat." She looked up at him and grinned. "The service starts at six. And I suppose if you're driving me, you may as well stay for the service."

He frowned, wondering if it were a test of some sort. "That sounds good to me."

She widened her eyes. "Well then. I guess we have a plan."

A commotion in the line ahead of them caught Cliff's attention. "Would you look at that?"

"My mama always told me it wasn't ladylike to raise my voice in public." Ruby's eyes were wide as she watched two women arguing loudly. "I guess their mamas didn't share that same opinion."

He shook his head. "I'll be right back." If there was one thing Cliff hated, it was seeing people fight. His parents used to call him their little peacemaker. Pushing the memory aside, he hurried toward the women. He glanced back at Ruby, who was standing on her tiptoes trying to see what was going on. She caught his eye and gave him an encouraging smile.

A church date hadn't been what he'd had in mind, but now that it was scheduled, he had to admit he was looking forward to it.

Very much so.

Chapter Five

....

From where she was standing, Ruby couldn't really see what was going on, but she could hear the commotion. Then the line shifted as everyone scooted out of the way, and she got a clear picture of the women yelling right in each other's faces. Their coarse language reverberated through the room, shocking Ruby. She'd heard bad language from time to time, but never from two women. This was just the kind of thing Papa and Wade had been worried about. But Ruby would never be like those girls. Independent was one thing. Unladylike was another.

She was surprised to see Cliff walk right up to them and clutch both of them by their elbows, all the while talking in a low voice. She couldn't hear his words, but it made her think of the way Papa would talk to a new colt so they could saddle it.

Ruby watched as Cliff skillfully calmed the angry girls down. In no time the situation was diffused and they went their separate ways, their argument forgotten—or at least put on hold.

"You'd better hang on to him, honey," the girl behind her in line said. "He seems like he'd be awfully handy to have around."

Ruby blushed. "Oh, he isn't my boyfriend or anything. We're just friends."

The girl snorted. "Right. And my lips are naturally this shade of red." She shook her head. "You may not see it yet, but that boy is smitten with you." She grinned. "Besides, he's a real looker. If you don't want him, why don't you send him my way?"

Ruby glanced toward Cliff one more time. He'd stopped to talk to a table of men who had clearly gotten a kick out of seeing the women argue.

She'd been taken aback by his offer to drive her to church on Sunday, and she wasn't sure if he'd really show up or not. She could tell he'd been surprised by her unwillingness to skip church to go on a date with him. He *had* been asking her for a date, hadn't he? Maybe he was only trying to be nice to her because of Hazel.

Regardless of Cliff's intention, Ruby knew her relationship with God had to be the most important thing. Any friend who couldn't understand that wasn't worth her time.

* * * * *

Ruby rushed to her room after her Sunday shift to change clothes. Her new green dress had been calling to her from the closet all week, and she just couldn't resist. She slipped it on and looked at herself in the mirror. Its fitted waist and flared skirt showed off her figure, and its color played up her eyes. She smiled at herself in the mirror. Not bad for someone who'd been working all day. She ran a brush through her hair, pleased it still held some curl. Lola had shown her how to tie up her hair using old rags to make it wavy.

She dabbed on some lipstick and stepped back from the mirror.

The door opened and Lola rushed in. "Wow, look at you." Lola grinned. "He must be something special."

Ruby blushed. "You know it isn't like that." She sat down on her bed and smoothed her skirt, enjoying the feel of the rayon beneath her fingers. She hadn't had a store-bought dress in such a long time. It felt like a real treat to wear something she hadn't sewn herself.

"Well, why not?" Lola asked.

Ruby sighed. "Remember when you asked me if I had a fellow back home?"

Lola nodded. "Sure. You said no."

"Well, I did have one. We met during our freshman year of college. His name was Joseph." His face came into Ruby's mind when she said his name.

Ruby had always loved the way Joseph's smile was a little crooked, the way his hair picked up flecks of red when the sunlight hit it just right. She'd told him right after they met that his brown eyes reminded her of chocolate, and he'd thought it was so funny he'd brought her chocolate bars when he picked her up for their first date. Even now she couldn't see chocolate without thinking of him.

She sighed. "After the bombing on Pearl Harbor, he joined the army. So instead of coming back to school after Christmas our sophomore year, he went off to fight. Before he left, he promised he'd come back for me. He even asked me to marry him."

"He never made it back?" Lola asked softly.

Ruby shook her head. "No. I never saw him again." She stood and picked up her Bible from the nightstand.

"But don't you think he'd want you to be happy with someone else?" Lola asked. "Surely Joseph wouldn't want you to be alone forever."

"Do you ever think about all of those men who are never coming back?" Ruby asked softly. "I think of them a lot. Of all those lives lost on a far-off battlefield—and of the lives forever changed back home." She sighed. "There are four war widows on my shift, and three more whose husbands are off fighting. After Joseph was killed, I realized I don't want to risk my heart again. I don't want to fall for someone who might not be there next week or next year."

Lola wrinkled her forehead. "Aren't you afraid of being lonely?"

Ruby shook her head. It was the same argument she'd had with Betty Jo last month after turning down Thomas Wilson's date invitation. "That doesn't matter. My mind is made up. I want to live on my own and make my own money. If I ever feel lonely, I just have to look at all those girls on my shift...or at my own cousin Lucille, who's stuck on a pig farm raising a baby by herself while hoping and praying her husband makes it back." Ruby shook her head again. "I will never let that be me." She'd protect her heart and maintain her independence. It was a perfect plan.

"I think you're making a mistake." Lola frowned. "This fellow you're seeing tonight may not be the right one, but there are others."

Ruby stopped in the doorway. "I will never forget how it felt when I found out about Joseph." She took a deep breath, steadying her voice. "The grief almost did me in. I can't go through something like that again." She managed a tiny smile. "Don't worry, though. I'll be fine on my own." She headed toward the stairs that led to the lobby. Lola would never understand, just as Hazel and Betty Jo didn't understand. Until you'd known the heartbreak that came from a loss like the one she'd experienced, it was impossible to know how it felt.

She stepped into the empty lobby. No sign of Cliff. Had he changed his mind?

She checked the wall clock. She'd need to leave now if she was going to make it on foot.

"You're not planning on leaving without me, are you?" a voice asked from the doorway.

She turned to face Cliff, a smile on her face. "Of course not."

Instead of the casual work clothes she'd seen him in before, he wore a suit and tie. It made him look like he belonged on the big screen rather than in an electrician's office. She was touched he'd gone to such effort to look nice for church.

Cliff held the door open for her and let out a low whistle as she walked past him. "You look nice tonight. I like that dress."

Heat flamed her face. "Thanks. It's new."

He opened the car door, and she climbed in.

"Well, it suits you."

She cleared her throat. "Do you need directions to the church? It's the one just over the railroad tracks."

Cliff cranked the car and headed toward the gate. The guard waved them through. "I know where that is." He slowed down as they went over the railroad tracks. "Thank you for letting me take you tonight," he said softly.

"You're welcome."

Ruby couldn't help but remember all the times she and Joseph had attended church services together. They'd sat side by side in the pew, and she'd imagined the years stretched out, a lifetime of Sundays. She'd always figured they'd finish college and he'd work at the bank like his daddy did. She'd teach school until they had kids. But the war had changed those plans and stolen those dreams. She glanced over at Cliff. He was a nice guy, she could tell. He had an air about him that told her he would take care of her. The way he opened doors and carried her suitcase. Even the way he'd refused to drop her off at the bus station or let her walk to church alone spoke to his character.

And if she were in the market for a boyfriend, he would be just the kind of guy she was looking for.

But she'd risked her heart once. And she wasn't prepared to do it again.

Ever.

* * * * *

Cliff pulled the car into the church lot. "Wait here." He hurried around to the passenger side and opened the door for Ruby. "Do you know many members here?" he asked as he offered a hand to help her out of the car.

"I've met a few." She grinned. "But since I've been walking, I usually get here just as the service is starting. So there hasn't been much time to visit."

Cliff followed her into the stone building.

She pointed toward a wooden pew near the back. "There's an empty spot."

Several churchgoers introduced themselves as they made their way to the pew.

Cliff settled into the seat and looked around. Aunt Ida and Uncle Fred went to a larger congregation closer to their home. They'd asked him repeatedly to come with them, but he'd managed to put them off by claiming he had to work. The plant was open seven days a week, three shifts a day, so there was always work to be done—but he knew that wasn't the only reason he'd stayed as far away as possible.

An older man in a suit stepped up to the podium. "Good evening," he said. "We're so glad you all could join us tonight."

Cliff willed himself to concentrate and to keep an open mind. Ever since Charlie's death a year ago, he'd avoided God, avoided church, avoided prayer. He was angry with himself for what had happened in that foxhole, but he was even angrier with the Lord.

His resolve to keep an open mind faltered as the preacher began to emphasize the importance of forgiveness.

"In Colossians 3:12, we are told to forgive as Christ has forgiven," the preacher said, reminding his congregants that although Christ has every reason to be angry with us, He forgives us instead. "When we harbor bitterness and anger," the preacher continued, "we are preventing ourselves from having happy, productive lives."

Cliff considered his own situation. He'd not been able to forgive himself after Charlie's death, nor had he believed his parents could ever forgive him. He knew he was angry and bitter. Was that preventing him from having a productive life?

But how could he possibly forgive or accept forgiveness? Any way he looked at the situation, he knew Charlie's death had been his own fault. If he'd just reacted differently, Charlie would still be alive.

As they stood to sing a hymn at the end of the sermon, Cliff glanced over at Ruby. She had no way of knowing how hard it had been for him to step foot in the church building tonight.

"Thanks for letting me come with you," he said as they walked to the car after the service was over.

Ruby smiled. "Thanks for driving me." She looked up at him. "And you're welcome to go with me again if you'd like."

He nodded. Tonight's sermon had bothered him, but strangely, he'd felt a glimmer of hope during the closing prayer. "I just might do that." Though he was not yet ready to forgive himself, and though he was still angry at God for letting his little brother die right in front of him like that, he felt that tonight might be the first step in a new direction.

They climbed in the car. "Are you hungry?" Cliff asked.

"I'm starved."

He grinned and started the engine. "I think I know just the place." He drove toward a diner not too far from the AOP. "How about burgers and fries?"

She nodded. "That sounds perfect."

Cliff turned the volume knob on the radio, and Jimmy Dorsey's "Amapola" filled the car. "Do you like this song?"

Ruby nodded. "I do. And it's nice to hear music again." She sighed. "My radio is on the blink."

"Oh no." Cliff looked over at her and grinned. "Not your prized possession. Also known as the cause of my poor aching back."

She giggled. "It wasn't that bad. I had a lot of shoes in that bag too."

"Would you like for me to try and fix the radio for you? I'm pretty handy with things like that." Cliff pulled into the parking lot at the diner and stopped the car.

Ruby smiled. "That would be wonderful. Do you really think you can fix it?"

If it made her smile at him like that again, he'd sure try. "I think so."

They went inside and placed their orders at the counter.

"Here you go, two Coca-Colas." The teenage boy working the cash register put two drinks on the counter. "The rest of your order will be right out."

Cliff led the way to a table for two. "So tell me more about yourself." He liked the way her green eyes matched her dress.

Ruby took a sip of her drink. "Well, I'm from a very small town in northeast Arkansas. So small it's not even on a map." She grinned. "Papa is a farmer and my brothers and I grew up working on the farm."

"I guess that was fun."

She nodded. "I used to complain about being the only girl in the family, but to tell you the truth, I kind of liked it. Besides, my cousin Lucille lived just down the road. How about you?"

Cliff shifted uncomfortably in his seat. "There's not much to tell. I grew up near Ozark, in a little town called River Bend. My parents still live there." He stirred his Coca-Cola with his straw. "I played football in high school and college. I went to Arkansas A&M down in Monticello. I haven't finished my degree yet though." He wanted to stop talking about himself and his past as soon as possible. "What else should I know about you?" he asked.

"Well…I played basketball when I was in high school. I like to roller skate. I love to bake, especially when I'm making up recipes." She grinned. "You've already heard about my famous molasses cookies."

"I'm still hoping to taste them someday." A smart, funny, thoughtful girl who could bake. Cliff might've found the perfect woman.

Ruby grinned mischievously. "I'll see what I can do about that." She raised an eyebrow. "If you're good."

He chuckled. "I'll do my best." He glanced up at the counter. "Looks like our order is up. I'll be right back." A minute later, he placed two heaping platters of burgers and fries on the table.

"This looks yummy."

He nodded. "It sure does. I'll say a prayer before we eat if that's okay."

"I'd like that."

Cliff bowed his head. He hadn't talked to God much lately, but considering their first date had been to church, he felt that it was only appropriate. "Lord, please bless this food we're about to eat. Thank You for giving me and Ruby this time to spend together. Please be with all of the boys in the military, and give our leaders wisdom to know what is best for our country. Watch over us, Lord, and keep us all safe." Once he said "amen," he raised his head and caught Ruby's eye. "Are you enjoying your time in Jacksonville, or do you miss home?"

She bit down on a french fry. "I really like working. I was a little nervous in the beginning, just because it was all so new. I'm not used to having to wear a badge or safety shoes and all. I'm used to being on the farm or sitting in classes." She popped the rest of the fry into her mouth. "But I've adjusted pretty well."

"That's great. I was a little worried about you at first, especially when you found out Hazel was getting married and leaving." He took a bite of his burger.

Ruby tossed her dark hair. "It would've been easy for me to be upset about that, but I figured there was no point. I'm happy Hazel is happy." She smiled. "And I really do believe this is the best place for me right now."

"Me too." He winked. "You've certainly livened things up. I think two of the old boys in the cafeteria on Friday had to be resuscitated just because you walked past."

She tossed a french fry at him. "You don't say? Well, I could say the same thing about you. The girl behind me in line was practically swooning while you were breaking up that argument. You should've heard her go on about how gallant you were."

Cliff laughed. "And what did you say?" He enjoyed the way their sparring brought color to her cheeks. "It made you jealous, didn't it?"

She rolled her eyes. "So jealous I gave her your number."

He frowned. "Did you really?"

Now it was her turn to laugh. "Of course not." She raised an eyebrow. "I don't know your number." She giggled again. "But if you want to write it down, I'll be glad to pass it along the next time I see her."

He grinned. She was quite a girl, this one. He liked the way she teased him back. It must be because she'd grown up with brothers.

Or maybe it was because she liked him.

Cliff quickly pushed the thought away. She'd be headed back to college in a month, and then they might as well live in different worlds.

But they could have a lot of fun for the rest of the summer. "How about a movie later this week?" he asked before he lost his nerve.

"That sounds like fun." Ruby smiled.

Cliff returned her smile. He hadn't even taken her back to her dorm yet, and he was already looking forward to getting together with her again.

Chapter Six

. . . .

July 25, 1943

Dear Lucille,

I hope this letter finds you well. Mama's last letter said your family had been hit by the summertime flu. I pray that everyone is well by now. I can't wait to see sweet Annie Sue in person. She probably won't even remember me. Have you heard from Donald lately? He's in my prayers every night, just as Jack and Raymond are. I will be glad when this terrible war is over and the three of them are safely home.

The weeks are flying by so fast I can't even believe it. I know you think I'm silly for wanting to live in the city and have a job, but I sure am enjoying being on my own.

I have a couple of pieces of exciting news. I will officially start a new position as line inspector on August 1st. I'll tell you a secret, and I trust you'll keep it between us because I don't want to worry Mama and Papa. I'm thinking about staying here for a few more months. Of course I'll go back and finish my teaching degree eventually, but surely postponing for a semester will be okay. I haven't decided for sure yet, but I'll keep you posted.

I've been spending time with Hazel's cousin Cliff. He's a neat guy, and we have a lot of fun together. Now, I know what you're thinking, but I assure you we're only friends. You know I'm not interested in a relationship.

Cliff and I have a lot of laughs together, and I like how easygoing he is. He's invited me to go with him to a Razorback football game in the fall, which sounds really fun. Of course, he has no idea I'm considering staying on at the AOP, so he thinks I'll be back at school by the time football season is here. I don't want to tell him what I'm considering, because I want to make the decision on my own, and I know he'll try to help.

My roommate and I are getting along really well, except that there's a guy she wants to introduce me to. I've tried to explain to her that I'm not interested, but she doesn't want to believe me. Some girls just can't understand why I'd want to stay single.

Even though I work long hours, there's still time for fun. I go bowling or roller skating with some of the girls from my shift. It makes me think of my freshman year in college when Hazel and I learned how to roller skate on the tennis courts. We got in so much trouble when we got caught—but it's still one of my fondest memories.

The only thing I don't like about my job is the safety shoes I have to wear when I'm working the line. They are so tight, my feet go numb after a few minutes. Sometimes I sneak in with my sandals on just so I can work in comfort. You know I don't usually break the rules, so that tells you how bad it is. I fear my feet will never be the same and in twenty years if I'm walking with a limp, you'll know why!

Overall, I'm happy here. It's been a bit of an adjustment, learning to live with people who are so different from me. Until now, all my time away from home has been spent at a Christian college around people who have the same values as me. I'm surprised at how "worldly" some of the girls are here. I haven't mentioned it in any of my letters to Mama, because I don't want her to worry. I'm still the same girl I always was.

And Cliff has been going with me to a church that's near the facility here. I didn't expect him to go with me every Sunday, but he does.

I think I've rambled on enough. I can't wait to hear from you and I'm already looking forward to Christmas when I'm hoping to come home for a few days. Show Annie Sue my picture and tell her that "Aunt" Ruby will see her soon.

Much love to you and your little family,
Ruby Jean

* * * * *

Cliff had been dreading the third day of August something fierce, and it wasn't just because of the humidity. It would have been Charlie's birthday, and this was the first year without him around to celebrate it. Cliff knew that if he was having a hard time with the occasion, his parents must be awfully sad.

Aunt Ida had encouraged him to send them a letter, but he'd declined and instead just passed on his love through her correspondence.

It was strange, though. Ever since he'd been going to church with Ruby, he'd started to wonder if perhaps forgiveness was possible. Last Sunday, the lesson had been about the prodigal son, and Cliff couldn't help but wonder if it wasn't divine intervention.

Would he be welcomed back with open arms like the son in the story? Or would the grief his parents felt over losing Charlie be too great? Cliff wasn't certain.

Uncertainty seemed to be the name of the game for him these days. Despite growing ever closer to Ruby, he wasn't any closer to figuring out whether she enjoyed his company or was just biding her time until she headed back to college.

"You aren't gonna get much work done just staring off into space like that." Harold chuckled from across the workroom.

Cliff nodded to his friend. "I didn't even hear you come in."

"You thinking about that pretty girl Andrew Wallace saw you with the other day? He said she had the kind of figure that could give Betty Grable a run for her money." Harold grinned. "He was quite impressed. Asked where he could find a girl like that."

Cliff hated to tell his friend that there weren't other girls like that, and it wasn't just because of her looks. It would give him away as being over the moon for her, and that's the last thing he wanted to admit. Especially to Harold. He was a nice guy, but he ran his mouth an awful lot.

"We're just friends. I give her a ride to church sometimes."

Harold raised his eyebrows and motioned at the radio in front of Cliff. "Is that her radio you've been trying to fix for the past two weeks?"

"Well, yeah. I can't figure it out. Sometimes it works, but others it doesn't."

Harold smirked. "You're working hard on her radio during your off time, but she's just a friend? That doesn't add up."

Cliff turned his attention back to the radio. "Let up, will you? I said we're just friends and we are."

"Well then, since you're still a free man, maybe you'll want to go out with a bunch of us tomorrow after work. There's some kind of get-together in the rec hall."

Cliff struggled to keep his expression from giving him away. He'd finally invited Ruby to see where he lived, and he was supposed to pick her up after her shift tomorrow. "I appreciate the invitation, but I need to get home after work."

Harold eyed him suspiciously. "Well, the offer stands. You're really missing out, though. There's a whole new crop of dames that just started in the admin building. They're from Louisiana, and you'd get a kick out of hearing their accents."

"Some other time." Cliff plugged in the radio and flipped through the dial. Frank Sinatra's smooth voice blared out of the speaker. "I'm not going to get my hopes up. Chances are the next time I plug it in, it won't work." It was becoming the thorn in his side. Just when he thought he had it fixed and he would get to play hero to Ruby, he would plug it in one final time and it wouldn't work. "I'm not taking it to her until I've gotten it to play two days in a row."

"Maybe you're missing a wire or something." Harold walked over and peered at the radio.

"Oh well. I'll look at it again later." Cliff stood and grabbed his tools. "I'd better run. There's a light flickering over at one of the detonator buildings. And if they can't see, they can't work." He hurried out of the maintenance shop and toward the building that housed the second detonator line. As luck would have it, it was Ruby's line. Cliff smiled to himself. This would be the first time he'd see her in action as a line inspector. He'd had to visit the building once right after she started, but she was too new then to even acknowledge him. She'd kept her eyes trained on the work station in front of her. Today would be different.

"Thanks for getting over here so fast," she said as soon as he walked in. Her dark hair was pulled back away from her face, and her green eyes sparkled. She pointed to a dim area in the corner of the room. "There's the problem."

Cliff walked past a row of women, each working intently as they measured just the right amount of black powder into the detonators. One false move and the powder could explode. He had to admire them for their fearlessness. "I'll get right on it," he said to Ruby.

She nodded and hurried back to the line where she peered over the shoulders of the workers, making sure they were measuring correctly.

Cliff glanced around. Posters on the concrete wall emphasized the importance of not discussing work outside of the building. He appreciated that. As someone who'd served in the military, he knew all too well the importance of keeping equipment and maneuvers quiet. He watched as Ruby walked the line, pausing a couple of times to offer encouragement or gently correct. She seemed so…capable. Maybe that was the thing that drew him to her.

She caught him looking and offered a smile and a raised eyebrow.

Cliff grinned. A few weeks ago he'd have been embarrassed to know she'd seen his obvious admiration. Not anymore. He turned his attention to the faulty light, pleased to find that it was an easy fix.

"Finished already?" Ruby asked once he'd gathered his tools. "That was fast."

He grinned. "I know you were hoping I'd have to stick around the rest of the day, but no such luck."

She wrinkled her nose. "Don't you flatter yourself. I've got plenty to do here without worrying about you falling off the ladder or electrocuting yourself." Her eyes danced with mischief.

Cliff chuckled. "Okay, okay. I'll get out of your hair. But I'm glad to know you worry about me." He winked. "Just as I suspected. I must fill your every thought in your waking hours. And probably your dreaming ones too."

Ruby burst out laughing. "You're too much. Now get out of here before you disrupt the line."

He turned to go but stopped. "We're still on for tomorrow, right?" Despite his flirting, he knew they weren't exactly on solid ground.

"Of course. I'm looking forward to it."

Cliff stepped out of the dim building into the bright sunlight. He was looking forward to it too.

So much so that it scared him.

And as someone who wasn't used to fearing anything, that was an unsettling feeling.

Chapter Seven
....

Ruby hurried down the stairs to the lobby, eager to see what Cliff had in store. He'd told her to wear dungarees and boots instead of her normal dress or skirt, but he wouldn't tell her the reason. "Just trust me," he'd said with a laugh.

She knew times had changed and it was appropriate for girls to wear pants now, especially since they were doing work that just a few years ago would've been reserved for men only. Even so, she had to wonder what Mama would say if she could see her going out in public in this outfit.

"There you are." Cliff grinned. "I was beginning to think you'd backed out or something."

"I got called over to the administration building after my shift."

He raised his brows and held the door open for her. "Are you trading your work boots for sandals again?"

She laughed. "Nothing like that. I think I've finally learned my lesson." She held up a foot encased in a cowboy boot. "Although if I could wear these my days would be a lot happier." She grinned. "Or at least my feet would be."

He opened the car door and she climbed inside, thankful for some time away from the dorm. The drawback to living just a few yards from where she worked was that she sometimes felt like she never had a break. Especially now that she was line inspector. It had been an adjustment for some of the girls on her hallway to get used to her being both their friend and their boss.

"What are we doing this afternoon? You never said."

Cliff waved at the gate guard and turned the car onto the main highway. "You asked me the other day what I do during my time off. I thought I'd show you." He glanced over at her with a grin. "We're going to do a little rabbit hunting this afternoon."

She wrinkled her nose. She'd gone hunting with Papa and her brothers a hundred times over the years. She understood that it helped put food on the table for their family, but she'd never been especially fond of it. "Hunting?"

"Oh, don't worry. You'll be fine. I'll be there to look out for you."

Ruby choked out a laugh. "Of course I'll be fine. I grew up on a farm."

He slowed down and turned the car down a dirt road. "You've met Hazel's parents before, haven't you?"

She nodded. "At the wedding. Mrs. Collins invited me to come out for dinner sometime."

"That's what I thought. I don't know if Hazel explained it to you, but Aunt Ida and my mom are sisters."

Cliff hadn't volunteered much information about his immediate family, only that he was staying with his aunt and uncle for a little while. And Ruby hadn't had much time to quiz Hazel before she and Troy left town.

"And you said your parents still live in River Bend?" She'd never been there but had heard of the place before.

He parked next to an older model car. "That's right."

"Do you see them often?"

Cliff shook his head. "Not enough." He motioned toward the white house. "Ready?"

Just as he had the last couple of times, he seemed to shut down at the mention of his family or where he came from. Ruby didn't know what to make of it. "Sure." She followed him to the house and smiled at the dog on the porch.

"Don't mind Old Blue. He's harmless."

She laughed. "I didn't think otherwise." She bent down and patted the dog's graying head. "He looks like he's already earned his keep and is enjoying his retirement."

"Something like that." Cliff grinned. "Actually he's a pretty good guard dog when it comes to strangers. When I first moved here, he'd howl and carry on every time I drove up. I think he's finally figured out that I belong here."

"And do you?"

Cliff stopped and turned toward her, his blue eyes serious. "As much as I belong anywhere I guess."

Before she had the chance to ask what he meant, the front door swung open and Mrs. Collins stepped out onto the porch. "Ruby, it's so nice to see you again." She ushered them inside. "I just got a letter from Hazel yesterday, and she asked if you'd been to the house. It sounds like she and Troy are settling in well in Pine Bluff."

Ruby followed her into the sunny kitchen. "I'm glad to hear it. I know y'all miss her, though." She smiled. "I owe her a letter. Hopefully I'll get to that soon."

"Well, it sounds like you'll be able to tell her all about your adventure here." Mrs. Collins grinned. "I'm so glad Cliff brought you by."

Mr. Collins walked in the back door, clad in mud-stained overalls. "I hear rabbit hunting is on the agenda." His face was still flushed from the August heat. "Are you sure you want to do that?"

She nodded. "Yes, sir."

"Okay," Cliff said, coming into the kitchen. "I've got everything we need." He held up a shotgun. "Let's go."

Ruby narrowed her eyes. "Wait a minute. What about my gun?"

Cliff chuckled. "You don't need one."

"Well, if we're going rabbit hunting, what am I supposed to do without a gun? Just stand next to you and watch?" She hated to admit it, but she rather enjoyed the startled expression on his face. Clearly he had expected her to just stand and watch.

Mr. Collins clapped Cliff on the shoulder. "She's got a point there, son. She can take mine."

Cliff sighed. "I'll go get it."

Ruby knew her mama would be appalled at her behavior, but she couldn't help herself. Sometimes Cliff acted like she was some prissy girl who couldn't do anything but stand around and smile. She'd show him. Her brothers might've been overprotective, but they'd taught her to shoot.

Cliff returned with a shotgun and carefully handed it to Ruby. "Here you go."

They stepped out the backdoor and started toward the thicket behind the house.

Ruby stopped. "Hang on a second."

"What's wrong?" Cliff turned to face her.

She held up the gun. "You gave me a gun but no bullets."

Cliff looked at her with wide eyes. "You sure are a lot of trouble." The grin that played at his mouth gave him away.

She swatted at him. "You did that on purpose."

He reached into his pocket and pulled out a bullet. "Here you go. I was just testing you to see what kind of outdoorsman"—he cleared his throat—"I mean, outdoors*woman* you were."

Ruby grinned. "I'm the kind that can probably hit a target as well as you." She knew she shouldn't be so sassy. She'd heard it plenty of times growing up that sometimes the best thing for a well-brought-up lady to do was stand to the side and cheer for the boys. But growing up the only girl in the family had likely made her a little more competitive than most girls. "How about we split up?" She motioned toward the left of the thicket. "I'll take that section. You take the opposite side."

Cliff looked unsure. "Well…if you say so."

That did it. "I'll see you in a bit. Holler if you need me." She tramped off, looking forward to showing him what she was capable of doing. She'd say one thing about Cliff Hamilton. He sure did know how to get a rise out of her.

And as much as she hated to admit it, she liked how alive it made her feel.

More alive than she'd felt in all of her twenty-two years.

* * * * *

Cliff watched her walk away.

Unbelievable.

He'd brought her out here so they could do something together, something away from the prying eyes of their coworkers. He was tired of the ribbing from Harold and the other guys who wanted to know all about the pretty girl he'd been spending time with.

So he'd thought they could get out in nature and look around, maybe see some wildlife. Honestly, he hadn't even meant to hunt much. He'd just wanted some time alone with Ruby away from everything else. And if he had to do it under the guise of hunting rabbits, he would.

Except that she'd turned it into some kind of competition.

Cliff sighed. He should probably have just been honest with her about wanting to spend time together. He'd always loved the outdoors, ever since he was just a small boy. Amid the trees and the wildlife, he always felt closest to God. And over the past few months, to Charlie. He and his brother had shared so many good times in the outdoors. Cliff had just wanted to share some of that with Ruby.

A gunshot rang out, breaking the silence.

He might've known she'd fire first. "Did you get it?" he called, hurrying in the direction of the shot. Since she only had one bullet, he was in no danger of sneaking up on her and being mistaken for a rabbit.

"I missed it." She stepped out of the thicket, a broad smile on her face. "But I guess you know now that I can handle a weapon."

She looked so proud of herself he had to laugh. "Tell you what, how about we leave our weapons behind and just go for a walk?"

Ruby nodded. "That sounds nice."

He took her gun. "I'll just lean these against that tree over there. We can get them when we head back to the house." He quickly put the guns down and motioned for her to follow. "It's a pretty place, isn't it?"

She grinned. "It sure is. It kind of makes me miss home."

"So you've really hunted before?" he asked.

"I really have. But it isn't something I make a habit of or anything. To tell you the truth, I'm a lot better at shooting at a target than at an animal. I think I'm way too tenderhearted for that."

"Yeah, Hazel mentioned that was the problem with your being a pig farmer for the summer. Said you'd end up turning them into pets."

She giggled. "You should hear my brothers tell the story about our pet cow. Her name is Spotty. She's not good for milk, but I made such a fuss when there was talk of sending her to a slaughterhouse that Papa finally gave in." She shook her head. "My brothers have teased me about it for years. After I went off to college, I think they were finally going to get rid of her, but they all felt too bad about it. So now we have this old cow who lives in one of our fields with no real purpose other than eating and sleeping."

Cliff grinned. "So underneath that tough exterior, you're really just a softie?"

"Something like that. I guess I've just always had a soft spot for creatures that can't help themselves. That goes for people too. You know how sometimes you meet someone and automatically feel protective? Maybe it's just me."

"No. It isn't just you." He motioned toward a log. "Let's go sit for a minute." He put his hand on the small of her back to guide her over and almost recoiled at the surge of electricity between them.

"Everything okay?"

He sat down next to her. "Yeah. But you know what you said about feeling protective of someone? I really understand that feeling."

"How so?"

It was time to tell her the truth. "I haven't mentioned this before, just because there never seemed like a good time, but I had a brother. Charlie." He smiled at the sound of his brother's name. "He was two years younger than me, and when we were kids he drove me crazy following me around."

Ruby grinned. "That was the role I played in my family. I followed my brothers around and tried to do everything they did, from climbing trees to skipping rocks."

"Charlie was the same way. But by the time we were older, we'd become best friends. No one understood me the way he did." He wiped a dirt smudge from his pants. "I went to Arkansas A&M to play football, and Charlie stayed home to work. Said he wasn't cut out for more schooling."

"Not everyone is," she said.

"Charlie was drafted. Army. As soon as I found out, I left college and joined up alongside him. No way was my little brother going without me."

She reached over and patted his knee. "Sounds like you were a good big brother."

"Not always, but I tried to be." He would do a lot different if he had the chance to do it over. "Charlie thought of the war as a big adventure. We were going to see the world." He shook his head. "I saw it as a mission to protect him at all costs. Charlie is—was—one of the most pure-hearted people I've ever known. He always wanted to do what was right. When the other guys were scared or homesick, it was Charlie who provided comfort. He'd pray with them or quote Scripture. It was really amazing. I realized while we were there that Charlie would make a great teacher or preacher. He just had such a way with people."

"He sounds amazing." She leaned closer to him. "Do you want to tell me what happened?" she asked softly.

Cliff looked into her green eyes and knew he could tell her

anything. He could tell her the true version, not the sugar-coated one. "We were in a foxhole together. There was heavy firing. All of the sudden, things got eerily quiet and then there was a huge explosion. It seemed like the end of the world. Just before we were hit, Charlie jumped on top of me. He caught the brunt of the force. I was injured." Cliff's hand went to his shoulder.

She grabbed his hand. "Oh, Cliff. I'm so sorry."

He looked down at their intertwined hands. "And he was killed. Saving me."

Chapter Eight

Ruby stared in horror. The grief on Cliff's face was enough to bring tears to her eyes. "I can't imagine how horrible that must've been for you. How horrible it must still be."

He gripped her hand. "Is it okay for me to tell you this? I was afraid it might be too much for you to deal with."

She managed a smile. "Now, Cliff. Haven't I proved to you that I'm tougher than I look? You can tell me anything, especially things like this that you obviously need to talk about."

"I wanted to tell you a few weeks ago. I know you probably thought I was avoiding questions about my family." He shrugged. "I just wasn't ready to talk about it until now."

"Of course. I understand. Sometimes we have to sort things out in our own heads before we can talk about them to someone else."

He nodded. "That sounds about right."

"What's happened to you—what you've gone through—is a terrible burden to bear alone. How are your parents?"

He let go of her hand and heaved a great sigh. "They blame me for his death."

"No. You can't think that."

"I don't have to think it. I know it. When I got back, I had to stay at their house while I recovered. I could see how much my being there pained them. I know that when they look at me, all they are thinking is that I let them down. That if I would've done a better job of protecting him, Charlie would still be with us." He sighed. "Today would've been his twenty-second birthday."

She reached over and took his hand again. "I don't believe for a minute that your parents place the blame on you. Cliff, this is an awful war. Nearly everyone I know has lost a family member or a friend." She sensed this wasn't the time to tell him about Joseph. Even though that experience had been hard on her, it wasn't as traumatic as what Cliff had gone through.

He nodded. "I guess. But I spent my whole life looking out for Charlie. He was the baby of the family. I remember once when we were kids and we went fishing. He went to dig for more worms but got lost in the woods. I think we were probably six and eight at the time. Once it dawned on me that he'd been gone too long, I was terrified. I yelled and yelled. He'd sat down under a tree. When I finally got to him, he just grinned. He told me when he couldn't find his way out, he just stopped because he knew I'd find him."

Ruby smiled at the sweet memory. "You were a good brother."

"He trusted me to keep him safe. Always. When we were kids. And then later in that foxhole, I should've been the one to cover him. I should've been the one to anticipate what was coming." Cliff looked at her with tortured eyes. "Not the other way around."

"Sometimes things happen. Things we don't understand or can't explain." Ruby squeezed his hand. "It's easy to place blame on ourselves or on the people around us." She shook her head. "But if there's one thing I've learned over the past few years, it's that we can't do that. We have to just trust that God will take care of us. That He is bigger than all of the bad stuff. Bigger than the wars or the hunger or the sadness."

Cliff shook his head. "I don't know. I used to believe that. But I'm not sure if I do anymore."

"Sometimes it just takes some time. Your grief is still fresh. In fact, I'll bet you moved here before your wounds even healed completely."

She remembered Hazel asking about his arm the day he'd carried her suitcase into the dorm. Now it all made sense. "Am I right?"

He nodded. "I couldn't stand to stay at my parents' house any longer. And my arm doesn't bother me that much anymore. Just every now and then it still aches."

"You've been through a lot."

Cliff shrugged. "No more than most. Like you said, there are lots of people who've dealt with loss."

Ruby frowned. "Don't do that. Don't try to act like what you went through with Charlie wasn't terrible. But you are going to have to let go of the guilt. It was *not* your fault. From what you've said, there was nothing you could do."

"Sure there was. I could've done for him what he did for me. I could've tried to save his life."

Ruby sighed. Nothing she could say would make it better or make his hurt go away. And letting go of the guilt was something he'd have to do on his own. But she could stand by him and help him however she could.

The thought came as a surprise. Because wanting to help him get through the toughest trial he'd ever faced meant one thing.

She cared about him.

And the realization terrified her.

* * * * *

Cliff felt as if a weight had been lifted. He'd hated feeling like he was keeping something from Ruby but hadn't wanted to admit his weakness. He wanted her, of all people, to see him as a strong, able man who could handle anything. Over the past weeks, he'd tried to steer her away from the topic of his family. But now, having told her what had happened and having heard that she was on his side—and seen the empathy in her eyes—he was glad he'd finally opened up.

"Thanks for being such a great listener."

She smiled. "I'll listen to you any time you want to talk."

"Any time?" He grinned. "Do you mean that? And do I always get to pick the topic?"

Ruby laughed. "Yes. And no."

"Fair enough." He looked down and realized he was still holding her hand. It felt nice.

"I have a confession." She grinned. "Earlier when I fired the gun, I didn't actually fire it at anything."

He burst out laughing. "Then what was that all about?"

"I guess sometimes I'm too stubborn for my own good. I really just wanted you to know that I knew how to use the gun. Sometimes my stupid pride gets the best of me."

Her honesty surprised him. "You realize I never would've known that you didn't fire at a rabbit."

Ruby nodded. "Yes, but I don't like the idea of being dishonest. Especially not with you." She grinned. "I think we should promise to always be honest with each other, even if it isn't pretty."

He stood up and offered his hand. "Sounds like a plan. Never hold back."

"Sounds good." She clasped his hand and allowed him to pull her up from the log. "You know how I told you that I had to go to the admin building after work today?"

He kept his grip on her hand as they started walking through the woods and was pleased that she didn't let go. "I'm still not convinced you weren't caught wearing sandals on the line again."

She stuck her tongue out at him. "I told you I learned my lesson about that. Actually I had to go over there to let them know that I'll be staying on through mid-December."

He stopped walking and turned to face her. "You will?" He knew she picked up on the excitement in his voice, but he didn't care. "What about college?"

"I think it's more important for me to stay here, where I'm actually making a contribution to the war effort besides just rationing or buying war bonds. You know? Every day when I go to work, I think about how what we're doing here in this little plant in Arkansas could be helping my brothers wherever they are stationed. And right now it's more important for me to do that than it is for me to go back to classes and do my student teaching."

Cliff didn't try to hide his grin as they started walking again. "Well, I can't say that I'm sad about your decision. I didn't even know you were considering it. I'm a little surprised you didn't say something sooner." If she'd gone to the trouble to schedule a meeting with the higher ups, it meant she'd been thinking about it for a while.

She shrugged. "You know how I am. I like to figure stuff out on my own. I guessed you'd think my staying was a good idea. Same with Lola. I didn't tell her either. I wanted to make sure the decision was mine and mine alone."

Cliff could respect her quest for independence, but it worried him some too. Would Ruby ever be able to let go of some of that and have a real relationship? The more he got to know her, the more he wondered. "Well, that's great. I'll be happy to have you around—for a few more months anyway. December, did you say?"

She nodded. "That's right. I'll work right up until Christmas, then I'm planning to go home to see my family. I can start back to classes in January." She shrugged. "If I were only taking myself into consideration, I'd probably just stay here until the war was over. But my parents are not going to take the news well. Papa has paid a lot of money for me to get a college education. I don't want to let my family down by dropping out, especially when I'm this close to finishing."

"You're a thoughtful daughter."

"I love my parents. I don't like the idea of doing anything they don't approve or aren't proud of. It wasn't easy for them to let me come here in the first place, so I know the idea of my sitting out of college, even just for a semester, is going to be a difficult one for them. But I think this will be a pretty good compromise and will make us all happy."

Hearing Ruby talk about her parents made Cliff wish he could mend his relationship with his. But maybe things would never be the same. Maybe the pain of losing Charlie would have a lasting impact. "That's wonderful."

They stopped at the tree where the guns were propped. "This was fun." Cliff grinned. "Despite your competitiveness."

Ruby blushed. "I don't know what makes me that way. I suppose it irritates me when I don't feel like I'm being taken seriously." She shrugged. "Just like the day we met. My brother came to get me, to try and convince me that working at the AOP was a bad idea and I should just come home."

"Maybe he was just trying to look out for you and keep you safe."

She nodded. "I know. And I'm grateful for that. But I don't want to be kept safe and sheltered. I want to have adventures and experiences that I can't get on the farm raising pigs."

Cliff smiled at the passion in her voice. She was unique. "Maybe the key is finding balance. You don't necessarily have to conquer the world by yourself, but I'm willing to bet that a lifetime of experiences awaits you."

"Let's hope so."

He winked. "I know so."

And he hoped many of those experiences would include him.

Chapter Nine

....

August 31, 1943

Dear Hazel,

I know you must think I'm a terrible friend, as I've received two letters from you since I've found time to write. I think of you often and selfishly wish Troy would be transferred back here. But I'm so glad to hear you like it there. It sounds like y'all have found a good group of friends from church.

I'm sure you've heard from your mama by now that I've been out to your house a few times with Cliff. Your parents are so kind to me, and your mama let me use her kitchen to bake. Cliff was thrilled to finally sample the molasses cookies. Have you given the recipe a try yet? I made some changes to it last week and added some pecans. You know how I love to come up with new recipes. It's a rare treat now that we're rationing sugar.

Cliff finally told me about what happened in that foxhole with his brother Charlie. Poor Cliff—I can't imagine losing one of my brothers, let alone feeling responsible for his death. I don't really know how to comfort him, other than to just listen and to pray. Charlie sounds like he was such a great kid. I remember how torn up you were last year over your cousin— now I realize it must've been Charlie.

Cliff and I spend a lot of time together. In fact, he's my best friend here. I've never had a boy as a best friend. It's kind of nice.

Last week, Cliff and I went to the skating rink, and the funniest thing happened. It turns out that my roommate, Lola, has been seeing Cliff's friend Harold. Lola has been trying for ages to fix me up with a certain boy, and Harold had been telling Cliff about a girl for him. It was us all along! They were so surprised when we walked in together, and we all had a good laugh. Of course, Cliff was full of himself on the way home, all puffed up and joking that they'd picked him out for me because they knew he was my dream man. I just laughed at him. He always jokes about us dating, so I know he's not really serious about it.

I hope it's okay to talk about Cliff like this to you, seeing how he's your cousin and all. But I assure you, we are only friends. He hasn't kissed me or anything, and if he tried, I'd tell him not to. My decision to remain single hasn't changed, and it never will.

It's strange to think that classes at Harding will be starting soon. I wrote to all my suitemates and let them know I won't be back until January. The only one I've heard from so far has been Betty Jo—you remember her, don't you? She's convinced that I'm having some great love affair and that's why I'm not going back. Some girls are so silly, aren't they? And my parents aren't exactly thrilled about my decision to stay on at the AOP, but they didn't put up much of a fuss. I am starting to get a little bit homesick, but I keep telling myself Christmas will be here before we know it.

Your mama told me that you and Troy will be here for Thanksgiving, and I am counting down the days! Your parents have invited me for Thanksgiving dinner. I've already promised Cliff I'll make a dessert. He sure does have a sweet tooth.

Well, I'd better end this. I'm about to go play baseball

*with a group of friends. It should be fun. I can't wait to see
the look on Cliff's face when he sees that I know how to catch
a ball!*

   *All my love,
   Ruby Jean*

* * * * *

"Batter up!" Cliff called from his spot on the pitcher's mound. Even though he'd gone to college on a football scholarship, he'd always loved to play baseball. So when Harold suggested an end-of-summer pickup game, he'd been the first to sign up.

Ruby clutched the bat and did a couple of practice swings. "Show me what you've got, Hamilton." She stepped up to the plate with a sassy grin on her face.

The upside to not being on her team, Cliff realized, was getting to face her from the mound. "If you want me to, I can pitch it slower for you since you're a girl and all," he called.

She laughed. "Just try to get it over the plate. I'll take care of the rest."

Cliff released the ball.

Ruby swung and missed.

"Strike one," Harold called from behind the plate.

She made a face. "I'll get the next one."

"Come on, Ruby!" Lola yelled form the sidelines, where she and some of the other girls waited their turns. "You can do it."

Ruby tapped the bat against the plate and hoisted it over her shoulder. "I'm ready." She grinned. "Try to put it over the plate this time."

He chuckled. "Keep your eye on the ball. Maybe that will help."

Cliff heard Andrew Wallace laugh from his position at shortstop. "Don't give her pointers, Cliff. Remember, she's not on your team no matter how pretty she is."

Cliff grinned. Andrew might not understand it, but even playing for the opposition, he was always on Ruby's side. He stood for a minute on the mound, then threw the ball over the plate.

Ruby swung and connected. The ball went flying toward left field, and she took off running. Her teammates cheered.

Cliff watched her go. She sure could run.

The trouble was, he wasn't sure if he could ever catch her.

* * * * *

"That was so much fun," Ruby said after the game. She plopped down on the grass next to Cliff. "I'm glad we did this."

Cliff nodded. "And congratulations on your victory." He leaned close to her. "Don't tell anyone from my team, but I was rooting for you," he whispered. His breath tickled her ear, sending shivers down her spine.

She grinned. "Thanks. You were the best player out there. And too bad that fellow struck out at the end or else y'all would've won." It had been a real treat to see Cliff in action. He'd told her about his years as a football player, so she'd known he was athletic. Getting to see it firsthand was fun. "You were a good coach too. Why, Lola could barely even swing a bat at first, but after you showed her what to do, she scored a run."

"Thank you, Ruby. Sometimes I think about what it would be like to be a coach. Maybe someday I'll get the chance." He smiled. "You never know what the future holds."

Ruby dusted off a smudge of dirt from the knee of her dungarees. "You're right. You never know." She grinned. "A year ago if you'd told me I'd be staying here for the fall, working instead of going back to school, I never would've believed it. But the decision just felt right."

"What did your parents say?" The concern in his blue eyes was evident. He knew how worried she'd been about broaching the subject with her family.

"It wasn't the easiest conversation. But they finally agreed." She shrugged. "Even though Papa made it clear he'd rather I return to school, he left the final decision up to me." She smiled. "I could tell he was proud of my promotion to line inspector."

"As he should be." Cliff grinned.

"Plus, I think they feel better about my being here since they know I have a good friend like you." She'd never admit it to him, but she was pretty sure he was a big part of the reason Mama had been on her side when she'd found out Ruby wanted to stay.

Cliff raised his eyebrows. "Your parents know about me?" His pleased expression made her laugh. "Well, no wonder they let you stay here."

She slapped him playfully on the arm. "And they also understand how much I want to contribute to the war effort."

"Well, I for one am glad you're here, regardless of the reason." His eyes twinkled. "I mean, think about how sad your life would be if you'd never met me."

She threw back her head and laughed. "That's right. I'd probably just be sitting in my dorm room, refusing to go outside except for classes or meetings." When he didn't say anything, she looked over at him. His normally sunny expression was serious. "Everything okay?" She nudged him with her shoulder.

"Maybe it's none of my business, but I'm kind of curious about something."

"What's that? You know you can ask me anything."

Cliff nodded. "I know that. But there's something we've never talked about before. I've been too chicken to ask."

Ruby's heart dropped. She wasn't ready to have this discussion. She only knew that she enjoyed spending time with him. But she couldn't give him more than that. "What?"

"Do you have a boyfriend back at college? I mean, is there a steady guy who'll be waiting for you when you go back in January?"

Relief washed over her as she realized he wasn't going to press her to talk about her feelings for him. "No. Nothing like that."

"But you must have fellows clamoring for your attention and asking you out for dates all the time."

She grinned. "I usually say no. Some girls always have a boyfriend. I've never been one of those girls." She sighed. "I've only had one steady guy, but it was a while ago."

"What happened?"

Ruby knew she'd avoided telling Cliff because she didn't want to remind him of his own loss. But there was no point in keeping it from him any longer. "Joseph and I met when we were freshmen and went steady for almost exactly a year. After the attack on Pearl Harbor, he joined the army. Said it was his duty as an American." She plucked a clover from the ground and twirled it between her fingers. "He didn't make it back." She tossed the clover to the ground. "He was killed at Guadalcanal." She shook her head. "Since then, I've kept to myself."

Cliff's jaw tightened. "Ruby, I'm so sorry. This war has brought so much grief. I hate to hear that you've suffered a loss too." He reached over and patted her on the back. "Was it very serious between the two of you?"

"Just before he left, he asked me to marry him. I said yes." Admitting it to Cliff was easier than she'd expected. "It was the last conversation we ever had."

Cliff let out a low whistle. "Wow, I'm so sorry to hear about this. That must have been a horrible thing to go through."

Ruby nodded. "It sure put things into perspective. I know lots of girls are happily engaged or married, but I can't imagine risking my heart like that again." She pushed a wayward strand of hair from her face and glanced over at him. "I just want to enjoy my independence."

Cliff nodded. "After what you've been through, that's only natural."

Ruby appreciated his understanding. "It seems like a lifetime ago—almost like something that happened to someone else."

He wrinkled his forehead. "What do you mean?"

"I was only nineteen when we met," she explained. "We celebrated my twentieth birthday together. It was one of our first dates. And in just a couple of months, I'll turn twenty-three. I know it seems like not much time has passed, but it has. When I met him, I was just a girl straight off the farm. But now...I'm grown up, living away from my family and working."

"So you're not the same person now that you were then?"

She sighed. "Yes, I think that's it exactly. I'm a different person now. I've watched my friends and my brothers go off to war. I've seen the world change around me." She shrugged. "I wonder sometimes if Joseph would even recognize me now."

Cliff reached over and squeezed her shoulder. "I'm sure he would. And he'd probably be proud of the woman you've become."

She blinked back tears. Was Cliff right? She'd often wondered what Joseph would think of her decision to work at the ordnance plant. Would he be proud of her service, or would he be more like Wade and think she was better off at home? She'd never know. "He was a good person. Sweet and kind."

What she didn't tell Cliff was how much turmoil accepting Joseph's proposal had created for her. She'd wondered if he'd only asked for her hand because he was headed to war. And likewise, she wondered if her acceptance had been for the same reason.

She'd loved him. But had she loved him in a happily-ever-after, soul mate kind of way? She wasn't sure.

But she knew that as long as she didn't give her heart away to anyone else, she would be safe from being hurt. She'd never have the kind of hard farm life that she'd seen Mama and Lucille have. She'd be her own boss and make her own rules.

The problem was that she couldn't quite figure out where Cliff fit into that plan.

Chapter Ten

Cliff tossed his screwdriver on the work bench with a clatter. "Jeepers. This radio is driving me crazy." Even though he was off today, he'd decided to come to the shop and spend some time working on Ruby's radio.

"That thing still on the blink?" Harold asked. He grinned. "I would offer to help, but I'm still a little sore that I'm not going to the football game today."

Cliff chuckled. "Sorry about that. Maybe next time." He rubbed his chin. "Must be a short in this thing or something." He sighed. "And I'm getting a bum rap. Ruby's starting to think I'm just hanging on to the radio so we'll have music in the shop." She'd teased him yesterday, accusing him of pretending he was Ol' Blue Eyes and singing along while he did his work.

"Don't tell me you're throwing in the towel. What will Ruby think?"

Cliff shrugged. "I just don't know what else to try. It seems like every other day I have it working, but then the next day it stops." He glanced up at Harold's freckled face. "You have any suggestion?"

"Maybe you have to hold your mouth just right." Harold snickered.

Cliff looked at the mischievous grin on Harold's face and realization dawned. "Have you been monkeying with the radio?"

Harold doubled over with laughter. "Me and Andrew have been taking turns disconnecting the wire after you're through fixing it." He wiped his eyes. "It's been the funniest thing to watch you toiling over that thing, not being able to figure it out."

Cliff shook his head. "You got me pretty good." He should've suspected something. Come to think of it, Andrew had been there the day Cliff brought it in. He grinned. "But the joke's over. And I owe you one."

"I look forward to your retaliation. It has been well worth it." Harold chuckled again.

Cliff unplugged the radio, grinning. At least he'd finally be able to give the radio back to Ruby. She'd be thrilled.

He tucked the radio under his arm, told Harold good-bye, and hurried toward his car. The whole day with Ruby stretched out before him, and he had to admit, he was really looking forward to it.

She had told him she wasn't ready to risk her heart again, probably because she needed to heal. He understood that. So he would give her time and be a great friend to her. But when the time was right, he couldn't wait to sweep her off her feet.

* * * * *

Ruby glanced in the mirror one final time. She'd chosen a red sweater today to match the team colors for the Arkansas Razorbacks. Cliff had assured her that many of the fans would wear team colors, and she wanted to fit in. Besides, every time she wore red, he told her how pretty she looked.

She dabbed on some red lipstick and slipped the tube into her purse.

"I'm so jealous that y'all are going to the game." Lola looked up from her bed where she was flipping through an old issue of *Modern Screen* that had Clark Gable on the cover. "Harold was going to get tickets, but he wasn't able to get off from his shift."

Ruby grinned. "I'll cheer loud enough for you."

"Thanks. I'm touched." Lola made a face. "It's okay, though, because Harold is supposed to make it up to me tonight. We're going to the dance, and he's promised me a jitterbug."

"That'll be fun." Ruby started toward the door but then stopped. "If you want to wear my green dress, it's hanging in the closet."

Lola jumped up from the bed and pulled Ruby into a hug. "Do you mean it? I know that's your favorite. But it sure is pretty, and Harold's already seen me in everything I own." She widened her eyes. "Are you sure you mean it?"

"I mean it. You'll look beautiful, and I know Harold will love it."

Lola snatched the dress from the closet and danced around the room. "Thanks. You're the best."

Ruby laughed. "You're welcome. I'll see you later." She closed the door on the image of Lola still waltzing the green dress around the room.

"Are you excited to go to your first Razorback game?" Cliff asked once she made it to the lobby.

She nodded. "I sure am. I thought Lola was going to steal my ticket and go with you until I loaned her one of my dresses to wear out tonight." She giggled and filled him in on Lola practicing her dance moves in the dorm room.

He chuckled as they walked out to the car. "I think those two might be a perfect match. Harold's been smitten with her ever since they met."

"I still think it's funny that they wanted to introduce us to each other." She grinned.

Cliff looked down at her. "Well, maybe that means we're a perfect match too."

Ruby never knew how to respond when Cliff joked about such things. "Maybe."

Cliff stopped at the car and pointed toward the backseat. "Guess what's waiting there for you to take to your room tonight?"

Ruby peered through the glass. "My radio!" She turned to face him. "You fixed it?"

He nodded. "I sure did."

She threw her arms around his neck and hugged him tightly.

"You're my hero. Thank you so much." His arms went around her and he embraced her back. He was so close she could smell his soap. Ruby let go and willed the heat to leave her face. She and Cliff were great friends, but she'd never hugged him before. It was kind of nice. Very nice. Something she wouldn't mind trying again.

Ruby climbed into the car, her heart still beating faster than normal. Maybe that hug hadn't been such a good idea. She glanced over at Cliff once he slid behind the wheel. "So tell me about today. What will we see?"

"We're in luck. The Razorbacks play only one game in Little Rock this year. Usually they play their home games in Fayetteville next to the university."

"Did I tell you that's where Lola is from?"

Cliff shook his head. "No, but Harold did." He grinned. "I'm telling you, he can't stop talking about her."

"That's sweet." Ruby was truly happy for her friend.

"The Razorbacks are playing Texas Christian University today. And just to warn you, they're supposed to be pretty good. I think they've got a pretty good defense." He frowned. "So we might be in for a fight."

Ruby laughed. "Oh dear. I had forgotten that you were some kind of football star. I hope you don't get annoyed when you have to explain the game to me. I may know how to play baseball, but I don't know anything about football."

"I'm sorry. I'm having a hard time believing what I'm hearing. Did you just admit to not knowing something?" Cliff chuckled.

She reached over and swatted him. "Are you calling me a know-it-all?"

"Now don't put words in my mouth." He grinned. "But maybe."

Ruby crossed her arms. "Cliff Hamilton. You take that back." She fought to keep her face stern, but a grin broke through. "Besides, you might be the same way."

He nodded. "You're right. We just might be two of a kind."

* * * * *

Cliff reached down and took Ruby's hand as they left the game. "Well? What'd you think?"

She smiled broadly. "That was so much fun. Thank you so much for taking me to my first college football game."

"You're welcome." He squeezed her hand. "Do you need to rush back to the dorm? It's such a pretty day I thought you might want to go for a walk or something."

She turned her face toward the sunshine. "It is a perfect fall day, isn't it?" She looked over at him and grinned. "A walk sounds wonderful."

They reached his car, and he opened the door for her. "Are you hungry? Do you want to go eat first?"

She shook her head. "Let's walk first and then decide."

Cliff started the car and headed toward Jacksonville. "We can always eat with Aunt Ida and Uncle Fred. If you want to, I mean."

"Oh, I hate to impose."

He chuckled. "I seriously doubt they'd see it as an imposition. They like you a lot. Uncle Fred is still talking about that pie you made a few weeks ago."

"I'm already looking forward to Thanksgiving with them. And Hazel." She grinned.

Cliff glanced over at her. "What about me?"

She laughed. "Well of course. That goes without saying."

He shook his head. "Nope. Too late now. I see what your priorities are."

Ten minutes later he turned the car onto the dirt road that led to the farm house. "If we're lucky, maybe we'll see a turkey or two. You know, I'm pretty good at giving out a turkey call."

Ruby raised her eyebrows. "Seeing a turkey would be neat, but listening to you practice your turkey call definitely sounds more entertaining."

They got out of the car and walked to the porch.

"Where's Old Blue?" Ruby asked.

Cliff grinned. "He's taken up residence in the backyard since last week. A towel blew off the clothesline, and he took it upon himself to claim it as a bed. He dragged it to the back steps and has been sleeping on it there the past few days."

She laughed. "Is your aunt going to let him keep it?"

"There was talk the other morning of swiping it from him, but that hasn't happened yet. Aunt Ida wouldn't want anyone to know, but I think she feels the same way about Old Blue that you do about Spotty the cow."

"I knew I liked her for some reason."

Cliff opened the front door and led her into the house. She'd been there a lot over the past few months. Just as she always did, she stopped at the collection of family photos that sat on the bookcase.

"I love this picture of you and Charlie and your parents." She picked up the photo for a closer look. "Y'all were so happy together." She caught his eye. "Have you talked to your parents lately?"

He bristled. Ever since he told her about Charlie's death and his guilt over what had happened, she'd been asking him that question. And the answer was always the same. "No." He shrugged. "They send letters, though. I think they're trying to give me some space, but they've made sure to tell me they love me and are praying for me."

She gently put the photo back in the right spot. "How about for Christmas? Will you at least go home and see them then?" Ruby had been encouraging him to go back to River Bend for a visit, but he wasn't ready to do it.

"I've been thinking a lot about that lately, and I don't think going home is the right thing to do. But I don't know that I want to stay here either. I love my aunt and uncle dearly, but sometimes I feel like they try too hard to make me feel better about Charlie and all." He shrugged. "There's a fellow from my regiment who told me I could visit him over the holidays. He was the one who helped carry me out when I was wounded, even though he was injured too. He sent a telegram not too long ago inviting me for a visit. I guess some of his family members are still serving, so he's afraid it might be too quiet this year."

Ruby nodded. "I know what he means. I'm looking forward to going home, but with Raymond and Jack still overseas, it just won't be the same." She frowned. "And my cousin Lucille's husband, Donald, has practically been a member of the family since we were kids. He's overseas too. I'm looking forward to seeing my parents, but sometimes I think we should just skip Christmas this year. I'm not sure how festive it can possibly be."

"You never know," he said softly. "Maybe the season will have a little magic in it, despite the turmoil our country is in."

She smiled. "I'm impressed by your optimism. And I hope you're right."

"You ready to go?"

She nodded. "I'm ready."

Cliff opened the door, and they stepped out into the backyard. He pointed toward a yellowed bath towel. "See that? There's Old Blue's new bed."

Ruby giggled. "He just wanted to be comfortable."

"I suppose so." Cliff reached over and took her hand again. When they were leaving the ballgame, he'd been prepared to claim he was holding her hand because he didn't want them to get separated. But now he'd have to own up to just wanting to hold her hand. Her skin was so soft.

"You didn't want to go hunting today?" she asked after a moment's silence.

Cliff groaned. "Not even a little bit. Besides, I was afraid that if I mentioned it, you'd want to have some kind of target shooting competition."

She burst out laughing. "You might know me a little too well."

Cliff led her to the same log they'd sat on all those weeks ago. "I do know you well. And you know me well too. Better than anyone else does."

She widened her eyes. "Really?"

"Ruby, I have a confession to make." He stared into her green eyes. "You know that day I brought you out here to go rabbit hunting?"

"Yes." She watched him expectantly.

He cleared his throat. "It wasn't even rabbit season. I was just looking for an excuse to get you away from work and have some time alone with you."

A smiled played on her lips. "Are you serious?"

"That's one of the reasons I wasn't really concerned with you having a weapon or a bullet. I knew we probably wouldn't see any rabbits. A squirrel maybe, but no rabbits." He grinned. "I thought Uncle Fred was going to give me away when I heard him ask you if you were sure you wanted to go, but he didn't. He probably saw right through my little plan."

"And then I had to go and make it into a competition."

He nodded. "Yes. But honestly, that competitive spirit is kind of attractive on you."

"Kind of?" She raised an eyebrow.

He chuckled. "You aren't fishing for a compliment, are you? Because I could definitely give you one."

"I'm listening." She grinned.

He cocked his head. "You already know I think you're beautiful. I mean, Betty Grable and Rita Hayworth don't hold a candle to you."

"Oh, Cliff. Don't be silly." Despite her words, the faintest hint of a blush on her cheeks told him she was pleased.

"I'm not. I'm being serious. But the more I've gotten to know you, the more I see that you're far more than just a pretty face. You're kindhearted and loyal. I see the way the other girls look up to you, and the way you're always friendly to everyone no matter who they are." He squeezed her hand. "I just want you to know that you're really special."

"Thank you," she whispered.

"When I met you, I was struggling a lot with my faith. I wasn't sure

I'd ever step foot in a church building again or talk regularly to a God who had allowed Charlie to die and me to live." He sighed. "But you've helped me find my way back. You make me want to be a better man."

Ruby's eyes shone like emeralds. "That is the kindest, sweetest thing anyone has ever said to me."

Cliff stood and pulled her up from the log, and then he enveloped her in a tight embrace. "I just want you to know what I think of you," he murmured.

She pulled pack to look him in the eye. "You are already a good man. I had nothing to do with it. It's obvious to everyone who meets you."

He held a finger up to her lips. "Shh. No more talking." He bent down and gently pressed his lips to hers, tentatively at first. As Ruby slid her arms around his neck and pulled him closer, the kiss deepened, and Cliff wished the moment could last forever.

Chapter Eleven

. . . .

October 17, 1943

Dear Lucille,

It was wonderful to get your letter last week, and I was so excited to find a picture of Annie Sue enclosed. I stuck it in the corner of my dresser mirror so I can see her sweet face every day. She sure is growing fast.

And I'm thrilled that you finally got another letter from Donald. I can only imagine the peace of mind it gives you to know for sure that he's okay.

You asked how things were going here. Well, work is going well. My shift is still accident-free, and I'm so thankful for that. And I've made some great friends here.

I still see Cliff regularly. We went to a Razorback football game a couple of weeks ago, and it was such fun to see the crowd and the team.

I'm going to tell you something in confidence now, so please tear this letter up once you've read it. After the game, we went for a walk in the woods. While we were there, he kissed me. Really kissed me.

Now you know I don't go around kissing boys for sport, so I don't have a lot to compare it to, but I think it was pretty good. In fact, it might be the most wonderful moment of my life. He tasted like peppermint, and for a few minutes, I was afraid I was going to faint I was so lightheaded.

When it was over, he just grinned, and we went back to his aunt's house and drank Coca-Colas like nothing had happened.

Oh, Lucille, I don't know what to do now. He hasn't come out and said he wants me to be his girl. He's never said he loves me, and we don't have any plans to see each other after I go back to school. And he hasn't made a move to kiss me again, not even the other night at the drive-in.

A few weeks ago I told him about Joseph, and I said I didn't want to risk my heart again. He seemed okay with it. So why would he kiss me? Sometimes I wish I knew what he was thinking. My job came with a handbook, and I'm beginning to think Cliff should've come with a handbook too!

Oh well. I supposed we'll work it out. My time here is getting shorter, and I guess it would be silly to get any more involved with someone when I know there's no future. Maybe he isn't kissing me because saying good-bye is already going to be hard enough.

I'll be glad to see you at Christmas—only a couple of months to go! It will be nice to see everyone, but I'll be sad when my time here comes to an end.

Much love,

Ruby Jean

* * * * *

Ruby sat in the dorm lobby, wondering why Cliff was running late. It wasn't like him. She pulled Mama's latest letter out of her purse and scanned over it to make sure she hadn't missed any news from home. It had been a while since they'd heard from Raymond, but sometimes no news was good news. Papa had written a note on the letter that said he was glad Ruby had made it to a football game. Lucille must have shared the news of the game with them, because Ruby didn't recall putting that in the last letter she'd sent her folks. She wondered what else Lucille had shared. Surely she hadn't told Mama about Ruby and Cliff's kiss.

"Everything okay?" Lola asked, coming through the door. "Why are you sitting here all alone?"

Ruby grinned. "I'm waiting for Cliff." She held up the crumpled letter. "And re-reading the letter I got from home today."

Lola plopped down beside her. "Anything interesting?" She grinned. "I hope they're telling you not to bother going back to school and they think you should just stay here."

"Not quite." Ruby was really going to miss Lola once she was back at school. "You'll have to come visit me some weekend. It's an easy bus ride. You can stay with me in the dorm."

Lola raised her eyebrows. "Or I can get a ride with Cliff. I'm sure he'll be making the drive as often as possible."

Ruby didn't answer. She still felt confused by Cliff's nonchalance about their kiss. On the one hand, it made things much easier for her. But on the other, she had to wonder if he hadn't liked kissing her. Or maybe he kissed lots of girls, and their kiss didn't mean anything special to him. "I'm not sure that we'll keep seeing each other after Christmas."

Lola rolled her eyes. "If you say so." She grinned broadly. "Guess what? Harold says he has a big surprise for me. We're having a special date on Friday night. Do you mind if I borrow your green dress again? Harold just loved it."

"Of course."

"Well, well. Don't you two make a pretty picture?" Cliff walked over to where they sat.

Ruby grinned. "You snuck up on me."

"It's from all that time I spend in the woods. I've learned to stay quiet. Stealth is my middle name." He chuckled.

Lola said her good-byes and hurried back to the dorm room.

"Sorry I was late," Cliff said once they were alone. "I hurried as fast as I could. We were tied up most of the day with an electrical problem over on one of the other detonator lines." He motioned toward the door. "You ready to go?"

She followed him out the dorm and to the car. "Lola told me Harold has something special planned for Friday," she said once they'd pulled away from the dorm. "Do you know anything about it?"

He looked over at her and grinned. "Can you keep a secret?"

She widened her eyes. "Of course. Do tell."

"Harold has tickets for them to go see a game in Fayetteville next weekend. He's never said for sure, but I suspect he'll be talking to her daddy while they're there and asking for her hand in marriage."

Ruby let out a breath. "Oh my. Really? Doesn't that seem awfully fast?"

Cliff laughed. "I thought girls were supposed to be all caught up in romance and weddings. Is that a hint of cynicism I hear?" He pulled the car into the parking lot at the diner.

"I don't think I'm your typical girl when it comes to stuff like that."

Cliff grinned at her, his blue eyes dancing. "Typical is definitely not a word I'd use to describe you." He got out of the car and came around to open her door.

She giggled. "Well, thanks. But I'm being serious." She took the hand he offered and let him help her out of the car.

Once they'd ordered and were seated, Cliff looked at her from across the table. "What do you mean when you say you aren't typical when it comes to stuff like that?"

Ruby took a sip of Coca-Cola. "You know how some girls are. They think their life doesn't start until they get married." She shrugged. "I'm not that way."

"No, you aren't. It's easy to see that you've gone out and grabbed the kind of life you want. I think it's really neat. You'll have a college degree soon, and you're getting great work experience here." Cliff grinned. "Those are things to be proud of."

She returned his smile. "Most people think I'm crazy, you know. Even Hazel."

"For wanting to have a little independence and your own job?" Cliff shook his head. "I can't believe Hazel would think that was crazy. Didn't she encourage you to apply at the AOP in the first place?"

Ruby frowned. "I mean, they think it's crazy that I never want to get married or have a family." She took a sip of her drink and watched the color drain from his face. Was he ill?

"Cliff, are you okay?" She peered at his ashen face, wondering what in the world was wrong.

* * * * *

Cliff didn't quite know what to say. And words usually came pretty easily to him. "Never?" He forced the word out of his mouth.

Ruby nodded. "I told you that before, remember?"

He stared at the beautiful girl across the table and wondered if this was some kind of practical joke. Maybe Harold was behind it. He glanced around, but Harold didn't pop out from behind the next table. "But I thought you just weren't ready for it *now*. I didn't know you *never* wanted to get married. Why ever not? Is it—is it because of Joseph?"

Ruby sighed. "It's true that I don't ever want to feel hurt like that again. But it's more than that. Have I told you before about what it was like for me growing up?"

"Just that you grew up on a farm and have three brothers. And you played basketball when you were in high school."

"We went through some pretty tough times, depending on the crops and all. Some years were better than others. Life on a farm can be hard. I watched my mama work as hard as any man." She sighed. "And I'm not afraid of hard work. That's not what I'm saying at all.

I don't mind work. I just…I saw how hard it can be to be the wife of a farmer and work hard on the farm while raising kids."

"So because of that, you don't *ever* want to get married?" How could she write off something like that just because of a limited experience? Ruby was usually open-minded, but he could see she had her mind made up about this.

"Cliff, do you know how close I came to being a widow? That terrifies me now. And that's the reality for so many women these days. I think I've told you about my cousin Lucille. She's three months older than I am. She got married right out of high school and has a baby now. I know I should look at her life and be envious, but I'm not. Not even a little bit." Ruby ducked her head. "It sounds so shameful and selfish when I say it out loud, doesn't it? I mean, she's married to a wonderful man who adores her and whom she adores. But all I can think is that she's never going to get off of that farm. She'll never live anywhere else. She'll just stay right there like her mama did and like my mama did." She sighed. "And her husband, Donald, was drafted last year. What if he doesn't make it back? What if she ends up having to run a farm and raise a baby all by herself? Never able to leave the farm, even if she wanted to."

"And you want something more," he said softly. "You don't want to end up stuck somewhere following someone else's dream."

Ruby managed a small smile. "Since the country went to war, there've been new opportunities for women. Just like me becoming the line inspector at the AOP. That never would've happened a few years ago. Even back when I met Joseph, that wasn't really an option. But now…there are doors open that didn't used to be. And I want to make sure I take advantage of the opportunities that come my way. I don't want to settle down right away and miss the chance to have an adventure and see things I've never seen before."

Cliff had never given much thought to stuff like that. He had to admit that some of what she said made sense—some, but not all. "No one says you have to marry a farmer." He took a sip of his Coca-Cola. "You might end up marrying someone who thinks like you do and who wants to have adventures too." He had himself in mind but didn't want to point it out. He was pretty sure he'd made his feelings for her clear. He might not have spelled them out, but surely she knew.

Ruby sighed. "I still say life would be much less complicated if I stayed on my own."

He flinched. Life might be less complicated alone, but it sure wouldn't be as much fun. He'd just have to show Ruby how nice it could be to have someone around. He'd change her mind. Cliff forced a cheerful expression. "Looks like our order is ready." He hurried toward the counter, already formulating his plan.

Chapter Twelve

. . . .

November 20, 1943

Dear ~~R.J.~~ Ruby Jean,

I guess you can see that I messed up and accidentally called you R.J. Sorry about that, but I don't want to waste paper and start over. I realize that since you're a grown-up now, we don't use your nickname anymore. It's been on my mind lately because Cousin Owen is staying with your parents for a few months to help out on the farm, and that's what he always calls you. I've heard your mama correct him a couple of times, and she made him promise that when you're home for Christmas, he'll call you Ruby. Old habits are hard to break, though. Wade still calls me Lucy sometimes—though of course, I think he only does it to get a rise out of me! You know how your brother is.

Speaking of your mama…she's been asking me an awful lot of questions about Cliff. She's sure that you love him and is afraid you're too stubborn to admit it! I told her that I wasn't sure about that and reminded her that you are adamant that your plans do not include marriage and babies.

That did not make her happy, and she said she thinks that is just a phase. Now, normally I would not get involved here, but I love you and don't want you to come home to any surprises. Besides, I agree with your mama on this one. She said that in one of your letters you mentioned something about moving off to Washington, DC, and working there after college, and I'll tell you, this has really got both of your parents worried. Your papa was about ready to drive to Jacksonville himself to pick you up, but thank goodness your mama always knows just how to calm him down.

Ruby, I hope you know what you're doing. I don't worry about you as much as they do, because I know you're just enjoying your life, and you always have been just a little bit stubborn. (It runs in our family—thank goodness I didn't get any of it. Ha!)

But this Cliff Hamilton that I've been hearing about all of these months sounds like a very good man. So if you're going to break his heart anyway, you should go ahead and do it. If you drag things out and keep him hanging on right up until Christmas, you're going to regret it, and it will ruin your holidays. And his. Mark these words from your older (though only by three months) and wiser (I like to think so anyway) cousin.

Love,
Lucille

* * * * *

"It's so wonderful to see you!" Ruby exclaimed. She pulled Hazel into a tight hug. "You look beautiful. Pine Bluff must really suit you." She grinned. "Or maybe it's just marriage."

Hazel grinned. "Thank you. Seems that something here agrees with you too." She raised her eyebrows. "I think I might know what that is." She leaned close to Ruby. "And I can't wait to hear all about it."

Ruby blushed. Of course Hazel would want details about her and Cliff. And her friend knew her well enough to know if she was leaving something out...so the story of their kiss would probably come out. "There isn't really much to talk about."

"Come on, Ruby." Hazel steered her into her old bedroom. A blue-and-white quilt was spread over the bed. Hazel sat down on the edge. "Are you and Cliff more than friends yet? Have you made it official?"

Ruby frowned. "It isn't like that. I told you he was my best friend. That's really all I know."

"Troy is my best friend." Hazel cocked her head. "In fact, I'd think that would be a quality you were looking for."

Ruby paced the small room. "That's just it. I'm not looking for anything. You know that."

"Do you mean to tell me that you don't have feelings for him? Because if you tell me that, I'll leave you alone about it."

Ruby wrinkled her nose. "I wouldn't exactly say that I don't have *any* feelings for him. But I'm choosing to ignore those, and I'm getting ready to go back and finish school. Then, who knows where I'll end up." She shrugged. "I may decide to move off to a big city. So there's no point in my getting involved with someone when I don't know what the future holds."

Hazel put her face in her hands and groaned. "Ruby McFadden, you are impossible. None of us knows what the future holds. We just pray about it and trust that we'll find the right path."

Ruby flounced down on the bed next to Hazel. "Well, maybe that's what I'm doing. I'm just not sure about things right now. Maybe everything will become clearer over the next month. My last day at the AOP is just a few days before Christmas, and then I'm going home until the spring semester starts."

Hazel sighed. "I'm only looking out for you, you know."

"I appreciate it, but I'm fine. I'll be fine." Even to her own ears, the proclamation didn't sound convincing.

"Will you? Are you sure about that, Ruby?"

Ruby sighed. "Can I tell you something if you promise not to tell me I'm silly?"

"Of course."

"I do love the idea of being independent and of living my own life. But sometimes I wonder if it's just because I'm scared." She traced the pattern of the quilt with her finger. "As long as it's just me, I'm in control. But the minute I let my life get tangled with someone else… anything could happen. There are no guarantees."

"But Ruby, you're *not* in control. And it doesn't matter if you're on your own in a big city or married with ten kids way out in the country. God is in control. Are you forgetting that?"

Ruby's own words to Cliff came back to her, the words she'd used after he told her how Charlie died. She'd told Cliff he had to trust that God had a plan. That God was bigger than all the bad stuff. Bigger than the wars and the sadness. She'd preached it to him, but she sure didn't practice it in her own life. "I guess I need to be reminded of that sometimes," she said softly. "But I'm still not sure the risk associated with love is worth it."

"It is," Hazel said. "Because without that, you're not left with much else." She smiled. "You just think about it for a few days, okay? I'm not saying Cliff is the fellow for you—although I do think there's something special between y'all. But I'm saying maybe you need to reconsider what's really important."

"Maybe so." Ruby could at least concede that much. She smiled to herself, realizing she must not be as stubborn as she used to be. Not too long ago she would've clung to her opinion no matter what.

Hazel stood up. "Daddy has been telling me about how good the molasses cookies are with the pecans added to them. How about you go show me how it's done?"

"I'd be glad to." Ruby linked arms with her friend and headed toward the kitchen. She caught sight of Cliff in the living room, playing cards with Troy. Just knowing he was near warmed her heart.

And she knew that on this Thanksgiving, he was one of the things she was most thankful for.

* * * * *

"Everything looks so delicious," Cliff said once they were all gathered around the table. "This is definitely a special Thanksgiving." Made even more special by the girl next to him.

Aunt Ida beamed. "I have to thank Hazel and Ruby for their contributions. We are in for a feast."

Cliff cast a glance in Ruby's direction. She looked beautiful in a rose-colored sweater and black skirt. The guys at the AOP had often joked that she looked like a pinup, but there was so much more to her than physical beauty. They had no idea.

"We're blessed beyond measure to be gathered around this table today," Uncle Fred said from his spot at the head of the table. "We've all suffered losses over the past few years."

Cliff felt a pang of remorse at the thought of his parents gathered around their table without either of their sons present.

"Even so, we have much to be thankful for," Uncle Fred continued. Then he bowed his head and offered thanks to God for the food and for the blessing of friends and family.

Cliff inhaled the sweet aroma of the food. Even though times were tough, Aunt Ida had managed to put together quite a spread. "This dressing looks delicious." He heaped a serving on his plate.

"The only available turkey was so small," Aunt Ida said. "So there's chicken and rabbit for those of you who'd rather have that."

"It all looks wonderful," Troy said, and then he winked at his wife. "I can see where Hazel gets her cooking skills."

Hazel beamed. "Thanks. And just wait till y'all try the dessert. Ruby outdid herself this year."

Cliff leaned close to Ruby. "What did you make?" he asked.

She giggled. "I made a batch of molasses cookies. Mama sent me some more sorghum and pecans last week." She plucked a deviled egg from the platter and passed it to him. "And I also made a pumpkin pie."

Cliff's mouth watered. He thought he'd detected the aroma of cinnamon and nutmeg earlier. "I can't wait."

She smiled and motioned toward his plate heaping with turkey and dressing. "I just hope you have room left over after you eat that. I'd hate for you to miss out."

"Don't you worry." Cliff patted his stomach. "I'll always have room for one of your desserts." He took a bite of dressing. It tasted just like his mom used to make. "This is very good."

"It's your mother's recipe," Aunt Ida explained. "She sent it last week. Said it was your very favorite."

Cliff took a sip of sweet tea and tried to wash down his guilt. The last time he'd had his mom's dressing, it had been the Thanksgiving before he and Charlie left for the war. They'd joked and laughed their way through the meal, then had gone outside and tossed the football around. He missed Charlie every day, but more and more lately, he'd been missing his parents and wondering how a visit to River Bend might go.

He quickly pushed the thought aside and turned his attention to Ruby. "I'm glad you're here," he said softly. With the conversations going on around them, no one else heard.

She gave him a tiny smile. "So am I."

* * * * *

"So what exactly do you think I should do?" Cliff asked Hazel after he'd taken Ruby back to the dorm later that night. "I can't force her to admit she has feelings for me." He grinned. "Even though I'm pretty sure she does."

Hazel nodded. "Me too. She's a tough one. Stubborn as the day is long. But honestly, do you want to know what I think?"

"You've known her longer than I have. So yes, please share."

"I think she's scared of her feelings. And the sooner you can get her to own up to that, the sooner she'll leave this silly notion of never marrying behind."

Cliff rubbed his jaw. "Scared? But why?"

"Losing Joseph really hurt her. It taught her that there are no guarantees in this life. And I think after his death, there was a fair amount of guilt—like she'd be doing something wrong if she moved on. Plus she saw how much having a broken heart hurt." Hazel filled him in on her earlier conversation with Ruby. "So I think as long as she remains on her own, she feels like she's in control. Let's just say that for someone who appears to be so adventurous, she's terrified of taking a risk."

Everything Hazel said made sense. The problem was, Cliff had no idea how to fix it. "So what should I do?" He'd tried to come up with a plan but hadn't had much luck so far. Things with Ruby had been the same as always.

"I think you need to make a grand gesture of some sort. Make sure she knows exactly how you feel." Hazel shrugged. "Just any old declaration isn't going to be enough for Ruby. She'd never admit to it, but she's a closet romantic. She reads *Gone with the Wind* every year and cries over the tragic ending. I asked her why she keeps reading a book that she knows is going to make her cry, and she just smiled and said that every time she hopes Scarlett and Rhett will realize how much they love each other." She shook her head. "So think of something that will really sweep her off her feet."

Cliff nodded. He could definitely do that. "I think I know just what to do." Ruby had mentioned more than once how much she loved Christmas. And he'd do everything in his power to make sure this was the best Christmas ever.

Chapter Thirteen

....

Ruby smiled as she read Mama's latest letter from home. Wade had scrawled a note at the bottom claiming to have emptied her room of books and clothes so Cousin Owen would have a place to stay. She refolded the letter and slipped it inside her Bible.

She knew better than that. Mama had already told her that Owen was staying in Jack's room. Wade simply couldn't resist picking on her, even across the miles.

The door burst open and Lola rushed inside. "You're never going to believe it." She gasped for a breath. "I had to run up here right away and tell you the news."

Ruby grinned at her friend's excitement. "What happened?"

"Harold asked me to be his wife!" She clapped her hands and jumped up and down. "Can you believe it?" She sank onto her bed. "I'm the luckiest girl in the world."

Ruby had been wondering if Cliff's guess was correct. It seemed it was. "Oh, Lola! I'm so happy for you. Tell me all the details."

"That weekend we went to Fayetteville for the football game was the weekend Harold asked my daddy for his permission. That stinker waited a month to ask *me*, though." She giggled. "We went to his grandparents' house for dinner with his entire family tonight. I guess he wanted to wait until everyone had met me before he popped the question." She beamed. "After we ate dinner, we went for a drive and he stopped the car at a park. We went for a walk and Harold led me over to a bench to sit down for a minute. The next thing I knew, he was on one knee, asking me to do him the honor of being his wife."

"That's so sweet." Ruby grinned at Lola's obvious happiness. "Cliff always says y'all are a perfect match."

Seeing Lola's excitement about a future with Harold gave Ruby an uneasy feeling. Even though she knew the future was uncertain, she couldn't help but wonder how it would feel to plan a life with someone. She quickly pushed the thought away. No way was she jealous of Lola.

"Oh. Cliff." Lola sat upright. "I almost forgot." She smiled. "Sorry, I guess I'm just too excited. Cliff is downstairs. I'm supposed to tell you that he wants to see you."

"Downstairs? We didn't have plans."

"Guess you do now," Lola said.

Ruby hurried to make herself presentable. She'd planned to stay in tonight and read and listen to music. But she'd rather spend time with Cliff. "See you later." She opened the door and glanced back at Lola. Her friend's dreamy expression made her smile. "And when I get back, I want to hear all about your plans for the wedding." Ruby grinned. "I know you probably have some ideas."

Lola giggled. "I sure do."

Ruby hurried down the stairs, anxious to see what Cliff wanted. It wasn't like him to just show up out of the blue.

Cliff sat in the lobby talking to a couple of girls who lived down the hall from Ruby. The petite blond girl named Irene threw back her head and laughed at something Cliff said.

Ruby had never struggled with jealousy before. But seeing those girls fawning over Cliff brought out a fierce desire to make sure they knew she was the one going out with him. She stopped herself before she sauntered over and took his arm. Lucille's last letter had warned her not to lead him on if she didn't intend for the relationship to go anywhere.

Still. The sight of him with other girls was enough to make her think. This is how it would be once she was back at school. He'd be here, surrounded by pretty, flirtatious girls clamoring for dates and dance partners. The memory of her was likely to fade fast when faced with that.

Her thoughts were interrupted by the sound of Irene laughing as if Cliff was the funniest man alive.

Leading on or not, enough was enough. Ruby marched over to where Cliff sat like he was holding court. "Lola said you were here to see me?" she asked sweetly. She reached out and touched his arm. "So here I am."

"We'd better run," Irene said. "Nice to see you again, Cliff." She and the redhead with her turned and walked away.

"Nice girls." Ruby watched Cliff's expression to see if she could tell how well he knew them. "Where'd you meet?"

"Irene and Dorothy are powder carriers in the detonator three building. I had to do some work over there last week and met them then." He raised his eyebrows. "Why? Jealous?"

"No," she mumbled. "Just wondering."

Cliff chuckled. "Sure you were."

"Did I forget that we were supposed to do something tonight?"

He shook his head. "No. But I have a little surprise for you and I couldn't wait to give it to you."

"You do? Oh, I love surprises." She clapped her hands. "What is it? Where is it?"

Cliff raised his brows. "Patience, my dear." He took her hand. "Now let's go."

She let him lead her out to the car. "Where are we going?"

"Nowhere. The surprise is in my car." He turned to her. "Wait here." He grinned. "And close your eyes."

She put her hands on her hips. "Close my eyes? What will people think if they walk past me and I'm standing out here on the sidewalk with my eyes closed?"

He laughed. "Do you want your surprise or not?"

She crossed her arms. "Fine." Ruby closed her eyes. "There. Happy?" she asked. She felt totally silly but couldn't keep from smiling.

"Very happy," he said from somewhere in the distance.

* * * * *

Cliff walked toward her carrying the surprise. He'd covered it with a blanket in case she tried to peek while he got it out of the car.

Ever since Hazel had suggested a grand gesture, he'd been considering how he could show Ruby how he felt. All these months, he'd thought they might be headed to forever until that night at the diner when she'd told him she had no plans to settle down.

Ever.

With anyone.

Now Cliff might not be an expert on the fairer sex, but he was pretty sure a girl who was falling for a guy didn't go and tell him that she never wanted to have a serious relationship. Hopefully Hazel was right and that wasn't the truth, and Ruby was just fearful of having her heart broken. So he wanted to do all he could to help her get over her fears.

Ruby stood by herself on the sidewalk with her arms crossed and her eyes closed. She looked so cute he had to fight the urge to walk right up and kiss her. But the last time he'd kissed her, it had been so intoxicating that he'd promised himself he wouldn't do it again until they'd talked about their feelings. He was too drawn to her, too attracted to her to keep up the friendly relationship she seemed to be comfortable with. After that kiss, his fingers itched to touch her and his lips ached to cover hers. And Cliff wanted to make sure Ruby knew that his interest in her was far more than just physical.

"Okay," he said. "Open your eyes."

Her green eyes popped open, and she grinned. "What's under the blanket?"

"Why don't you take it off and see?"

She whipped the blanket off and squealed. "You got me my very own Christmas tree?" The little cedar tree would be perfect for her dorm room.

"I found it out in the woods and knew it was perfect." He lifted it up. "I made a little stand so it can go on your dresser."

She beamed. "I love it! It's perfect."

Cliff hoped this would be the first step in making Ruby his girl, hopefully for good. Hazel had said to show Ruby how he felt—and surely this would do the trick. "I'm glad you like it."

"I'll have to find some tinsel and some lights to put on it."

Cliff held up a box. "Actually, I have one more surprise."

She snatched the box from his hands and opened it up. "Lights!" she exclaimed. She looked at him, her green eyes filled with wonder. "But these aren't normal lights." She pulled them gently from the box. "How did you do this? I've never seen Christmas lights that had red, white, and blue bulbs like this."

Cliff didn't embarrass easily, but his gesture was so over-the-top, he felt that "I love you, Ruby" might as well be written on his forehead for all to see. "I had to put each light on the strand. I found some old bulbs that were colored and realized that you needed special lights for your special tree." He grinned. "So that's what you've got."

Ruby walked over and grabbed him with a force that surprised him. She hugged him tightly and kissed his cheek. "Thank you," she murmured.

Cliff pulled her tightly against him, and she rested her head against his chest. He kissed her lightly on the forehead before he let her go. "I'm glad you like your surprise."

"I do. I love it." She smiled. "It's the best surprise anyone has ever given me."

Cliff felt certain that the best surprise he'd ever been given was that he'd had to give a girl a ride from Searcy to Jacksonville, and she'd turned out to be Ruby.

But the more he learned, the more he wondered if that wasn't a surprise at all, but a divine plan finally coming together.

Chapter Fourteen

....

December 10, 1943

Dear Lucille,

Can you believe I'll be there in two weeks' time? I can't wait to see everyone, but I'm getting really sad about leaving here. And not just because of Cliff, although he's the biggest part. The girls on my shift are so much fun. I've promised them a night of bowling before I leave. And there's a big Christmas party with a dance and everything on the day before I leave. I'm not a good dancer, but I don't want to pass up the chance to waltz with Cliff just once.

How was your Thanksgiving? Mama's letter sounded like she was planning a modest affair. She promised that Christmas would be more festive, but I wrote her back to say it was okay to just pretend like it was a normal day. With Raymond and Jack off at war and all, I'm not sure we should do much celebrating. Will our lives ever go back to normal again?

We had a wonderful Thanksgiving at Hazel's parents' house. Hazel and Troy came in, and guess what! She's going to have a baby. She waited until they were about to leave to spill the beans because she didn't want to be fussed over too much.

Cliff found me a little cedar Christmas tree in the woods, and he brought it to me as a surprise tonight. It's just perfect. Can you believe he'd also strung a set of red, white, and blue lights himself, because he knew I'd want to have a patriotic tree? He said my tree needed to be special.

Well, Lucille, I could hardly contain myself. I hugged him so tightly I think he almost lost his breath, and he kissed me on the forehead. *The forehead.* It was awfully nice of him to bring me the tree, but I'm starting to think maybe he really does just think of me as a friend.

I know what you said in your last letter about my stringing him along if I knew we didn't have a future. And you're right. The last thing in the world I'd ever want to do is hurt Cliff. But since he still hasn't mentioned wanting to see me again after I leave, maybe I don't have to worry about it. Lola thinks I should just flat out ask him what's going on, but I think that sounds like a terrible plan. I don't want to have to ask him; I want him to volunteer the information.

I had a long talk with Hazel at Thanksgiving that made me think about things. You'll be shocked to hear this (ha!) but I'm afraid I've been stubborn. I've not been trusting God the way I should. I told Cliff once that God was bigger than war or sadness. Well, maybe He's bigger than my fears too.

I know you'll be happy to hear this next part, but lately I've been wondering if I should reconsider my position on marriage. Hazel is happier than I've ever seen her. My roommate Lola just got engaged, and she's over the moon. And you and Donald have been perfect for each other since you were kids. Maybe there is hope for me yet. (Please don't tell Mama any of this, because I still have some thinking to do.)

Well, I hope this letter finds everyone there happy, healthy, and full of thanks.

All my love,
Ruby Jean

* * * * *

Ruby shivered and pulled her wool coat tightly around her. "It sure is getting colder." She grinned up at Cliff. "Do you think it might actually snow?"

He shook his head. "I don't think so, but it sure would be nice." He'd always loved how fresh the snow made everything. And the way it cast a silence over the outdoors, like all of God's creatures were standing still and enjoying the beauty. But it rarely snowed in Arkansas.

They walked along the sidewalk in downtown Jacksonville, pausing every now and then to look in a shop window and admire the Christmas lights and displays.

"Are you frozen yet, or should we keep walking?" Cliff asked.

She stepped closer to him. "I'm a little cold, but I want to keep walking."

"We'll go to Aunt Ida's in a bit and have some hot chocolate by the fire." He grinned. "Doesn't that sound like a swell idea?"

"It sure does." She clutched his arm. "Oh, look!" she exclaimed. "They have a Christmas tree in the window." She pulled him toward the window. "It's nice, but not as pretty as my tree." She grinned up at Cliff.

Cliff smiled. "I'm glad you're still enjoying it."

"Oh, I am. Lola is too. And I think all the girls in the dorm have come by to see the lovely lights." She nudged him with her shoulder "You're quite famous in the women's dorm."

"Well, I don't like to brag." Cliff hooked his thumbs through imaginary suspenders. "But the ladies do love me."

She burst out laughing. "Oh, look at that ornament." Ruby pointed to a round, red ball with a snow scene depicted on the front. "Isn't it lovely?"

He looked at her profile, her slightly upturned nose, long lashes, and full lips. The chilly afternoon had turned her creamy cheeks pink. "It sure is."

"It reminds me of a Christmas a long time ago. I think I was five." Ruby continued to stare at the ornament. "It was the only Christmas I can ever remember it snowing. Mama and Papa came outside and played with us kids. We had so much fun. That snow, and the time we all spent playing together in it, was better than any gift that year. I remember seeing Papa sneak up behind Mama with a little bit of snow in his hand and sprinkle it over her head. She laughed harder than I've ever heard her laugh before. Me and my brothers watched them chase each other around the yard like teenagers." She smiled at the memory. "It was perfect."

Cliff grinned. He'd had success with the tree and the special lights. But now he knew exactly how he was finally going to tell Ruby how he felt once and for all. And with a little luck and a lot of prayer, hopefully she would return those feelings.

* * * * *

December 14, 1943

Dear Mom and Pop,

I know I haven't responded to many correspondences over the past several months, and I should apologize. Actually, I should apologize for a lot more than that.

Looking back, I see that I probably didn't make things very easy on the two of you when I was recovering at your house. I say it that way because for the first time in my life, being at your house didn't feel like home to me. Seeing Charlie's empty room with his old pinup posters on the wall and his baseball glove in the corner was just too much. And I knew that whenever you walked past that room, all you were thinking was how I'd failed him. And failed the two of you.

I joined the army because it was the right thing to do for the country. But I also joined because I wanted to protect Charlie. And for the first time in my life, I failed miserably at something.

And now we all have to suffer the consequences.

These past months, I've returned to church, and in doing so, I've found a peace that I can't explain. I know in my heart that Charlie is in a better place. He's gone on to a reward that is so wonderful, we can't even imagine.

Even so, I know the two of you will never be able to look at me the same way. And I can hardly blame you for that.

I've decided to go visit a buddy over the holidays. He was in our regiment and I know he's had his share of grief too. He's invited me to have Christmas with his family, and I accepted. I'll be coming back to the AOP the week after Christmas and returning to work.

I love you both, and not a day goes by that I don't long for the past, when Charlie and I were home with you and our biggest worry was which lake we'd choose for fishing.

Your son,

Cliff

Chapter Fifteen

....

This had been one of those days when the extra pay for being the line inspector wasn't nearly enough. Mae Adams had come in with a cold so bad she could barely get anything done for all of the coughing and sneezing. And then at the end of the day, two of the girls had gotten into a big argument over a borrowed dress that was returned with a rip. Ruby had been nurse, counselor, and inspector all at once.

She walked into her room, looking forward to relaxing for a little while before she had dinner with Cliff.

The cedar tree sat on the nightstand next to Ruby's bed. The red, white, and blue lights were lit up even though she'd turned them off when she left that morning. A tiny box, wrapped in silver paper, sat beneath the tree. The tag on the box had her name on it, written in Cliff's handwriting. How had he managed this?

She picked up the box, smiling at his thoughtfulness. Had he meant for her to go ahead and open the gift? Or should she wait?

She grinned. Definitely open.

She gently tore the paper away and took the lid off the box. Sitting inside was the red ornament she'd admired in the store window.

Ruby carefully took it out of the box and held it in her hand for a long moment. She would cherish it always. Cliff had even looped a string through the top so she could hang it on her tree.

She placed it right in the middle of her little tree and smiled. Her bad day melted away. And making it even better, she'd get to see Cliff later and thank him properly.

And she couldn't help but hope that would include a good night kiss.

* * * * *

Cliff paced the floor in the lobby. It had been a risky move to have the gift waiting for her under the tree rather than giving it in person. But he'd weighed the options and decided the element of surprise was the best way to go. He could just imagine her walking into her room after a long day and seeing the lights of the tree and the little silver box waiting underneath it.

And now he waited.

And worried.

He'd been trying since June to get close to her. And he'd thought they were on the right track until she'd informed him that she never wanted to marry. By that point, he'd made his feelings pretty clear. The kiss alone should've been enough to tell her that he wanted to be more than just pen pals after she went back to college.

No. He wanted much more than that.

And he should have his answer tonight. He tried to steel himself to the possibility that this would be their last date.

But no matter how much he tried to imagine that, he couldn't fathom Ruby not being part of his life. Forever.

Ruby stepped into the lobby, looking beautiful in a red sweater and black skirt. She smiled broadly. "You'll never guess what someone left in my room today."

"Someone was in your room? That's a little scary, don't you think?" he teased.

She made her way to him. "Do you think I should report it to admin? One of the girls on my hall said she heard someone yell out 'man on the floor' and saw an electrician go in my room." She giggled. "That's a violation of my privacy, don't you think?"

He couldn't resist a quick hug. "I had the full support of your roommate, who had informed me there was a light out in the closet." He grinned. "So really I was just doing my job." He searched her face for evidence that the answer she'd give him tonight was the one he was hoping and praying for, but she wasn't giving anything away by her expression.

"It was so sweet and thoughtful of you," she said. "I thought nothing could top the tree and lights, but this did." She smiled up at him. "The ornament is so beautiful, and it will always remind me of that Christmas when I was a kid. I just love it. It's something I will cherish forever." She placed a hand on his arm. "It was such a wonderful surprise, Cliff. Thank you."

Cliff waited for more, but nothing came. He furrowed his brow. "So...what did you think? I mean when you opened it up? How did you feel?"

Ruby's eyes widened for a moment, as if in surprise. "Well, of course I felt like the luckiest girl in the world that you'd want to surprise me like that—and with such a lovely gift. At first I wasn't sure who'd done it. I thought it might've been Lola. But then I saw the little note in your beautiful penmanship." She raised an eyebrow. "You know, you have prettier script than I do. I'd never really thought about it until tonight."

Cliff fought to keep the disappointment off of his face. It just didn't make sense. He'd all but poured his heart out, and she was acting like it was no big deal. Unless it wasn't a big deal to her. Had he meant nothing to her after all? "That's it? Pretty script?"

Ruby drew her brows together. "What do you mean?"

Cliff sank onto the lobby chair and put his head in his hands. "Ruby, I think we need to talk."

* * * * *

Something seemed off with Cliff tonight. She'd come down the stairs expecting that he might kiss her again tonight, especially since he'd given her such a sweet Christmas gift. But he'd only given her a quick hug and now…something was wrong. Ruby couldn't quite put her finger on it. But their entire conversation felt forced. That wasn't normal. Usually the two of them could banter back and forth, and it was the easiest, most natural give-and-take she'd ever experienced.

As soon as he said the words, she had a bad feeling in the pit of her stomach. "Okay. Do you want to talk here?" She gestured around the lobby. It was empty now, but at any given moment someone could show up.

Cliff set his jaw. "Let's go outside for some privacy. I know it's chilly, but it won't take long."

Was that anger flashing in his eyes? She'd known him for all these months and never seen him angry. No matter what dumb prank Harold or the guys pulled or how many times the kid at the diner put lettuce on his hamburger even though he always asked him not to, he'd always just taken it in stride. Always just laughed it off.

But right now he looked as if he could spit nails.

She followed him out the door and into the cold December night. She could see the Christmas lights strung in the window of the rec hall. Normally she loved to see those festive lights, but tonight she felt sad for some reason. She had a bad feeling about whatever it was Cliff had on his mind.

She pulled her coat tighter around her, wishing Cliff would wrap her up in his arms and block out the cold. "Okay. What do you want to talk about?"

Cliff held her gaze for a long moment. For the first time, his blue eyes didn't have that mischievous twinkle in them that she'd grown to love. "Do you know how foolish you've made me look?"

She flinched as if she'd been slapped. "What?" Her heart began to pound against her chest, but not in the good way like it did when Cliff hugged her or when she thought about his kisses.

"I have followed you around like a puppy dog. Driving you to church so you wouldn't have to walk, fixing your radio even though the guys poked fun, taking you to the Razorback game with me. You've even become a normal fixture over at Aunt Ida's. We've had Thanksgiving together, countless dinners at the diner, long drives, church services, movies at the drive-in, and conversations about everything under the sun." He shook his head. "And through all of that, I've kept trying to get closer to you."

Ruby didn't know what to say. What had she done to upset him so? The sudden chill that overtook her body had nothing to do with the December night.

"When you first told me you didn't want to risk your heart again, I thought it was just because you needed time to get over Joseph. I was willing to let you heal, willing to be your friend and wait until you were ready for something more. But then that night at the diner when you said you *never* wanted to settle down with anyone, it was a real eye-opener. Because after all the time we've spent together, why would you say that to me if you weren't trying to send me a message? And you told Hazel the same thing. And Lola, because she told Harold, who told the whole department, that you are headed back to college and then you plan to go live a glamorous life somewhere in a city." He frowned. "The guys laughed at me for falling for a girl who saw this as a temporary stop on her way to someplace better. You even told me that you were glad you worked here so you'd have work experience." Cliff shook his head.

Ruby swallowed. She'd never meant to cause him this pain. Never. "You kissed me once, a long time ago. But never again. How was I supposed to know what was going on in your head? You spent time with me, but we never discussed the future."

Cliff snorted. "It's hard to want to discuss the future with someone who has made it perfectly clear to anyone who would listen that she never plans to settle down. You know what, Ruby? I do plan to settle down. I do hope to have a family someday." He sighed. "And I feel certain I can find a girl who'll want those same things."

Ruby felt the heat rise up her face. She stood up, fists clenched. "I'm sure you can. In fact, if you sit right there in the lobby of the women's dorm, I'm sure one will come along directly." She gestured toward the dorm. "I thought I made it clear that I wasn't interested in another relationship, and it didn't bother you. You were still my friend. Had I known you were so disappointed in our friendship, I'd have wondered why you wasted your time with me." She shook her head. "If it was so terrible for you to be spending time with me, and if it was such a burden on you to do all of those things, then why did you?"

Cliff frowned. "I thought you just needed time to heal, Ruby. I thought I could change your mind about marriage. And I figured that after you opened the gift tonight, you would know how I felt."

How was an ornament—not matter how lovely or thoughtful—supposed to tell her exactly how he felt? Why wouldn't he just tell her himself rather than leave her to guess? "Right." She felt the sting of tears in her eyes. "Well, I guess not."

He stood up, and the hurt in his eyes was unmistakable.

And she'd somehow put it there.

"So this is it." Ruby said it as a statement, not a question. "I guess we won't be going to the Christmas dance next week. But like you said, I'm sure it will be easy for you to find a replacement for me."

Cliff hesitated for a moment and then nodded. "Yep."

She watched him walk off and wasn't sure if she'd have the strength to make it up the stairs to her room. How had a night with so much promise turned out so badly? She wasn't sure what had just happened. But she was sure of one thing.

For someone who hadn't planned to risk her heart, hers sure did ache.

Chapter Sixteen

···················

"Are you sure you won't go with us?" Lola paced the length of their tiny room, looking beautiful and festive in a red and white dress. "It's the Christmas party."

"I'm not going to be a third wheel." Ruby frowned. The idea of tagging along with Lola and Harold didn't appeal to her, but knowing Cliff would be there with another girl absolutely turned her stomach. "Besides, I have to pack."

Lola stopped pacing and stood in front of the mirror fluffing her hair. "If I were you, I'd put on my best, most figure-flattering dress and go flirt with every able-bodied man there. Cliff will wish he'd never even laid eyes on that Irene Stillfield." She frowned. "I thought she had a boyfriend, but I guess I was wrong."

Ruby threw herself across her bed, and she didn't care how dramatic it looked. "It doesn't matter. If not Irene then it would be somebody else. You know, there've practically been girls lined up at the maintenance building ready and willing to accompany him to the party. And I all but gave him permission."

Lola turned away from her reflection and faced Ruby. "Well, you'll get no argument from me there. I know you're bound and determined to keep your independence, but couldn't you have waited until after tonight to tell him?"

"It doesn't matter anymore. Cliff thinks I was just leading him on all that time. He said I made him look foolish." She sighed. "I'm not that kind of girl."

Lola sat down next to Ruby and patted her leg. "Anyone who ever saw the two of you together never thought that. Including Cliff, if he were honest with himself. But you can't change what you want out of life, and if you know for sure what that is, then you have to go after it."

Ruby didn't want to mention that the more she thought of Cliff actually going out with another girl, maybe hugging her and laughing with her and kissing her—the less she knew about what she did or didn't want. "I just wish…well, I wish I could have it all. I wish I could keep seeing Cliff but also keep my independence."

Lola laughed. "Honey, it doesn't work like that. There comes a time when you have to choose." She stood up and grabbed her clutch. "And I guess you've chosen."

Ruby watched her go and turned her attention back to her suitcase. Memories flooded back of the first time she'd seen Cliff, there on the sidewalk in front of her college dorm. The way they'd laughed and teased one another. The serious talks they'd had about their families and their faith.

She unwound the string of lights from her little cedar tree and couldn't stop the tears that flooded her eyes. Cliff had strung these lights for her, one by one, because he knew they would make her smile each time she saw them. But now they only made her sad.

She plucked the lone ornament from the tree. Her early Christmas gift from Cliff. She held it up for a long moment, relishing the thought that Cliff had chosen it just for her. He'd gotten it as a reminder of the Christmases past that had been filled with happiness, and as a promise of happy Christmases yet to come. And she'd turned him away.

Ruby carefully wrapped the ornament in paper to keep it safe on the bus ride home. Someday, just as the green dress would be a reminder of her first paycheck, this ornament would be a reminder that she'd once had a best friend named Cliff.

She could only hope that one day, she'd be able to look at it and remember the happy times they'd shared. Because right now, she wasn't sure if she'd ever be happy again.

* * * * *

As the faint strains of Christmas music played in the background, Cliff tried to concentrate on the story Irene was telling him. It was no use though. His eyes kept wandering to the door. This was probably a bad idea. He should've known not to take advice from Hazel, but she'd been so certain Ruby would come to her senses if she found out Cliff went out with another girl.

And he'd been very clear to Irene that he was only interested in being friends, so he'd figured there was no harm.

Except that he felt pretty miserable.

"Have you heard anything I just said?" Irene asked. She put a hand on the hip of her petite frame. "Or are you just pining away for Ruby and hoping she'll show up?"

Cliff sighed. "Guilty. I'm sorry, Irene. I never should've come here tonight."

She slapped him on the arm. "Nonsense. I knew when I invited you that you and Ruby were going through a rough patch. She's a great girl." Irene grinned. "But dates are hard to come by. I'd rather be here with someone preoccupied than not at all."

He chuckled. "That's a good attitude to have."

"Besides, my Aub is somewhere in Europe right now. He wouldn't want me to sit home alone and miss the party." She tossed her blond hair. "So I figured you'd be a safe date and all, since we're both wishing we were with someone else."

The opening bars of "Boogie Woogie Bugle Boy" began to play, and Irene grabbed Cliff's arm. "You promised me a dance. I'm cashing in."

Cliff chuckled. "I must warn you, I can dance a mean jitterbug."

"Well, let's see you prove it." She led him onto the dance floor, and Cliff tried to get lost in the music and forget all about Ruby.

And the fact that she'd be leaving tomorrow.

For good.

* * * * *

"Tell me everything." Ruby had waited up for Lola to return from the dance just so she could hear all the details. She might as well get used to the idea of Cliff with someone else, so she wanted every single move he'd made.

Lola grinned. "It was such fun. We really missed you though."

"Did Cliff ask about me? Did he look like he was having a good time?" She gripped her pillow. "Did you see him kiss her or anything?"

Lola sat down on her bed and took off her shoes. "I didn't get to talk to Cliff. Harold did, but he didn't mention what they talked about. And I didn't see him kiss her, but it did look like they were having a good time." She rubbed her foot. "They did a jitterbug that was pretty entertaining. He's a good dancer and seemed to really enjoy it when the crowd cheered for him."

"I'll bet he turned on the charm when he realized everyone was watching, didn't he?" Ruby had seen it happen. He had a flair for the dramatic and could always play to the crowd.

Lola smiled. "Kind of. He has kind of a star quality. People are just naturally drawn to him." She took a pin out of her hair and tossed it on the nightstand. "But you do too. I've always thought that was what made y'all so perfect together."

"Do you think I'm making a mistake by walking away from him?"

Lola sighed. "I can't answer that for you. If you really think you're never going to be ready for marriage and all, then I guess it was the right decision. No one knows what's in your heart but you."

"But Cliff looked happy tonight? With Irene?"

Lola nodded. "From what I could tell."

Ruby leaned back against her pillow and pulled the sheet up to her chin. Maybe that was all she needed to know. Cliff was happy. Wasn't that what she wanted for him? To be happy. To heal from the guilt of losing Charlie. To find a place to call home.

Lord, help me to move on. Show me the path that will keep me closest to You and allow me to have the most happiness possible.

Chapter Seventeen

....

December 23, 1943

Dear Hazel,

I'm trying to get this in the mail before my bus leaves, so please excuse the poor penmanship. It was so nice to see you and Troy at Thanksgiving. And I'm still in shock over your news. You'll be such a terrific mother.

Hazel, I thought I'd better drop you a note of explanation just in case Cliff ever mentions anything about me to you. Your cousin is truly the best man I've ever met, and these past six months wouldn't have been the same without him. I never knew it was possible to be such close friends with a guy.

Now that I'm about to get on the bus and leave here for good, I can confess that my feelings for Cliff grew by leaps and bounds over the months. And he did some awfully sweet things for me. The Christmas lights he strung for me were so pretty, and a week ago he gave me a beautiful ornament that he knew I'd admired. He said it was my early Christmas gift.

Then we had a big fight and honestly, I'm not sure what it was even about. He seemed awfully upset about something, but he wouldn't come out and tell me what it was. Please don't tell him I said this, but if he'd have come out and told me how he felt, it might've made a difference. We've talked about everything under the sun, but he's never expressed his feelings.

*So we parted ways, and last night he went with another girl
to the Christmas dance.*

*It's okay though. I'm still considering moving out of
state once I finish my degree. Now that I have some real work
experience, I can try and find a job somewhere glamorous like
Washington, DC.*

*Okay, the bus should be here any minute. I'll stay in
Searcy tonight with one of my college suitemates, and then
Wade is going to pick me up there tomorrow. It's hard to
believe I'll be seeing my family so soon. I can't help but feel
a little sad that Cliff and I didn't even say a proper good-bye.
If you hear from him, please give him my best.*

Much love and Merry Christmas,
Ruby Jean

* * * * *

When Cliff had agreed to go visit his friend Owen Sanders over
Christmas, he hadn't realized how far of a trip it would be. The directions Owen had sent via telegram had taken Cliff as far as a gas station
in a little town called McCrory. Owen was supposed to meet him there
and lead him the rest of the way.

Cliff pulled in to the station and spotted Owen standing beside an
old farm truck. He raised an arm in greeting. "Owen," he called.

Owen's face broke out into a wide grin. "I'm glad you could come.
My aunt and uncle are really excited too. Their house has been quiet,
especially these past years. So when I mentioned inviting you, Aunt
Sallye thought it was a wonderful idea."

"Well, I appreciate it more than you know." The closer it got to
Christmas, the more Cliff wished he'd tried one more time to tell Ruby
how he felt. Maybe he should've just said the words out loud instead
of trying to be clever. He kept trying to push her out of his mind, but

it seemed like her memory had set up a permanent address. "This has been a tough year, and I'm thankful for a few days off to relax."

"This is a great place to do that. My aunt and uncle's farm is really peaceful. Uncle Earl will put you to work if you want him to, or if you'd rather just relax and explore or whatever, that will be fine too." Owen motioned toward the truck. "Just follow me. It's not too far, but I'll warn you, once we get out of town, the roads might be a little rough."

Cliff chuckled. "Dirt doesn't scare me." He climbed back in his car and followed Owen out of the parking lot. He wondered again about Ruby. She'd probably be on a bus headed home by now. He'd asked her once the name of her town, and she'd just laughed and said it was so small it wasn't even on the map. Still, she'd mentioned living in the northeast part of the state. He wondered if she was close by.

What he wouldn't give to be able to show up at her door, take her in his arms, and tell her how he felt. Except that she'd seemed pretty certain that she wasn't interested in a life with him—or with anyone.

That independent streak he'd so admired from the day they met had turned out to be the thing they couldn't get past.

Thirty minutes and three dirt roads later, he parked his car next to Owen. "This is a nice place," he said, getting out of the vehicle. "Nice, flat land." River Bend had more hills than this, that was for sure.

"Makes for good farming." Owen gestured toward Cliff's sedan. "Do you need help with your bag?"

The unspoken question came through loud and clear. Cliff circled his right arm around a few times. "I'm much better than the last time you saw me. Still gives me some pain sometimes, but nothing I can't handle." He grinned. "Thanks, though."

Owen shrugged. "Come on inside then. I'm sure Aunt Sallye has fixed something good to eat."

Cliff followed Owen into the large farmhouse.

A striking woman in a flowered dress met them at the door. Despite her graying hair and lined face weathered from years in the outdoors, she still held on to the beauty of her youth. "Come in, come in." She smiled at Cliff.

"This is my aunt Sallye," Owen said. "She and Uncle Earl have been kind enough to take me in and give me a job for a few months."

"Our house is much too empty these days, and Earl can use all the help he can get," she said. "So we've been happy to have him here." She turned her gaze on Cliff. "And we're happy to have you here too." She motioned down a hallway. "You can stay in one of the boys' rooms."

Cliff followed her down the hallway adorned with family photos. He gave them a cursory glance as he walked past. One in particular caught his eye. He paused to look closer.

The girl in the picture was beautiful.

And also very familiar.

"Who is this?" he asked, already knowing the answer.

Owen walked up behind him and glanced over his shoulder. "That's my cousin R.J. I asked you if you knew her. She's been working at the ordnance plant for the past few months."

Cliff's bag fell to the floor with a clatter. "You asked if I knew an R.J." He shook his head. "You never said R.J. was a girl."

Owen chuckled. "Yeah, I guess we're not supposed to call her that anymore. She's just Ruby Jean now." He peered at Cliff. "Why? Do you know her or somethin'?"

Cliff nodded. "I do," he whispered. "I sure do."

Mrs. McFadden raised her eyebrows. "Ruby will be here before long. Why don't we get you settled in Raymond's room and give you a chance to relax a bit?"

Cliff picked up his bag and numbly followed her into a small bedroom. He set his bag on the bed and looked around. It reminded him a lot of Charlie's room back home. "Thank you."

"It won't be a problem that you and Ruby know one other, will it?" Mrs. McFadden asked softly.

He shook his head. "No, ma'am. I'll be glad to see her."

She smiled. "And I'm sure the feeling will be mutual."

Cliff wasn't so sure, but he didn't think it appropriate to say so. On the drive over, he'd been wishing he could show up at Ruby's house and surprise her. It looked like he was going to get his wish.

Except that he had no idea what to say to her and was pretty sure she didn't care to see him.

* * * * *

"Ruby Jean McFadden. What exactly do you have in this suitcase?" Wade groaned as he lifted her bag out of the car.

Ruby giggled. It sure was nice to be home. "Don't poke fun. I've been gone for six months." She followed Wade up the path that led to her childhood home. Even though the place wasn't fancy, there was something comforting about its familiarity.

Mama met her at the door and pulled her into a hug. "I'm so glad you're home."

"Me too."

Mama stepped back and looked at her. "You look beautiful and so grown up."

"I am grown up." Ruby grinned. "I might be the baby of the family, but I'm an adult now."

Mama laughed. "You may think that, but you'll always be my baby." She winked. "Just wait until you have children of your own, and then you'll understand."

Ruby frowned. She'd told her mother time and again that she had no plans to ever settle down. Even though she'd been rethinking that decision lately, Mama didn't know it. "Is there anything to eat? I'm starving."

Wade poked her from behind. "There's always something to eat. You know that. Now move out of the way before I collapse from holding this suitcase for so long."

"Come on in the kitchen. There's a surprise waiting." Mama's eyes sparkled.

A surprise in the kitchen could only mean one thing—her favorite food. "Did you bake a pecan pie?" Ruby's mouth watered. She'd been so upset over Cliff for the past week, she'd barely had any appetite. But just the thought of her mama's cooking was enough to make her stomach start growling.

Mama laughed. "I think this surprise is even better than pie." She winked.

Ruby rounded the corner to the kitchen and her mouth dropped open.

There, at the wooden table where Ruby had eaten countless meals with her family, sat Cliff. A slow grin spread over his handsome face, and his blue eyes twinkled like they always did when he teased her. He stood up as she came into the room.

Ruby's feet felt stuck to the kitchen floor. Nothing had ever seemed more out of place than Cliff did sitting in her family's kitchen talking to Papa. Acting like he belonged there. Acting like he was part of her family and part of her life.

"Ruby," he started.

She shook her head. "I don't understand. How did you find me?" She couldn't help but feel a little flattered that he'd tracked her down like this. After the way things had ended between them, she'd been sure she'd never see him again.

Owen chuckled. "Oh, R.J., he didn't come to see you. He came to visit me."

Ruby's face flamed. "What?"

"We were in the same regiment." Cliff wore an uneasy expression. "Owen sent me a telegram inviting me for Christmas. I didn't know it was your house I was coming to until I got here and saw your picture."

"Well, that's nice." She forced a smile. "How's Irene? I hope she's doing well."

Cliff frowned. "Fine."

She could tell he wanted to say more, but not in front of her family. That suited her. The less they said to one another, the better.

There had been a moment when she'd first walked in and seen him sitting there that she'd actually imagined he was there to tell her he loved her. To say that he couldn't live without her. And in that moment, her desire to keep her independence had flown out the window. But now that she knew he hadn't come for her, she felt foolish for having those thoughts in the first place.

Chapter Eighteen

Cliff wished the floor would open up and swallow him. When Ruby had walked into the kitchen and seen him at the table, her face had lit up just like it used to when she'd spotted him across the cafeteria or seen him waiting for her in the lobby.

But now she was looking at him like she barely knew him. "It's nice that you were able to come visit Owen for Christmas," Ruby said. "I'm sure y'all have a lot of catching up to do." She turned her attention away from him and to her family.

Cliff stood awkwardly next to the table as Ruby made the rounds to hug Owen and Mr. McFadden.

"Cliff, can I get you a slice of pecan pie?" Mrs. McFadden asked kindly. "It's Ruby's favorite."

He shook his head. "No, ma'am." He cleared his throat. "I think I'll go out for a walk and let y'all catch up with Ruby." He looked over at her, but she refused to meet his eyes. "I know it's been awhile since she's been home." He hurried toward the front door, eager to get away from the family scene unfolding in the kitchen.

The family scene that shouldn't include him.

Mrs. McFadden followed him to the door. "Enjoy your walk, Cliff. Do you need a hat or gloves? It's getting chilly out there."

He smiled. It was easy to see where Ruby got her looks and her ability to put others at ease. "I won't be long. Maybe I'll head out to see Spotty." He chuckled.

She smiled. "Go behind the house and you'll see the barn. Spotty's probably set up camp there."

"Thanks." He walked out the front door and headed toward the barn. He had the sudden urge to put as much space between himself and Ruby as possible.

Because seeing her was stirring up emotions he'd just as soon forget.

* * * * *

Ruby stood in her bedroom, pulling things out of her suitcase. The action irritated her because every article reminded her somehow of Cliff. There was the green dress she'd worn the first time they'd attended church together. The red sweater she'd worn to the Razorback game. The gingham dress she'd been wearing on the day they met.

She heaped the clothes into a pile and tried to figure out the best way to handle the situation. What were the odds that Cliff would show up here, an old buddy of Owen's? She couldn't wait to tell Lucille this news.

There was a tap at the door and Mama poked her head inside. "You have a minute?"

Ruby grinned. "Sure." She motioned toward the growing pile on the bed. "Sorry about the mess. I'm just getting my bag unpacked."

Mama began sifting through Ruby's bag. She pulled out the strand of red, white, and blue Christmas lights. "Well, these are neat." She looked curiously at Ruby. "Did you have your dorm room decorated?"

Ruby managed a smile. She might as well give credit where it was due. "Cliff surprised me with a little cedar tree, and he strung up these lights for me."

Mama raised her eyebrows. "That was awfully nice of him." She sat down on the bed. "Is there a reason you're hiding out in here instead of sitting in the living room with everyone else? It was very rude of you to get up and walk out as soon as Cliff got back from the barn."

Ruby didn't want to explain the situation to her mother. "Sorry."

"We don't treat guests that way. We make them feel welcome." She held up the strand of lights. "Especially guests who are good friends."

Ruby nodded but didn't say anything.

"And he has been a good friend to you, right?" Mama's knowing gaze seemed to see right through her. "Your letters to me and Lucille have been full of stories about Cliff. You've depended on him and laughed with him and spent time with him all these months." She frowned. "Now, I don't know what happened to hurt your friendship, but maybe you need to do some thinking before you cut him out of your life for good."

Ruby sighed. "Okay."

"Now come on out and visit." Mama rose from the bed and smiled at Ruby. "It's almost Christmas." She walked out and shut the door behind her.

Ruby's eyes fell on the box that contained the ornament Cliff had given her, and she softened toward him. She knew how much he'd dreaded the holidays—so much that he was willing to visit a guy he barely knew to avoid the pain of going home and facing his parents and Charlie's empty room. Her heart hurt for what he must be going through in this strange place—and to think she'd acted like she barely knew him.

Cliff deserved better than that. And she knew just how to make him feel welcome.

* * * * *

Cliff sat by the fire in the den, trying to concentrate on an old Zane Grey western he'd picked up off the bookshelf. Owen and Mr. McFadden had already said good night, and he hadn't seen Ruby since she went storming out as soon as he came in from the barn.

A Christmas tree in the corner filled the room with the smell of the season, and yet Cliff felt none of the happiness that was supposed to come with it.

This had definitely been a mistake. He had half a mind to load up and leave tomorrow morning.

"Cliff?"

He nearly jumped out of his chair in shock to see Ruby standing in the doorway. A red and green Christmas apron covered her dress, and she had a smudge of flour on her cheek. And she'd never been more beautiful.

"I have something for you."

"A peace offering?" He raised an eyebrow.

She smiled. "Something like that." She motioned toward the kitchen. "Now come on."

He folded the page corner to mark his place and put the book on the table. As soon as he stepped out of the den, he could smell something delicious. Ruby had baked several times at Aunt Ida's, and it had always been tasty. In fact, the desserts she'd made at Thanksgiving had been some of the best he'd ever had. "What have we here?" He stepped into the kitchen and watched as Ruby pulled a cookie sheet from the oven.

She set it on the stove top and turned to face him. "I realized that I never gave you a Christmas gift." She gestured toward the cooling cookies. "So I came up with something edible."

"Please tell me they're your chewy molasses cookies." He grinned. "They're my favorite."

Ruby returned his smile. "I know. That's why I chose to make them for you. I even made a few different versions—some plain with just our home-raised sorghum molasses, some with pecans, and some with raisins." She set a plate full of cookies in front of him. "Here you go."

He bit into one of the still-warm cookies. "Perfection." He grinned. "Thank you so much."

She smiled. "I'm glad you like them."

"I'm sorry I ended up here of all places," he said. "I nearly fell over when I walked down the hallway earlier today and saw your picture."

Ruby sat across from him at the table. "It's okay. I was rather surprised, that's for sure, but I'll get over it. After all, tomorrow is Christmas Eve." She stood up. "I'm heading to bed. Help yourself to as many cookies as you'd like and stick the rest of them in the cookie jar." She set the jar in the middle of the table. "See you tomorrow."

Cliff watched her go and mulled over her peace offering. He didn't expect her to have a change of heart or anything. And he was sure they couldn't be just friends. There was too much between them for that.

But maybe for the next two days, he could enjoy the Christmas season and try and make the best of the situation.

Chapter Nineteen

....

Ruby didn't sleep well. She tossed and turned, and her dreams were plagued with images of Cliff. To know that he was right there, under the same roof, unsettled her. Yesterday, seeing how well he got along with her parents and brother, had given her an idea of how their lives might have been, had things worked out differently.

She still didn't understand the argument they'd had or why he'd seemed so angry. There was no longer anger in his eyes, but it had been replaced by something far worse—indifference.

She pulled on a sweater and skirt and padded down the hallway. She could smell bacon cooking already. Mama had always been the earliest riser in the house, and it was nice to know that even though years had passed, and even though her brothers were off fighting a war in far corners of the world, some things hadn't changed. "Good morning," Ruby said as she walked into the kitchen.

Mama turned from the stove. She had on the same Christmas apron that Ruby had worn last night to bake Cliff's cookies. "Morning." She smiled. "How did it feel to sleep in your own bed for a change?"

Ruby grimaced. "I had a hard time sleeping." She walked over to the counter to pour herself a cup of coffee.

"Something heavy must be weighing on your mind," Mama said. "And I have an idea of what it might be."

Ruby took a sip. "You do?"

"That boy sleeping down the hall from you." Mama raised an eyebrow. "Am I right?"

"It doesn't matter. Whatever used to be between us isn't there any longer." Ruby wished she hadn't been so forthcoming in her letters to Mama and Lucille about all the time she'd spent with Cliff. "He's going to move on, and I'm going to finish my degree and be an independent woman." She perched in one of the chairs and looked up at her mother.

Mama sat down across from Ruby. "Lucille and I were talking about that very thing just a couple of weeks ago. She mentioned that you might want to move to a big city after graduation. She also says that she's afraid you're hiding behind your dreams of independence to mask your fear of getting your heart broken." Mama's green eyes bore into Ruby's. "Is that true?"

"She's just mad because I told her I didn't want to wind up stuck on some old farm like her." The words sounded hollow, even to Ruby's own ears. "Besides, so what if I'm a little scared? The whole world is in turmoil. We don't know what tomorrow might bring. How could I be anything *but* scared?"

Mama shook her head. "Listen to yourself, will you? You'll hear how misguided you sound." She reached across the table and rubbed Ruby's hand. "We've raised you to be independent and think for yourself. You were the smartest one in your class, and you had a curiosity that we encouraged. And your papa and I are so proud of you for doing well in your college courses and in your work at the ordnance plant." She smiled.

Ruby had always aimed to please, so hearing that her parents were proud made her feel good. She'd worked hard her whole life to try and be the kind of daughter they could be proud of.

Mama continued. "You are quite a girl, Ruby Jean. But you are way off the mark about one thing."

Ruby frowned. "What's that?"

"This idea that women like me and Lucille are living in some kind of prison. Honey, I wouldn't trade my life here for anything." She took a sip of coffee. "The greatest pleasure of my life has been being married to your father and raising you kids. And Lucille will tell you the same thing. When she and Donald and little Annie Sue are together, the three of them positively radiate happiness. And when he comes back from overseas, they'll have the happiest of reunions."

Ruby swallowed. "But he might not come back. Joseph didn't come back. Plenty of the girls on my shift at the plant are either in mourning or waiting to hear whether their husbands are still alive."

Mama nodded. "It's not an easy time, I'll give you that. But we have to put it in the Lord's hands and let it go."

"That's really hard, Mama." Ruby looked down at her hands. "Because bad things still happen. Even to people who put all their trust in God."

Mama gave her a small smile. "Honey, trusting in God doesn't mean that everything will always be perfect. It just means that you have a faith that will get you through those tough times. You can't control the world around you, Ruby Jean."

"I know."

"Do you?" Mama asked. "And do you also know that by failing to put your hope and trust in the Lord, you're letting your fear win?"

Ruby sighed. "Maybe I've used my quest for independence to cover up my fears. But it's a whole lot easier to keep my heart to myself and know it can't get broken than to give it away and know I might get hurt."

Mama patted her arm. "That's right. You might get hurt. You might lose a husband just like you lost Joseph. But honey, by closing yourself off and resolving to be alone forever—you're missing out on a wonderful part of life."

"That's what Lucille says. She says that even if Donald never comes back, she's blessed to have had him for as long as she did. And Hazel and Troy are so happy together as they're getting ready to start a family. She says he's her best friend." She managed a tiny smile. "There was a time when Cliff was my best friend. Mama, I was so afraid of losing someone else that it made me lose Cliff."

"Ruby, honey, let's not forget you're probably not the only one afraid of losing someone you love. Cliff has dealt with a lot over the past year."

"You know about Charlie?" Ruby hadn't told Mama about Cliff's guilt.

Mama nodded. "Owen filled me in. I suspected something terrible must've happened to make Cliff choose to come here instead of enjoying Christmas with his own family."

"I guess I didn't consider that Cliff might be a little scared too. He seems so confident." She sighed. "I think I messed up, Mama. With Cliff I mean. Y'all are right about me. I've hidden behind my stubbornness and independence out of fear. Nothing else."

Mama smiled. "Have you prayed about it?"

"All summer. And every time I'd pray that I'd know what to do, Cliff would do something wonderful to surprise me." She shook her head. "I think I might've been a little bit blind."

"But you've figured it out now." Mama smiled. "And I don't think it's too late."

Ruby sighed. "You don't understand. Cliff has yet to come out and tell me he has feelings for me. And I want him to do that without my prompting him."

"That doesn't sound unreasonable. But did it occur to you that maybe he's a little nervous about doing that? You're not a simple girl, Ruby. You've always challenged your brothers. You can play sports and shoot guns as good as them. You're good at your studies and a hard worker." She reached out and tipped Ruby's chin up. "And you're beautiful." She smiled. "That's a lot for even the most confident man to handle."

Ruby grinned. The idea that she somehow intimidated Cliff struck her as funny. "You really don't think it's too late to fix things?"

Mama stood and pulled Ruby to her feet, drawing her into a hug. "There's only one way to find out. But I certainly think Cliff is the kind of man who is worth the risk. Your feelings for him have been evident through the letters you've sent these past months. That kind of bond doesn't come along too often."

Her mama was exactly right. Now that she'd realized the error of her ways, the paralyzing fear was gone. And in its place was a bunch of big old butterflies. Because the next conversation she had with Cliff could change her life forever.

"Thanks, Mama." Ruby kissed her mother on the cheek. "We'd better finish getting breakfast ready." She smiled. "I think I have a big day ahead."

* * * * *

"This is the best breakfast I've had in a good while," Cliff said, eating the last bite of his scrambled eggs. "Thanks again for the hospitality."

Mama smiled. "I'm glad you enjoyed it. What do you have planned for today, Cliff?"

Ruby froze as she waited for his answer. Now that she'd decided to have an honest talk with him, she was nervous that he might up and leave.

"I offered to help out on the farm today, but Mr. McFadden wouldn't hear of it." He took a sip of coffee. "So I guess I'll go for a walk and maybe come back and read a little." He grinned at Ruby. "I thought I might go out and see what Spotty is up to today."

She smiled. "That sounds nice."

"It does sound like a lovely way to spend the day." Mama wiped her hands on her apron. "Please take your time. Lunch will be ready around noon."

Cliff excused himself and left the kitchen.

Mama shot Ruby a knowing glance. It was now or never.

Ruby put her coffee mug next to the sink and hurried after Cliff. She rounded the corner from the living room to the hallway and ran right into him.

Cliff's hands went around her waist to steady her. "Sorry about that," he murmured.

Her breath caught as his hands seemed to linger on her waist. "That's okay," she said softly.

She started to walk past him, but he caught her hand. "Would you like to join me on my walk?" he asked.

"Yes, I would. Let me go get my coat." She rushed to her bedroom, relieved that he wanted to spend time with her. She shrugged on her coat and glanced in the mirror. Not too bad considering her fitful sleep. She fluffed her hair and squared her shoulders. She could do this.

She hurried down the hallway to where Cliff waited and saw Mama peer around the corner. "Everything okay?" Ruby heard her ask him.

"Yes, ma'am. Ruby and I are going to go for a walk. We'll be back soon," Cliff said.

Mama looked pointedly at Ruby, and the gleam in her eye was unmistakable. "Take your time. And have fun." She grinned and turned back to the kitchen.

"Let's go." Ruby led the way out the front door. "I haven't been out to see Spotty yet."

Cliff chuckled. "I'm sure he'll be happy to see you again."

They walked in silence for a long moment.

"Is it weird for you that I'm here?" Cliff asked finally. "Because I can go back to Jacksonville today if it would make your Christmas better."

Ruby stopped walking. "You know, I thought it was going to be weird. When I first saw you in the kitchen and found out why you were here, I expected it to be really uncomfortable." She grinned. "But last night eating cookies and this morning having breakfast, I didn't think it felt weird at all." She gave him a tiny smile. "It felt normal."

"I'm glad you think so." He led the way into the barn and motioned toward a hay bale. "Let's sit for a minute. There's something I want you to see."

Ruby sat down next to him, surprised that she should feel nervous around Cliff. "What's that?"

He pulled a crumpled letter out of his pocket. "I got this yesterday before I left to come here." He handed it to her. "I finally wrote my folks a few weeks ago."

Ruby reached over and squeezed his arm. She knew it was a big step for him. "I'm so glad. I know they were relieved to hear from you."

He motioned at the letter in her hand. "This is their response. I thought you might want to read it."

Ruby was touched that he would share something so personal. "Are you sure?"

He nodded.

She unfolded the letter.

Dearest Cliff,

We have hoped and prayed you would contact us. After our attempts to reach out to you through Ida didn't go so well, your dad thought it best to give you some space. Now, giving a hurting child space is one of the hardest things a mother can do, but I did it. I wanted so badly to talk to you, but I knew it would have to be on your terms. So you can imagine how thrilled I was when your letter arrived in the mailbox.

It brought us joy that you are doing well, but incredible sorrow that you think we hold you responsible in any way for Charlie's death. Cliff, you have always taken care of your brother. From a very early age you looked out for him, and as a mother I always found it beautiful to see. You even used to try and take Charlie's punishment for him when he got into mischief (which he often did!), because you didn't want anything bad to happen to him.

I cannot imagine what you must've gone through over there, what you must still be going through. But mark my

*words: we love you now and always. We have lost one son,
and we do not intend to lose another.*

*As for our place not feeling like home any longer, well,
I suspect that is because you are an adult now. You will
someday find your own home, and you will rediscover those
feelings of love, safety, and security that our home provided
you as you were growing up.*

*We love you and look forward to seeing you whenever
you decide you are ready to come for a visit. Many times over
the past months your father has had to talk me out of taking
the bus to Jacksonville, because I ached to see you. Thankfully
Ida has kept us informed of your well-being. She mentioned
that you'd taken up with a wonderful girl, Ruby, whom Ida
believes has made all the difference for you. If that is true,
please give Ruby my best and tell her I look forward to meeting
the girl who won and healed my son's heart.*

Love you always,
Mom and Dad

Ruby's eyes filled with tears. Was it true? Had she won his heart?
She felt his eyes on her. "Oh, Cliff, it's wonderful. I'm so glad you contacted them."

"Me too."

Cliff sat so close that she could see the faint stubble on his jaw. She
fought the urge to reach out and run her fingers over it. "Are you going
home for a visit?"

He nodded. "Soon." He grinned at her. "And Mom was right. You
were all the difference. You're the reason I finally contacted them in
the first place. Right after I got you the Christmas tree, I realized that
one of the things I wanted most was for my parents to know you. So
I wrote them that letter." He sighed. "Of course, soon after that, we
stopped speaking."

"You wanted me to meet your parents?" She was unable to keep the surprise out of her voice.

He grinned. "Of course. I figured you knew."

"I had no idea."

Cliff took the letter from her hands and folded it back up. "I wanted you to read this because I wanted you to know that even if nothing else came from our relationship, it at least prompted me to reconnect with my parents." He smiled. "And for that I'll be forever grateful."

Ruby sat, speechless, trying to process the turn of events. She'd come to the barn expecting to reveal her heart. Instead, Cliff had managed to surprise her again. She took a breath. It was time to come clean about her fears and her feelings.

Before she could speak, Cliff stood up from the hay bale and began to pace. "I need to apologize to you, Ruby. You made it perfectly clear that you weren't looking for a relationship. You told me in no uncertain terms that you never wanted to marry. And yet, I said those words anyway. I never should've put you in that position, and I'm so sorry."

She wanted to correct him and tell him her stance on marriage had changed. But she was too confused. "It's like you're speaking a foreign language." Ruby looked up at him. "What 'words' did you say? Am I missing something?"

Cliff sat down next to her again. "The ornament. The note." He raked his fingers through his hair. "I never should've done it."

"Note? What note? What are you talking about?"

"The note. Inside the ornament." He widened his eyes. "There was a little string I'd attached so you could pull the silver top off of the ornament. And inside was a note I wrote telling you how I felt."

Realization dawned on Ruby. His reaction that night when she went downstairs. He'd expected her to say something about the note he'd written. But she hadn't seen it. "I—I never read it. I saw the string but thought it was just for hanging it from the tree."

"But you said you read the note. You said my penmanship was better than yours."

She tried to process what he was saying. "I was talking about the tag with my name on it that said 'open me.'"

"So you didn't read it? You don't know?"

Ruby thought of the ornament sitting in her bedroom right now. "I didn't. But I'm going to." She jumped up. "You wait here. I'll be right back." She took off running toward the house, not even caring how silly she must look. If Cliff had gone to such elaborate trouble to send her a message, she couldn't get to it fast enough.

152

Chapter Twenty

Cliff paced the length of the barn. It wasn't far from there to the house, but the seconds seemed to be ticking past in slow motion. She hadn't seen the note yet. Unbelievable. And he thought he'd been so smooth by hiding it like that.

He tried to shake off the nerves. He'd never had feelings for anyone like he had for Ruby. And once she read the note, there would be no turning back.

Ruby ran into the barn, a grin on her face. "Two minutes flat."

"Must be some kind of record," Cliff said with a grin. She didn't need to know that it had felt more like two hours to him.

Ruby fought to catch her breath. "I'm pretty fast for a girl, huh?" She grinned and held up the ornament box. "Here it is."

Cliff's eyes twinkled. "Are you sure you want to read what's inside?"

"Are you sure want me to?"

He nodded. He'd never wanted anything more. Even though he had no idea how she'd react, he knew he'd never rest again until he was sure she was aware how he felt.

"Before I do, there's something I need to tell you." Ruby sat down next to him and took a breath. "Something I need to apologize to *you* for."

Cliff enjoyed the way the brisk run had put color in her cheeks. He'd missed her so much. "What's that?"

"Telling you that stuff about how I never wanted to marry was silly. There was truth to it, because I do enjoy being independent, and I do like the idea that I can pick up and move somewhere after college.

But at the same time, I hid behind it." She sighed. "I never expected to meet a guy like you. It scared me. The life I wanted with you was the very life I've been saying for the past year that I never wanted. I was confused and terrified of losing you and of getting my heart broken."

He reached out and swept a strand of hair from her forehead. "I never would've broken your heart."

She smiled. "But you never told me you wanted to keep seeing me after I went back to school. I look back now and see that maybe you assumed I knew. Or maybe you thought your actions spoke louder than words." She shrugged. "But I needed to hear it before I could believe it."

"And you never heard it." He understood. "You might not believe this, but I was scared too. Kissing you was unlike anything I've ever experienced. But I didn't want our relationship to become just about that, and I could see how easily that could happen. I've never been attracted to another girl the way I am to you. And it isn't just your looks. You keep me on my toes. We talk about everything from politics to pig farming." He grinned. "And most importantly, you've shown me that a relationship with the Lord is the most important one I can have."

Ruby's eyes filled with tears. "What are you saying?" she asked softly.

He lifted the ornament from the box. "Open it," he whispered.

She took the ornament with trembling hands and pulled on the string he'd attached to the top. "I can't believe I missed this."

Cliff chuckled. "My grand gesture was a dud. I put a little slip of paper inside the box that directed you to pull the string, but I guess you didn't see it."

Ruby handed him the silver top and held her eye up to the hole in the ornament. She grinned. "I see the note."

"Told you," he said with a grin.

She turned the ornament upside down and shook it. A little piece of paper fell onto her lap.

* * * * *

Ruby carefully unfolded the note and began to read.

> *I love you, Ruby. I've waited months to tell you, because I wanted to be sure and I wanted to find the right time. You are the answer to my prayers and the best thing that has ever happened to me. All my love, now and forever, Cliff.*

Her heart pounded as she read his sweet words. She looked up at him. "Oh, Cliff—"

He held a finger to her lips. "Shh. Let me finish." He knelt before her. "Words have always come easily to me. I've never gotten nervous about speaking, no matter how many people are in the room. In fact, I don't usually get nervous at all."

She grinned. His confidence was one of the things she loved the most.

"But you have made me nervous since day one. When I saw you on the sidewalk with your big old suitcase"—he smiled—"you made me nervous, because for the first time I was faced with something that I knew was too precious to lose. You are everything I've ever dreamed of, ever hoped for, ever prayed for. And I was terrified I would mess it up. You bring out the best in me. I should've told you I loved you when I first realized it. It was the day we went rabbit hunting." He chuckled softly. "Not only did you prove to me that you're no ordinary girl by the way you handled that rifle, but you were so kind when I told you about Charlie. You put me at ease that day, and I realized that I could talk to you about anything." He shook his head. "But instead of telling you right away, I wanted to wait until the perfect time. And then when you told me that you never wanted to settle down, I started to fear that I'd misread things and missed my chance. That maybe you didn't feel the same way." He reached up and stroked her cheek. "I told you a while back that I felt like I didn't have a home. Well, that's not true anymore. You are home to me. I love you with all of my heart." He stood up and pulled her to him.

Ruby wiped a tear from her cheek and looked into his eyes. The twinkle she loved so much was back. She'd never imagined anyone would say such sweet words to her. "I love you too. I have for a long time. I'm so, so sorry that my stubborn pride got in the way."

Cliff kissed her on the forehead. "I might have a little bit of that stubborn pride too. Maybe we can work on it together."

"Together," she repeated. "That sounds wonderful." She grinned. "Because you are home to me too. I've told everyone who would listen that I wanted an adventure. It's occurred to me that *you* are my adventure. And it wouldn't matter if I lived in New York City or on an Arkansas pig farm. As long as I'm with you, it will be the greatest adventure of my life."

He tipped her chin toward him. "It sure will."

Ruby shivered in anticipation of the kiss she knew was coming.

Cliff bent down and touched his lips to hers. She circled her arms around his neck and pulled him closer, losing herself in a kiss that was even more perfect than their first.

When she pulled back and looked into his bright blue eyes, she knew without a doubt that this would be the best Christmas she'd ever had.

Epilogue

....

December 31, 1943
River Bend, Arkansas

Ruby turned on the radio in the living room of Cliff's parents' house. She had the place to herself, since Cliff had gone to lunch with his folks. Ruby had insisted on staying behind. She'd known they needed some time alone with their son.

It was nice to look at the collection of family photos on the mantel while Irving Berlin's "White Christmas" played softly. After all the excitement she'd had over the past days, it felt good to relax and reflect.

The past week had passed in such a blur of happiness. Once she and Cliff had confessed their love, her whole world seemed to change. Mama had been so thrilled at the turn of events, she'd made Christmas dinner even more festive by stringing up the patriotic lights Cliff had made and hanging some mistletoe in the doorway.

Even better, Cliff had come to her on Christmas morning and asked if she'd go with him to River Bend to visit his parents for a few days after Christmas.

She'd balked at first, not wanting to impose. But Cliff had convinced her that she was a large part of the reason he'd finally healed enough to face his home.

"You okay?" Cliff asked softly from the doorway. "You look like you're a million miles away."

She turned toward him and smiled. "I was just thinking about how happy I am. I finally see that even though I don't get to control everything that happens to me, it actually feels pretty great to trust that God has a plan for my life."

He pulled her to him in an embrace. "And I hope I'm part of that plan."

She smiled against his chest. "Oh, I think you are."

He tipped her chin up. "My parents adore you, by the way. We had a nice visit and a really good talk." He played with a strand of her hair. "It's time for me to let go of my guilt over Charlie. I can see that now."

She nodded. "I'm glad you've finally forgiven yourself. And I know your parents are happy to have you back." She reached up and touched his cheek. "And so am I."

Bing Crosby's new hit, "I'll Be Home for Christmas," began to play on the radio.

Cliff grinned and turned up the volume. "I never did get that dance you promised before the AOP Christmas party." He held a hand out. "How about it?"

She giggled and went into his arms. "I love this song."

"And I love you." Cliff held her close, and they swayed to the music. "As long as you're with me, I'll be home. No matter where I am."

Ruby's heart fluttered. He said the sweetest things to her.

Once the song ended, Cliff took a deep breath. "Ruby, I've already told you how much you mean to me. And I know you're headed back to school next week."

She frowned. Now that she and Cliff were a real couple, the thought of being separated made her feel sick. "I'll write often. And I can take the bus to visit and stay in the dorm with some of the girls."

He nodded. "That all sounds wonderful. And it will get us through a few months until your graduation." Once her student teaching was finished at the end of the semester, she'd graduate in May. "But there's something I need to know."

Ruby furrowed her brow. "What's that?"

"I talked to your Papa last week about the future. He gave me his blessing to ask you a question." Cliff dropped to one knee.

Tears sprang to Ruby's eyes.

"Ruby Jean McFadden, will you make me the happiest man in the world and marry me?" he asked.

"Yes. Yes! A million times yes." She bent down and kissed him on the lips.

Cliff rose and took her hand. "My parents are waiting out back." He chuckled. "We'd better go tell them the verdict. I think they were as nervous as I was."

Ruby clung to his hand as he led her through the house and to the back door. Her desire to be in control of her own life suddenly seemed very silly. Because once she'd relinquished that control and let go of her fear, such wonderful things had happened.

Things she knew were part of a better plan than she could've ever imagined.

Tomorrow would begin a new year, and soon she'd begin a new life with Cliff. And she had no doubt it would be the biggest adventure possible.

Ruby's Chewy Molasses Cookies

....

1 cup sugar*
1/2 cup shortening
2 cups flour
1 1/2 teaspoons soda
1 cup oats
1 egg
1/2 cup sorghum molasses
1 teaspoon salt
1 teaspoon vanilla

Combine all ingredients in a large bowl and mix well.
Drop by teaspoonfuls onto a greased baking sheet.
Bake at 375 degrees for 12 minutes.

*Ruby would have used less sugar and more sorghum
molasses due to the fact that sugar was rationed.*

Author's Note

....

Sweet Southern Christmas is very special to me, because I wrote it with the participation of my grandmother. Just like the heroine in the story, she worked as a WOW during World War II at the Arkansas Ordnance Plant in Jacksonville. That's where she met my grandfather and where their real life love story—one that would last more than sixty-five years—began. When I created Ruby and Cliff, I knew I wanted to use some of the stories from my grandparents' courtship, and it was such fun to blend a bit of truth into the fictional story.

About the Author

. . . .

 Annalisa Daughety is the award-winning author of ten novels and novellas. Her previous works include *Love Finds You in Lancaster County, Pennsylvania* and *Love Finds You in Charm, Ohio.* A graduate of Freed-Hardeman University, Annalisa has spent the past twelve years working in the nonprofit sector in marketing and event planning. She is an active member of American Christian Fiction Writers and loves to connect with her readers through social media sites like Facebook and Twitter.

A native of Arkansas, Annalisa has lived in many states and traveled to many countries. However, she recently moved back home to her hometown of McCrory, Arkansas, where she lives in a house in the middle of a cornfield with three spoiled dogs. More information about Annalisa can be found on her website, www.annalisadaughety.com.

Small-Town Christmas

BY GWEN FORD FAULKENBERRY

To Stella Jane Faulkenberry,
the biggest—and best—surprise of my life.

Acknowledgments
....

Thank You, Jesus, for being grace and extending it to everyone.

Thank you to my wonderful family, without whom I'd never be able to write books.

Thank you, Annalisa Daughety, for your refreshing spirit of camaraderie in writing. I'm honored to have my name on the cover with yours.

Thank you, editor Rachel Meisel, for being a genius and having the heart to go with it.

And thank you, Ozark, Arkansas, for being the community of people I love coming home to.

Prologue

....

The altar was filled with ferns. Their earthy green color provided a simple and elegant complement for the hundreds of white candles that illuminated the sanctuary and produced a romantic if hazy glow. Cedar branches, laden with blue-white berries, decked the window ledges, sheltering more soft candlelight that flickered like rubies in the stained glass. Jon smelled the woods and thought that the cedar was a good idea. If only he could say the same about the wedding itself.

Looking around, he wondered why he was there. But it was no wonder, really. He was there because Sophie had asked him to come. In town the other day, they'd bumped into one another at the check-out counter of the grocery store. They'd wished each other a merry Christmas, and then she'd looked at him with her dancing blue eyes and said, "You'll be there on New Year's Eve, won't you?" And he had answered yes. He had always been there for her.

Jon and Sophie met on their first day of second grade at River Bend Elementary. He was a bus rider and had arrived early to Mrs. Sigman's class. He was settling into his desk when through the door walked Sophie with her red satchel and blond pigtails. She plopped down in the seat beside him and said, "Hi. I'm Sophia Grace Harper. I know how to write cursive already. Who are you?"

"Jon," he had answered simply.

"Jon who?"

"Jon the Baptist," he'd responded, trying to be funny and feeling rather clever after learning about John the Baptist in Sunday school. Sophie carefully studied him for a minute and then burst out laughing.

"You'd better be careful not to lose your head then," she declared. Being a preacher's daughter, she knew the story well.

They had been best friends ever since. That is, until the last few years.

College had been rough on their friendship. They'd chosen the same school and studied together often. They'd also spent some of their time together watching movies, going out for dessert, playing a little music, occasionally jogging. But somewhere along the way, Jon had realized he loved her—a suspicion he'd suppressed for years because it complicated everything. He never told her, because he knew she didn't love him. At least not in the same way.

She was in love with Stephen, a dark-haired, green-eyed musician who was everything Jon wasn't. Stephen was a performer. His presence on stage and off was magnetic—a little dangerous, in Jon's opinion— and he had most of the girls at school swooning over him. In the end, from the stage of a concert at their college, he had asked Sophie to be his bride, and she had giddily accepted. Or so Jon heard later.

He had seen less of Sophie this past year than he had any year since second grade. And now she was walking down the aisle to become Stephen's wife.

Jon caught his breath when he saw her enter on her father's arm. Sophie looked like a fairy-tale princess, and no doubt felt like one. She seemed to Jon to be caught up in a dream. Her elaborately detailed veil could not hide the excitement—no, enchantment—in her blue eyes. As she came toward his pew, she stuck her foot out playfully and showed him that she wasn't wearing shoes. For just a moment their eyes met, and he thought what a child she was.

"Don't ever change…," he said softly to her back as she floated past, doubting that Stephen was worthy even to kiss that foot. Jon watched her the rest of the way down the aisle till her father gave her away and she joined her hands with Stephen's.

Jon fought back a wave of nausea. Air. He needed air.

He had seen Sophie, and she'd seen him as she walked down the aisle. He'd been there as he said he would be, and that was going to have to be enough. He knew he'd never make it through the rest of the ceremony. So he slipped out of his pew as inconspicuously as possible, lingering just a moment at the door.

"If any man can show just cause why this man and woman should not be joined, let him speak now…" Dr. Harper's sonorous voice was intoning to the expectant congregation. A formality.

"Because I love her?" Jon whispered to himself. Then he stepped outside into the cold, dark night, tears streaming down his face as the snow began to fall.

Chapter One

....

Present day

Sophie groaned as she looked in the mirror. The dark circles under her eyes fanned out like shadows on the pale white landscape that was her face. She splashed water over it, as if to wash away the shadows and wake herself up. But the ghostly figure in the mirror just stared back at her, bleakly, like a dead person who could not be awakened.

A single tear rolled down her cheek, and then another followed, hitting the sleeve of her white terry-cloth robe and sinking silently into its softness. She lay back down on the bed where Spot, her Boston Terrier, was nestled in the pillows. She stroked his warm, satiny fur. It felt good. He lazily opened one eye to acknowledge her, rolling over for a full belly rub. Inching closer, he realized Sophie was crying and began to lick the tears off her face. She hugged him.

"You're right," she said. "No more tears!"

Spot's nub of a tail wagged as Sophie sat up and wiped her eyes. Pulling herself together, she got up and padded to the back door, her oversized slippers making a squishing sound on the old hardwood floors. Spot followed, toenails clicking, and went out to do his business in the yard. Sophie started the coffee pot. When Spot came back in, she went to her room briefly, threw on some clothes, and then sat down at her desk with a cup of Southern Pecan and her To Do list. She was grateful it was a long one. That list would take her all day.

Before the divorce, Sophie never thought she'd end up back in River

Bend. That was never part of the plan. As far as she was concerned, it was a good place to be from—truly—but she'd had bigger fish to fry.

Opening her laptop, she typed in "Catfish Fillets," smiling weakly to herself at the pun. Rubbing her temples, she scowled at the clock. The menu had to be at the printer's by five o'clock to be ready for opening day on Thursday, and even though she had worked and reworked it for the past few days, it was still as unfinished as the rest of her thoughts. She forced herself to focus on the short list of her specialties, carefully wording each item. Spot went in and out, and Sophie drank the whole pot of coffee in lieu of lunch. Finally she finished the menu, ending it with the salad and sandwich options. Grabbing her sunglasses and leaving her dog staring out the window after her, she dashed off on her bicycle to the print shop.

Sophie parked her bike on the sidewalk next to the window boxes that spilled over with English ivy and all colors of petunias still in bloom. There was no place to lock the bike, so she left the chain lock in the basket that hung between the handlebars.

The print shop was located on the corner of the town square, behind the courthouse and conveniently tucked in an old building along with the offices of the *River Bend Record*, the newspaper Harvey's family had run for years. Sophie knew the place well from high school, when her friend Jon worked there.

The ancient door creaked and a bell jangled when she opened it and stepped in. She inhaled the musty odor of the building—burning wood, melted plastic, and fresh paper and ink. Some things never changed.

Harvey Weinberg, the owner, rose from his desk when he saw Sophie. His face lit up with delight. Like the shop, Harvey looked the same as he always had, except that his hair was now gray. He still wore it brushed back, and his blue eyes twinkled over round spectacles. Sophie had always thought he resembled pictures she'd seen of Benjamin Franklin.

"Everybody's excited about your new eatin' place," Harvey told her when she handed him the menu, requesting fifty laminated copies. "It's the talk of the town."

"Uh, yeah." Sophie tried to smile at him from behind her glasses. She squeezed his arm. "Thanks, Harvey."

"Say, are you going to have food from all those exotic places you been?"

"Maybe I'll try them once in a while as daily specials," she told him. "I'm just open for lunch for now—kind of playing this by ear."

"Well, you always been good at that." He smiled warmly at her, and she felt his kindness wrap around her like a blanket. She remembered all of those Sunday mornings when she'd played the piano while Harvey led the singing for the senior adult Sunday school class. Playing by ear wasn't intimidating when your audience could barely hear you in the first place. And Harvey was so good-natured and fun. She'd been just a kid, and he a step away from the senior adults. Looking into his wrinkled face, she supposed he'd joined the class by now.

"Come see me, Harvey," she told him as she turned to leave.

"I'll see you on opening day."

Sophie walked out of the print shop and into the breezy sunshine of a perfect October day in the Ozarks. She hopped on her bike and pointed it toward River Bend's town square.

Being back at the print shop made her think of Jon. Throughout high school, he'd spent a few hours there most days after school, writing, editing, tinkering with the press, and getting covered with printer's ink. She'd stop in sometimes with a vanilla Diet Coke, Jon's favorite drink from the Dairy Freeze, and keep him company. He always liked to have her proofread his stuff, even though—or perhaps especially because—she could be brutal. Her mother was an English teacher, and she'd inherited the gene for perfect grammar. She loved catching Jon in a rare mistake.

Sophie remembered the funniest mistake she'd ever seen him make—and how lucky they were that she discovered it. Her dad had paid Jon to run an ad in the paper for the church's annual pancake breakfast. Just before he printed it in the *Record*, she happened to drop by, and he showed it to her. It read:

> *The First Baptist Church will hold its annual free*
> *Pancake Breakfast this Saturday morning, December 12, at*
> *8:00 a.m., in the Fellowship Hall. All townsfolk are welcome*
> *to attend.*

And then, in fine print:

> **A reminder to the ladies of First Baptist: Please drop*
> *off your girdles at the church Friday night and be ready to*
> *demonstrate your love in action!*

Jon had almost died from embarrassment, quickly changing the typo to "griddles" while Sophie rolled on the floor laughing at him. She had never let him live it down. She could still see his face blushing in horror before he finally joined her laughter.

Chuckling at the thought and feeling a little more lighthearted, Sophie turned her bike in the direction of the Dairy Freeze. She needed a Dr Pepper. She had it on her drink fountain back at the restaurant, but as Jon always said, the Dairy had the best ice.

Cycling around the square before heading up Main Street, Sophie almost felt like she was sixteen again. The crape myrtles were still blooming in their places along the sidewalk. The "pocket park" between two buildings was there with its lamppost, wrought-iron benches, and shady trees. There was the hardware store, where her father's friend Mr. Worley worked, and where she'd been sent on countless errands for pieces of pipe, or wire, or screws, for whatever project her father was in the middle of and couldn't leave. Next door was a law office, which adjoined Turner Abstract Company. Sophie remembered going there with her parents and her younger brother, Tom, when they signed the deed to the Harbor House. Mr. Turner was a family friend, but he had shaken his head at their plan to restore it.

"If there ever was anyone who could make something nice out of an old pile of boards, it's you, James. I just hope you know what you're doing."

Her father had smiled at him. "We won't hold you responsible for the outcome of this transaction, Ralph."

On the corner was Milton's barbershop, where the only black man in town had been cutting hair for as long as Sophie could remember. As she pedaled toward it, she thought she saw Tom's white truck parked at the curb, right in front of the candy cane barber pole mounted on the side of the building. She pulled over just as Tom was coming out the door with Milton close behind him.

"Sophia? Sophia Grace Harper? The homecoming queen and the smartest girl in school is back in town?" The sound of Milton's voice was as comfortable and warm as an old quilt. "Gonna start yourself a business, I hear. You come over here and give ol' Milton a hug. Girl, you're a sight for sore eyes."

Sophie felt the same way about Milton as he hugged her underneath the barber pole. "Hey, Milton. If you and Clara can get away from the shop, come see me on Thursday. I'd love to treat you to lunch."

"We might just do that. I haven't been in the Harbor House since your daddy finished working on that place."

Sophie returned his kind smile.

"Thanks for the haircut, Milton." Tom rubbed the back of his head, where the hair was now an inch long. "Where are you headed, sis?"

"Just up to the Dairy Freeze for a coke, then home."

"Wanna ride?"

Tom slung her bike into the back of his truck, and they drove through town toward the Dairy Freeze.

"I'll pick up a milkshake for Madeline, and that will win me some good husband points," he joked.

"How is Madeline feeling?"

"Good, overall. Sometimes she's a little more emotional than usual"—he grinned mischievously—"and she gets pretty tired. But heck, who wouldn't? It's a pretty big deal making a baby."

"And you?"

"I'm good. A little scared, but mostly pumped. I figure by the time the baby gets here, I'll be ready—well, as ready as you can ever be for a huge life change. What about you?"

"Oh, I'm excited about being an aunt. I can't wait."

Tom narrowed his eyes at her. "I don't mean what about you and the baby, I mean how are *you*?"

They pulled up to the window and ordered their drinks and Madeline's milkshake. When they pulled away, Sophie sipped her Dr Pepper and tried to answer.

"I don't know, Tom. I want to be fine, and I should be. I am so thankful to be home, near you and Madeline and Mom and Granny. In the puzzle of my life, this is the first piece that has fit in a long time, and it feels really, really good."

Following the strand of crape myrtles, they passed the flower shop, the bank, the bookstore, and then the square again, with the old courthouse and veterans' memorials flanking each side of the lawn. In a few minutes they pulled up to the Harbor House, and Tom stopped the truck at the back door.

"But...?" Tom prodded. He had always done this. He had always cared.

"Oh, I don't know. I still feel a lot of guilt about leaving in the first place...and Daddy dying. It's like I traded everything that really mattered for something—some crazy dream I had about life—and someone who was so wrong. And now I can never get it back. I have to live with that forever." There was a long pause while Sophie looked down. "And this is really stupid, and not near as important, but on another level I'm also really embarrassed. I feel like a fool. I think people here expected me to really be somebody when I grew up, and I let them all down—the ones who like me, that is. And the ones who don't, well, they're probably all gloating. The preacher's daughter—divorced. I just feel like my life doesn't have any credibility in this town anymore. And yet, I don't want to be anywhere else, because you guys are here."

She could barely look at him. She knew the last part sounded self-absorbed and stupid, and she knew he'd probably tell her that.

Tom sighed. Then he looked at her. "Well, we could all move somewhere else."

"Huh?"

"I said, we could all just move somewhere else. It sounds like that would make things a lot easier for you."

"Are you mocking me, Tom?"

"Not at all. Just think about it—would it really be easier if we were all somewhere else?"

Sophie looked out the window toward the square and tried to imagine it. "I wouldn't have to face all these people. And I wouldn't have to face all the memories I have here...of Dad, and growing up..."

"Do you think that would be easier or better?"

"I don't know..." Sophie was feeling something begin to unravel. When had her brother become so wise? "Actually, no. I think it might be easier at first, but not better in the long run. Because I would still have to deal with these issues within myself. Otherwise there would never be any peace."

Tom smiled at her. "You know, sometimes it's hard being the brother of someone so special." He looked into her eyes and let his words sink in before he continued. "Especially if I compare myself or worry about what others think. But one thing I've learned through the years is to look inside and see what God has for me...what He wants to make out of my life. All we have to offer is ourselves—our strengths and also our failures. In His hands, even those can become something beautiful." He gestured to the building outside the window. "Kind of like this house."

She leaned her head on his shoulder and hugged him for a long moment before she slipped out of the truck. She felt his protective brother eyes on her as she walked up the steps, and only when she was safely through the door did she hear him drive away.

* * * * *

Sophie stood with her hands on her hips and stared at the box like it was full of copperheads. Spot sauntered into the room and sat down beside it as if he knew she could use the moral support. It was the box she dreaded most, the one she'd saved to unpack for when she finally had some privacy.

Even if she'd had the energy to face it before now—which she hadn't—it wouldn't have mattered, because she hadn't really been alone since she returned to River Bend. Her mother, grandmother, and sister-in-law had seen to it that she had plenty of help cleaning and getting set up…and plenty of company.

And even though she still didn't really have the energy to face this, she knew in her heart it was time. A part of her was ready. So she sat down on the floor next to Spot and opened the box.

It was closed very securely, and breaking the tape unleashed a floodgate of emotions. The first thing she pulled out was her wedding album. It was embossed with the words WEDDING MEMORIES OF MR. AND MRS. STEPHEN HUNTER. Her smiling face next to Stephen's, behind hard plastic and framed in gold on the cover of the leather volume, seemed to mock her, daring her to look inside. She took the dare and felt a sort of queasiness creeping over her as she opened the book. She hesitated. Maybe now wasn't the time to deal with this. But if not now, when? She needed to put it behind her.

Sophie looked down, skimming through the pictures. In this one, she was getting ready in the dressing room with her bridesmaids, all of them looking radiant, laughing, and having fun. In another she saw her family—her mom and dad, Granny, Aunt Stella, and Tom. They all looked festive in the picture. Everyone but Tom.

"He knew even then," she mused aloud, causing Spot to raise his pointed ears. He gave her a quizzical look and then settled back down, curling his sleek black-and-white body into a little crescent beside her.

She thumbed through the album, finding an individual shot of the groom in his black tuxedo, standing in front of a stained glass window. The vibrant colors behind him matched the look in his eyes, which sparkled with the thrill of their adventure. For a moment Sophie felt a flicker of the old tenderness she'd once had for Stephen. At a glance it was easy to see how he'd swept her off her feet, with his intelligent green eyes and the dark raven hair pulled back in a neat ponytail. That ponytail had scandalized her mother, but Sophie had thought it so attractive, like everything else she knew about him at the time.

He was really two people, she'd come to discover, but the one who stared at her from the page in the album was the one she'd loved. They'd had what seemed to be such a deep connection, it was hard even now to believe it hadn't been real. Sophie still didn't understand. Maybe she never would. She turned a few pages to move on.

The next picture her eyes rested on was a view of the whole sanctuary. Regardless of how the marriage had turned out, it *had* been her dream wedding. From the balcony of the church, the photographer had managed to capture the whole scene in one neat frame. There were the candles—scores of them—and the cedar and the ferns. The wedding party formed a *V* fanning outward toward the crowd, and at the center stood her father. He was tall and strong with his Bible open in front of her and Stephen, and they were holding hands and looking into one another's eyes through her gossamer veil.

"Repeat after me," her father's booming voice had commanded. "I, Stephen…"

"I, Stephen…"

"…take you, Sophie…."

"…take you, Sophie…."

They made so many promises that day. At least he'd kept that one,

Sophie thought bitterly. He'd been a taker all right. She slammed the book shut, having her fill of the pictures. Spot jumped a little, startled out of his sleep, and she patted him, noticing that a bundle of letters had fallen out of the album. She untied the string.

Dear Sophie, one letter read. *Of all the stars in my universe, you shine the brightest. Light my way forever, my forever love. Stephen.* And another: *My darling Sophie, my dream, my passion, I feel so alive since you said you love me. Have I been dead without knowing it all these years? The songs we will sing, the places we will go, the adventures we will have. I am invincible with you by my side! Stephen.* And finally, *Sophie Girl, I love you madly. This waiting is killing me. Let's go away together and do something crazy like get married. Your Stephen.*

Her Stephen. Forever love. My universe. Something crazy like getting married. She'd been over these letters, like the pictures and the whole experience of their relationship, so many times before. There were times when the words had cut like knives through her stomach and she'd cried so hard she got sick. There were times when she had actually laughed at their stupidity—his sheer audacity and hers—for what those words had once meant to her. And then there were times she'd actually pitied him and felt an almost motherly compassion, as though he was a prodigal son. But now she just felt numb. And felt a deep sense of regret for all she had wasted of herself on the wrong person.

Setting the letters aside, she picked up a picture in a small frame. As she took it out to examine it, she felt a nick and noticed blood dribbling from her finger and onto the picture, blotting out the image. The glass had been broken in the move, and there, exposed, were she and her old friend Jon. The picture had been taken at their high school graduation ten years ago. His mother had snapped it as he stood with his arm around her, both of them in purple robes with gold cords. Sophie stared at it a moment, remembering, and tried to smooth away the blood from their exuberant faces. But the picture was ruined. She tossed it into the trash, broken glass and all, and went to get a Band-Aid.

Chapter Two

. . . .

Jon Anthony stepped out of the French doors onto his cedar deck, holding a cup of coffee, and peered at the Arkansas River five hundred feet below him. His dog, a Great White Pyrenees named Aslan, was sitting with his head erect on the edge of a rock that jutted out over the bluff, like a king surveying his kingdom.

And what a glorious kingdom it is, thought Jon. The leaves on the trees were just starting to turn, hinting at the change that would come to the landscape later in the fall. The sky was cloudless and blue, the perfect backdrop for the birds that soared at his eye level. The river was a dull gray-green color today—loden, he thought—as he watched it twisting and bending through the mountains he called home. Jon sighed. *This is why I can never leave here*, he thought to himself. *This river flows through my veins.* So no matter where his work took him, he always landed back where he felt most comfortable—in a cabin he had built himself, with the help of a friend, on a bluff that overlooked the river.

Jon had bought a hundred acres of land with the proceeds from his first book. With an unused cattle farm on the front and mountains butting up to the river on the back, the whole place was wild. Aside from cutting a road up to the bluff and pushing out just enough brush to build his cabin and have a small yard, he'd made no effort to tame it.

He gave a few lectures a year, went to the required meetings with his editor, publisher, and agent, and attended occasional conferences and book signings. Occasionally he'd have to spend a chunk of time somewhere else doing research. But the bulk of his life was spent right here on this bluff—drinking coffee on his deck, reading by the fire with Aslan at his feet, or writing at his computer desk by the window. He went into town as little as possible. On Tuesdays he had breakfast with his mom at her house, and on Thursday mornings he drank coffee at the bakery with three pastor friends. He would usually try to sneak into the grocery store on one of those days to buy his supplies. If he had other errands at the hardware store, library, or post office, he did them then as quickly as possible. He also went to church some Sundays, visiting different congregations as he felt led and occasionally treating his mom to lunch afterward. He wasn't a member anywhere.

This particular Wednesday morning as he stood on his deck, Jon was in a quandary. He had been since breakfast the day before at his mother's. Always abuzz with the latest news from Patsy's Kut and Kurl, where she got her hair done every week, Margaret had told him about the grand opening of Sophie's new café in the old Harbor House. He knew about it already, of course, but he hadn't mentioned the fact to his mother, nor that he contemplated going.

Jon paced. Should he go or should he not? Was there any harm in it? After all, they were still good friends, right? She might be expecting him. It was logical to think she might be. She knew he lived in River Bend, didn't she? But what if she wasn't expecting him? What if she hadn't even thought about him over the past ten years? Should he take his mother? No, too awkward. He couldn't ask one of his friends. What if they figured him out once they saw Sophie? Maybe he should just go by himself. Or maybe not at all. Maybe he was making a big deal out of nothing.

The phone rang and interrupted this mental dialogue. He poked his head through the open door and listened to the machine in case it was important.

"Jon? Oh Jonny Boy, are you there? Pick up."

Recognizing his friend David's voice, Jon jogged to the phone. "Hey."

A plastic-sounding voice. "Are you a homeowner? Is your house wood or aluminum? You have been selected—"

"David?"

David was the builder-turned-preacher who had helped Jon build his house.

Now he was imitating an old woman's voice. "Brother Jonny, could you come over right now? My cat Fluffy is up in a tree and I can't get her down. I know it's dinnertime, but—"

"And you wonder why I screen my calls?"

"Not really. You've about got me convinced to do it too. My wife's all for it. But I just can't get over the guilt factor that a preacher should actually be available to his parishioners. You know what I mean?"

"That depends on your definition of available."

"Okay, thesaurus man. I'll think about that one. We can discuss it over lunch tomorrow."

"Lunch? Don't you mean breakfast?"

"No, I mean lunch. We're changin' plans just for tomorrow. There's a new place openin' up. Jim and I decided we might as well see for ourselves what all of the fuss is about. He's callin' Danny. So what do you say? Meet us for lunch?"

"Um…"

"It's in that old Harbor House…the one Dr. James fixed up. I think it's his daughter that's runnin' the new joint. You ought to know her… I think she's about your age. Anyway, how about eleven? Maybe that way we can beat the noon crowd."

Jon was silent.

"Jon? Is that all right? I mean, does that sound good?"

What could he say? "Uh, yeah. That's fine. See you there."

"Okay, bye."

They hung up, and simple as that, he was going.

Chapter Three

· · · · · · · · · · · · · · · · · · · ·

The tired evening sun reflected how Sophie felt as she dug deeper into the box. *I will finish this box or perish,* she thought, remembering a phrase from *Anne of Green Gables,* which had been her favorite movie as a child. Her fingers moved more carefully now, treading softly over what could be more broken glass.

The next framed picture she found was intact, but she felt her heart break into a thousand pieces when she looked at it. Her dad was holding up a stringer full of river catfish and grinning from ear to ear. The fish were heavy, and her finger traced the outline of his arm muscles, which were bulging under his white T-shirt. How many times had those strong arms enfolded her? Squeezed her in bear hugs that made her back pop? Scooped her up for a ride on his broad shoulders? Held her tight as they danced around the living room floor?

It was his arm she had leaned on as she walked down the aisle to marry Stephen. His arms that lifted to bless their union. And as she and Stephen walked away from him as man and wife, she'd had no idea how far that path would take her, and what—or whom—she'd lose along the way.

After the divorce, she had gone abroad, not knowing why. She just knew she didn't want to go home. So she wandered. She ended up in Italy, in a village called Vernazza, one of the Cinque Terre.

In Vernazza, Sophie found a measure of peace as she lay on its rocky beach and let the sun burn away her pain. She walked and prayed along the Via dell'Amore, going village to village and getting lost, then finding her way again. For money she worked in a trattoria on the water, serving wines from local grapes and fresh-baked bread with local olive oil. She lived in a little room above the trattoria.

There had been a beautiful simplicity about her life in Vernazza. An acceptance she felt among the people there, especially Mamma and Papà Gemme, who owned the trattoria. There was a wide range of children in their family, with three away in college and then the twins, who Papa winkingly said were a surprise. Valentina and Luca, who were eight, had charmed Sophie with their big brown eyes and golden hair, and she'd charmed them. At first they were shy with the strange American girl, but it wasn't long before they were running into the trattoria every day after school looking for her, begging her to take them down to the beach.

With a nod from Mamma they'd be off. The beach was just a few yards—though a treacherous few yards—from the trattoria. Sophie would help the twins climb down the small rocky ledge to the water, then stretch out on a flat boulder close by while they played and splashed in the sea. They liked to look for fish and shells and other wonders in the little tide pools that would come up between the big rocks that lined the shore. Every few minutes they'd shriek with delight at a discovery and demand that she come see their treasures. If she didn't come, they'd usually bring whatever it was to her, sometimes plopping it on her belly and laughing hysterically at her reaction. The innocence of the twins touched her. Sophie loved to close her eyes and listen to them laughing. It was a healing sound.

During slow times at the trattoria she would quiz them on their English, and they would quiz her in Italian. It was from them that she learned to say "sei bellisima," "you are beautiful," and "Dio è amore," "God is love." She loved the way they said thank you, as though everything was a gift of grace: "grazie."

Mamma had taught her the secret of her wonderful pomodoro sauce. And Papà had taken her fishing in his rickety little boat, teaching her how to find the right fish in the right parts of the sea. They had caught some fantastic dinners. But the salty Mediterranean was too clear, too revealing for Sophie. Though it healed some of her wounds, it also forced her to see the truth. And the truth was that she couldn't stay there forever. In her deep heart's core, she wasn't home. Comfortable as it was for a while—even happy at some level—it was sort of like treading water. Her life was going nowhere.

And then the call came.

"Sophie?" She had been scared the instant she heard Tom's voice. They usually scheduled their calls.

"Tom?"

"Sophie, I don't know how to tell you this…." Tom had been crying. "Daddy died this morning. An hour ago…he was killed in a car crash. Can you get home?"

Sophie had felt the floor give way beneath her. She was falling. Some darkness in the center of the earth had opened, and its great throat was swallowing her down. She was blank. Shocked. Sick. Chilled to the bone. She dropped the phone, then scrambled to pick it up and hold it in her trembling fingers.

"How?"

"He was on a visit…on his way to see someone in the hospital… some trucker…we think…fell asleep and crossed over into Dad's lane and hit him. He was killed instantly."

The flight from Florence had been pure hell. Never had time stood so still, never had she felt so far away from her own life. For the first time, it seemed, she could look at herself as though a mere observer and see that she was an utterly lost person. Bereft. Suspended in space. She was floating, devoid of meaning and purpose. Squandering her time. Without direction and without hope. Despair descended on her like a thick fog.

She had called Tom, and he and Madeline picked her up at the airport. Their eyes told a tale of tears, and their faces showed the strain of sleeplessness. They put their arms around her, and she fell into them. Holding each other, the tears flowed for them all. No one said anything. But it was comforting somehow just to be together and to share the awful load of grief. Even under that crushing weight, perhaps especially because of it, Sophie had been glad to be home.

* * * * *

Home. If there was one thing Sophie knew as she sat on the floor unpacking her box of broken memories, it was that it was good to be home.

She'd dreamed up the idea of a little café on her plane ride back to the States. There had been nothing she could really imagine herself doing in River Bend besides hanging around, visiting her family, as she'd done briefly at Christmas and Easter the last few years. She knew if she was going to stay, she had to do something, but what? What did she have to offer other than perhaps teaching music lessons? What was a degree in liberal arts going to do for her in River Bend?

Somehow the thought of the yellow house came to her mind. Her mom and daddy had bought it one summer as an investment and a "ministry opportunity" when she was a child. She remembered the first time she saw it and how they laughed when she said it was a "broken house." And so it was. But they had worked away steadily on it, doing most of the restoration themselves, and it had become a beautiful home. They renamed it the "Harbor House" and opened it as a bed-and-breakfast, drawing a few people a month as they passed through River Bend on their way to the wine country a few miles west.

It had a commercial kitchen, and her mother had used it for catering jobs and special events, like ladies' teas and wedding or baby showers and anniversaries. And occasionally a family, or perhaps a battered woman who had no place else to go, would shelter there for the night, or several nights, while the preacher and his wife attended to their needs before returning to their own home, the parsonage.

They had planned to live in the Harbor House and expand its ministry potential after Daddy retired and left the parsonage, but as things happened, they lived there only six months before her newly widowed mother moved in with Granny up on the mountain and the yellow house was empty. It would work for Sophie.

She picked through the rest of the box. There were a couple of old yearbooks from River Bend High School, where she'd been the homecoming queen. She leafed through one of them, reading a few corny entries her friends had written on the signature pages and finding her face and long hair with bangs plastered everywhere in a section under the heading "Who's Who?" Miss River Bend High School: Sophia Harper. Most Likely to Succeed: Sophia Harper. Class Favorite, Most Talented, Best All-Around: Sophia Harper. The list went on.

I'm certainly none of the above, thought Sophie. *What about Biggest Loser?* The list didn't include categories for Divorcee or Wanderer either. Cursing herself for letting it matter even a little, she suddenly felt the impulse to flee her hometown.

Jon's picture on the same page caught her eye as he was voted Most Studious, Most Courteous, and with her, Best All-Around. *That's the truth*, she thought. *He's the best friend I ever had.*

She set the annuals to the side and reached into the box again. This time she pulled out her old Bible. It was in an easy-to-understand translation and had been a gift from her parents when she was a kid. Her dad had read it to her, cover to cover, one story at a time as he tucked her into bed. She could still hear the sound of his voice as he read and remembered how simple and coherent all of the stories had seemed to her then. In those days she could have told you almost anything about the Bible. But it had been a long time since she'd looked at it without pulling down the veil of doubt over her eyes. It wasn't simple anymore.

When did everything become so complicated? But she had no answers, only more memories. A memory of the time Stephen sat across from her at that coffee shop in the Bay Area and told her he'd lost his belief in God. As unsettled as it had made her, she'd foolishly believed him when he said it didn't really matter. Their love, he said, was all that mattered.

In the end, however, Sophie's adventure in love outside of faith led to disaster. A few months later she found Stephen and another woman in bed together in their apartment. He had cried, said he was sorry, begged her not to leave, the works. But in that moment she had seen him for what he was. Stephen was an utterly lost person. And though she didn't know it then, leaving him was the first step Sophie made, herself, toward being found.

Sophie noticed a marker in the old Bible and turned to it. Someone (she?) had underlined the last part of Galatians 5:6: "...*all* we need is faith working through love."

She took Spot outside and sat on the porch, watching him and pondering that thought. It was a lot different from Stephen's philosophy, and frankly, a lot different from hers. She didn't know exactly what she needed, but she didn't think faith would be enough. It never had been for her. Or had it?

Sophie couldn't remember. She was tired of thinking, and she had cheesecake to make. Spot came back up on the porch and led her to the door. They went inside, and after two long hours in the kitchen, Sophie finally turned out the light in the yellow house. Falling into bed, she snuggled underneath the covers with her dog, and slept.

Chapter Four

. . . .

When Jon arrived at Milton's at ten o'clock, the place was packed.

"Hey man!" Milton called when he stepped through the door. His smile looked like ivory piano keys set in an ebony grand. "Be right with ya!"

Jon had been coming here since he was a kid, and he knew what that could mean. Glancing at his watch, Jon nodded at Milton and grinned at Clara Belle, his wife. A capable and no-nonsense type of woman, she was working with Milton that day so Jon had hopes he could still get his hair cut without being late to meet the preachers.

He took the last seat, near his old boss, Harvey, and after shaking Harvey's hand, he opened a book. Jon was roused from the page by Milton's friendly voice asking the crowd who was planning to go to Sophie's grand opening.

"I am," Ralph Turner said, "although it makes me feel old to think that girl's old enough to be running a business. I gave her her first swing set. I can still see those blond pigtails flying through the air. She sure was a cute little thing."

"Was?" Colby Clarkson spouted. "You seen her lately? Ain't no *was* about it."

Jon cringed behind his book.

"I'm goin', too." J. T. Spencer puffed on a cigarette from outside the door under the barber pole. Not wanting to miss out on gossip, he called out, "But can you believe that child's mother run off and left her at a time like this? It's opening day of Sophie's restaurant, and Janie done flew the coop and gone out of town! And to go someplace like Ireland. What've they got over there that we don't have right here in River Bend? That's what I'd like to know. I don't get why anybody'd want to go across that shark-infested ocean to see a place like Ireland, anyway."

"Well, I can tell you." Mildred Cooper, the county clerk recently retired after thirty years in office, was an expert on everything that happened in River Bend, and she'd been dispensing her knowledge to anyone who would listen for years. She was waiting on her husband, Bob, who sat in Milton's chair. "They're going because Ruby wanted to go—she always has. I remember her talking about it years ago when we worked together down at the courthouse. She's into all that ancestry stuff." Mildred blew her nose into her hankie. "Anyway, Milton, to answer your question, yes, we'll be there. We're going right after we leave here, to try to beat the crowd."

Milton lathered Bob's neck for a shave. "I'm glad Janie's getting out. That's a good woman, been through a hard time these last years. I'll bet a little change of scenery will do her some good." As proprietor of the shop, he was ever the diplomat.

Earl Mabry, clad in overalls and a work shirt, looked up from his farming magazine. He'd been a deacon at his church for over fifty years and spoke as an authority. "I agree. And anyway, talkin' 'bout runnin' off and leavin' somebody, Sophie's the one that run off and left her family with that long-haired hippie she married. Why, she's been 'round the world and back while her folks was sittin' here worryin' 'bout her. What with Sophie gettin' a divorce and all, and then gala-vantin' all over Europe, and then Brother James up and dyin' in a freak accident like that...well, I'd say it's Janie's turn to have a little fun."

Jon felt the blood running to his head. Pressing his knuckles into the wooden arms of his chair, he took a deep breath, preparing to tell them all off, but Harvey Weinberg piped up.

"I think it will be good for all of them," Harvey offered. "Ruby's not getting any younger, so if that's one of her life's dreams, I say go for it! And Earl's right that Janie's due a vacation. Besides, Sophie can handle it. I hear she's got some good help, and anyway, that girl— for whatever problems she's had—is smart. She's a good kid too. It takes a lot to come back home after going through what she has. I, for one, admire her guts. And I'm glad we might be finally getting a decent place to eat around here."

Jon stood. "Harvey's right. Sheesh, sometimes I wonder why anyone would want to come home to this town." Nodding to Milton, he walked out, letting the door shut somewhat loudly behind him.

Chapter Five

....

Sophie's "good help" was late, and she was getting nervous. She'd made the cheesecake the night before so it could chill, and Mamma Gemme's sauce was out of the refrigerator and simmering on the stove. Half-cooked pasta soaked in a pot of cold water, ready for a quick boil when ordered. The pinto beans, with their ham hocks and dash of sugar, were almost done, and she had turned them down to low. Brown rice for the daily special sat in a steamer, and shredded chicken with peppers and onions were staying warm in a slow cooker. The catfish fillets were thawing in salted water. Two fresh apple cobblers bubbled in one oven, and a coconut pie and a chocolate pie were toasting their meringues in the other. Sophie was making pecan cornbread to go with the beans when the telephone rang.

"Hello? I mean, Harbor House Café, can I help you?"

"Hi, sweetheart. How's it going?" It was her mother calling from Ireland, where she was on vacation for two months. No telling what time it was there.

"Well, so far so good. I'm going to be in trouble if Shannon doesn't show up in a minute, though. How are you guys?"

"We're doing well. Granny is having a great time, and I think it's going to be good for me, too."

"How's Aunt Stella? Is she behaving? Getting on your nerves?"

"Stella and I are getting along fine. I'm really glad we all came together. I feel terrible about missing your big day, though. I trust it is the right thing that we went ahead and did this…?" Her voice sounded unsure.

"I'll be fine, Mom. I'd never have let you change your trip. Who knew I would be doing this back when you made those arrangements? And Granny didn't need to put it off anymore anyway. It's the right thing. Don't worry about it, please."

"I can't help but worry a little. But I know you'll do a great job. I've been praying for you all day! How is Tom?"

"Good. I saw him yesterday after I got my menus printed. He was at Milton's. And Madeline is great—just tired all of the time, I think. They'll be here later."

"Well, tell them Granny and I said hi. We're off to Sligo in the morning. Cousin Bridget wants to show us Yeats country. It should be interesting."

"Oh, I've always wanted to see the Lake Isle of Innisfree. Take lots of pictures if you go there. Listen, Momma, I've got to go, but thanks for calling. I'll e-mail you all about the day when it is over. Oh good, here comes Shannon."

"I'll keep praying, hon. I love you."

"I love you too. Be safe."

Shannon hurried in the door with a flushed look. "I'm so sorry I'm late," she said. "Katie had a science project due today and she dropped it on the way to the bus so we had to fix it and then I had to run her by the school."

Sophie managed a chuckle. "That's okay. I'm sure glad to see you. Come on in here and get chopping."

While Shannon chopped the lettuces, bell peppers, cucumbers, broccoli, cauliflower, onions, radishes, and carrots for the salad, Sophie sliced sandwich meats and cheeses on the slicer. She was shaving smoked turkey when she heard a knock and saw the back door opening.

"Yoo-hoo!"

Sophie was trying to register the nasally voice from some mental archive when a woman her age stepped through the door. She was clad in a tight tank top and very short running shorts that showed off fabulous tanned legs. Her hair was tied in a ponytail on top of her head, and her makeup, a little thick for a morning jog, Sophie thought, was immaculate.

Sophie had to turn off the slicer to keep from cutting herself, and she forced a smile as she recognized the face that matched the voice of Misti Lane.

"Misti. Nice to see you. Uh, can I help you?"

"Oh, Sophie—I was just out running and just *had* to come by and check on you. I heard you were back in town. I just haven't had the chance to get by here. But I wanted to come say hello."

"Well, that's nice. You look great." Sophie hated to admit it, but it was true.

"Thanks...so do you." Misti smiled a little too sweetly as her eyes traveled quickly over Sophie's appearance, and Sophie felt suddenly uncomfortable as she saw herself in her mind's eye. Her hair was back and her face was free of makeup. She wore a tie-dyed T-shirt and ripped jeans underneath her red apron, which was already covered in stains. Her feet were in red Crocs.

Misti continued. "I know it's your opening day—everyone's talking about it. I'm coming for lunch. A lot of old friends are. We all just can't *wait* to see you and get caught up."

Sophie could. She felt a knot forming in her stomach.

"I mean, we all thought you were living the high life with your rock star husband. Who'd have guessed you'd end up back in River Bend?"

Sophie cringed.

"This is such a charming old place," Misti continued. "How perfect that you would come home and work here." She surveyed the kitchen. "So...quaint. Such a perfect thing for you to do, especially since you don't have any kids or anything. I mean, you don't, do you?"

Sophie took a deep breath. "Nope, just a dog."

Misti laughed. *Like a horse*, Sophie thought.

"A dog. Oh, how sweet. Sophie, you're just so funny. You always were."

"Do you have any?" Sophie asked her.

"Kids? Yeah. We have two, a boy and a girl."

"I'm sorry, Misti, I guess I don't know who you married." Sophie went back to slicing.

"Well, you know I dated Michael forever in high school, but I ended up marrying Colby."

"Colby Clarkson?" Sophie tried to keep her voice neutral, but mentally she cringed. Colby had been quite the womanizer in high school.

"Yeah. I'm Misti Clarkson now."

"Well—congratulations. Are your kids in school?"

"They're four and two. But they go to daycare. I have lots to do with helping Colby in his business and around the farm."

"I'm sure that keeps you busy." Sophie was trying to sound interested, but she really didn't have time for this conversation. "Hey, Misti, I'm sorry I can't really talk much right now, but I have a lot of prep yet to do. Thanks so much for stopping by—I'll look for you later."

"Sure, yeah. I better finish my run. I've got to shower and everything before I come back."

Misti turned to walk out the door. "See ya later," she called.

Sophie shivered a little, then she shook her head clear and shrugged at Shannon, who was looking at her, questioning.

She washed her hands, drying them on her apron, and went out on the porch to write the daily special on the chalkboard she'd mounted by the front door.

THREE CHICKEN TACOS, BEANS, AND RICE. $6.00. It was a specialty she'd tasted and perfected while living in California, different from any other version of tacos one might get in River Bend. They were delicious—at least she thought so and hoped others would too.

"Watch that spelling."

A voice behind her made Sophie drop the chalk. But as she turned around, she realized the voice was familiar.

As if out of the past, Jon Anthony walked up the steps and onto the porch, picked up the chalk, and placed it in her hand with a warm smile.

Sophie squealed and threw her arms around his neck. After a second, Jon's arms encircled her, and he returned her hug.

Sophie pulled back to look at his face. "Jon Anthony. Is that really you?" She surveyed the changes in her friend since she'd last seen him at her wedding. He seemed taller, more muscular, his face more chiseled. It had lost that baby roundness, and the glasses were gone from his brown eyes. His dark hair was shorter.

Looking at him with her older, wiser eyes, Sophie realized with a surprising warmth in her face that Jon was good-looking.

Really, really good-looking.

Suddenly uncomfortable, Sophie stepped out of his arms as nonchalantly as possible and tried to keep the blush out of her cheeks.

"In the flesh," he said, his voice deeper than she remembered. "You don't think I'd miss the second biggest event in River Bend history, do you?"

"Actually," Sophie said, staring at him, "that's exactly what I'd expect of you. Who twisted your arm?"

Jon laughed. "I guess that's why I'm here early, to beat the crowd."

His reference to the crowd jolted Sophie back into business mode. "Oh, uh, I'm sorry I can't talk much right now, Jon. I am so happy to see you, but you can't imagine how much I have to do. Would you like to sit on the porch? Maybe I'll get a break later—I really would love to catch up with you. I can't believe you're here!" She laughed, a little nervous.

He grinned at her. "The porch would be great. It's a beautiful day. Just put me in the quietest corner. Oh, yeah—and I'm meeting someone, so how about this table?" He pointed to a four-top on the far end of the porch.

"Sure, that's fine." Sophie surprised herself by feeling a little pang of—what? Possessiveness? That was weird. She hadn't seen the guy in years, and he was free to eat lunch with whomever he liked. Hurrying back toward the kitchen, she almost ran into one of her servers, René, who was carrying a tray of drinks out onto the porch.

"Oh my goodness, is that Jon Anthony?" René whispered.

Sophie nodded.

"You *know* him? He's River Bend's most eligible bachelor. Kind of like a town celebrity." René giggled.

Sophie glanced back to where Jon was now sitting, then quickly turned her head, giving René a look of bewilderment.

Her heart beating fast as she returned to the kitchen, Sophie wondered why in the world she should be nervous around Jon Anthony.

Chapter Six
....

By noon, Sophie was out of the special and almost out of dishes. There was no commercial dishwasher in the Harbor House, just two deep sinks that were now full of plates, glasses, and silverware. And there was no sign of Andy, the kid she'd hired to wash dishes.

At twelve thirty, Sophie bent over one sink and was frantically washing a few plates so she could fill her next order when Jon poked his head in the door of the kitchen.

"I just came to say good-bye. Everything was really good...." His voice trailed off as he took in the situation.

Sophie glanced up at him and tried to smile her thanks. She felt strands of hair in her eyes as sweat beaded on her face. Like the kitchen, she was a complete mess.

Jon let the door swing shut for a minute, and then he came back in while rolling up the sleeves of his white button-down shirt.

"Can I have a job?" He beamed, nudging her from the sink.

Sophie was dumbfounded. But realizing he was serious, she gathered herself.

"You're hired!" she exclaimed with relief. Tossing him an apron, she turned the dishes over and dashed back to the stove.

For the next two hours they barely said a word. Sophie, Jon, and Shannon worked like a well-oiled machine, filling orders and sending them out of the kitchen via the servers, who whisked them on to the tables of their happy customers. It seemed the whole town had come out to try her café, and Sophie was touched by the reception. She hadn't expected it to be so kind. Or so overwhelming.

A little after two o'clock—closing time—the last diners left and René locked the door behind them. The kitchen was almost clean, and while the servers worked on sweeping and re-stocking the front, Sophie invited Jon and Shannon to fix themselves plates and have a little rest.

"I can't today," said Shannon. "Thanks, but I have to pick up Sam early from school. He has a doctor's appointment."

"Oh, okay," said Sophie, "but please take something with you—and for Kyle, too." She mustered a smile. "You did an awesome job today, by the way. I appreciate it so much." She felt like she'd just come out of a whirlwind and knew Shannon and Jon were the reasons she survived.

"I actually enjoyed it." Shannon scooped some food into a to-go container and held it up. "Thanks for this. See you in the morning!"

Sophie turned to Jon, who was taking off his apron. As he rolled down his sleeves, she noted that the bottom of his shirt and the top of his jeans were drenched.

"Jon, you are soaking wet!" Then she noticed a red tomato sauce stain on his sleeve. "Oh no, I hope that shirt isn't ruined."

"Nah, it's all right. Nothing Margaret can't get out."

"Since when do you call your mother 'Margaret'?" Sophie asked, grinning.

"Since she's not here," he said, and they both laughed. She knew Jon would never call his mother "Margaret" to her face.

"Well, do you want some dessert or anything? Or how about a coke with me on the back porch?" She smiled. "I think I've even got some vanilla."

"No food, thanks. I had a really good lunch." He grinned. "But a drink sounds good. I haven't had a vanilla Diet Coke in a long time."

* * * * *

Jon stretched out his legs on the low porch, which was really more of a stoop, and leaned back against the house. His lower back ached from bending over the sink, but otherwise he felt good. And he was touched that Sophie remembered his favorite drink.

He closed his eyes for a moment and heard the door creak, then the fast clicks of tiny feet trotting across the porch. He opened his eyes to see a little black bulldog plop down from the porch, run over to the hedge to do his business, and then look back at Jon, just realizing he was there. The dog lifted his ears to attention, focused his eyes, and began to growl at Jon suspiciously.

Sophie came out of the house then. "Spot, it's okay," she said, and the growling ceased. Spot resumed sniffing and poking around the yard. She handed Jon his drink and sat down beside him with a salad.

The servers began to file out the back door, stopping a moment to say good-bye to them both.

"We're finished inside," Debbie said. "Everything's done and set up for tomorrow."

"Thanks again!" Sophie told them.

"It was fun," answered René, and the others agreed.

"I didn't know Jon Anthony was going to be working here today, though," declared Rhonda.

"Neither did I." He grinned, and they all laughed.

"Did you forget your wallet or are you really that nice?" Debbie grinned.

"You certainly came to the rescue in the kitchen," René acknowledged with a sigh. "Whew—I don't think we'd have gotten all of those orders out without you."

"That's for sure," Sophie added, then she teased him. "He might have to stay on full time!"

"I don't think my back could take it." He rolled his shoulder. "But you can keep me on your reserve list."

When the servers had all gone, Jon and Sophie were finally alone. He relished the quiet. She munched some of her salad, and he took a long swig of his drink. In the stillness it seemed to dawn on them both, for the first time in hours, that it had been years since they'd been together. There was a pregnant silence. Then, as if on cue, they looked at each other at the same time.

Sophie said with gravity, "Thank you."

"Thank you for the job." He smiled playfully, shaking off her seriousness.

"Really, Jon, thank you."

He wanted to act like it was no big deal but was moved by the feeling in her voice.

"You're welcome."

They both looked away and were silent again. The moment felt surreal to Jon. It had been so long, and everything had changed. But seeing Sophie again—it was as if nothing had changed. He reached for a blade of grass to ground himself.

She said, "Well."

He laughed and turned to her, back in the present. "That's a deep subject."

They both smiled.

"Here we are," she said, looking away.

That's a deep subject too, he thought, but he didn't say it.

Sophie set her salad plate down off the porch for Spot to inspect. He came over and sniffed, then carefully picked out the grilled chicken slices and bacon crumbles. He kept one eye on Jon as he ate.

"It's kind of weird being here—home, I mean," she said.

"Is it? How so?"

"It just is. But, I wouldn't want to be anywhere else. At least I think that's one thing I've learned after ten years living everywhere else." Sophie pulled her knees up under her chin and hugged them.

"So tell me about your travels," Jon said gently, looking in her eyes.

The wistful sound left her voice and she said clearly, "I think I'd rather talk about you."

* * * * *

Spot came back up on the porch, and Sophie gathered him in her lap, where he curled up in the shape of a crescent.

"What do you want to know?" Jon asked.

"Oh, you can start anywhere. Bad friend that I am, I don't know much except that you went to graduate school in Fayetteville, became a writer, came back home, and now you're rich and famous…and yet you're still humble enough to wash dishes for a damsel in distress."

Jon laughed. "Well, I guess that sums it up. What more is there to tell?"

Sophie's eyes bored into him.

He tossed the blade of grass.

"Well…let's see. I doubled up that last semester of school after you got married so I could finish in December. I spent a little time here with Mom, and then I took the student loan money I had saved and went to Europe for about three months, backpacking. You know, like we always used to talk about doing."

Sophie nodded, rubbing Spot's back with her fingers.

"I sort of planned a whirlwind tour—starting in London, making my way down, and then flying open-jaw out of Athens. But by the time I got to Athens in June, I had hooked up with some people who were going from there to Israel and Egypt, so I changed my flights and tagged along. I'm glad I did. It was really cool—and totally different from Europe, of course. After that I figured I might as well see more of Africa since I was there, so I flew down to Nairobi and traveled around Kenya—and actually across the borders of Uganda and Tanzania—before finally coming home. It was quite a trip. Really changed my perspective."

Sophie nodded, soaking it all in. She realized how little she really knew about Jon's life since they had gone separate ways. "Wow—then you came home and started school?"

"I had been accepted to law school, so I got my stuff together and moved to Fayetteville. I started school a few days later."

"Law school? I didn't know that was the plan."

"Well, it wasn't, really. That last semester of college I just took the LSAT sort of on a whim. By some fluke, I scored well enough to get a scholarship and decided I might as well go."

"'Might as well go' to Kenya, and then 'might as well go' to law school? That really doesn't sound like you. It's hilarious." But even as Sophie said it, she remembered some of her questionable reasoning for decisions she'd made.

Jon grinned at her. "Now it seems so. But at that time I had no idea what I wanted to do. I was drifting."

"I thought you always wanted to be a writer."

"Well, yeah, I did, but...I guess I just wanted something more secure to fall back on if that didn't work out. Margaret's advice."

They both grinned at that.

"So...you have a law degree?"

"Uh, no. I have thirty-six hours of law school and remain in 'good academic standing' in the unlikely event I should ever choose to return."

You quit? Sophie almost burst out. But something in Jon's eyes, a look of vulnerability, stopped her from saying it. She just looked at him in amazement. "So where did the first book deal come in?"

"Well, I was working as a waiter in this cool restaurant in Fayetteville and writing on the side. I got to know a writing professor who came to eat there often, and through a friend of a friend, she ended up helping me connect with an editor who read my manuscript and actually liked it. It was a big break. I was really, really lucky."

"I doubt luck had a lot to do with it."

"Well then, the grace of God."

"So what is your book about?" she asked, ashamed that she didn't know.

Jon was very unassuming. "Oh, it's kind of a coming-of-age story...

about this guy who grows up without a father. He thinks his father's dead—and then his dad shows up and he has to come to terms with all of that...."

Knowing how closely this mirrored Jon's personal background with his own father, her heart swelled with pride. "Oh, Jon, how cool—and how brave of you to take that on. Does it end happily?"

"Well, yes, sort of. That's actually something I'm not real comfortable with. The editor had me change the ending to make it happier, tidier—and I did need help—but it seems sort of cheesy, especially from where I am now.... I don't know. I was a kid, it's my first book. What could I do? And she was right, it sells. But it doesn't really represent my highest aspirations as a writer. Let's just put it that way."

"I'm very proud of you. You've certainly done well for yourself, my friend." Sophie smiled at him. "What's next?"

Jon grinned sheepishly and shook his head. "I am *really* tired of talking about myself. Will you please tell me something about you now?"

Sophie looked at him and then looked down. "I don't know what to say." Spot was snoring in her lap.

"You must have been through a lot...I'm sorry. You don't have to talk about it if you don't want to."

"Oh, it's not that. It's just, well, things sure haven't turned out like I thought. I've really made a lot of mistakes, Jon. And there's no excuse for it. I was raised in a great family, given lots of opportunities, even had good friends like you—and I just blew it. That's all I can say. I'm not a victim or anything. I had every reason to make the right choices and I just didn't. There's no excuse. It's really humbling—embarrassing."

"Well, you are human. That's excuse enough." Jon's eyes were kind. "Anyway," he went on, "you're here—and it's a time of new beginnings."

"What an encourager," she said, and leaned over to bump against him. "I'm sorry, Jon, that I ever let our friendship go."

"Maybe we can begin again," he said softly, bumping her back.
Maybe so.

Chapter Seven

....

That evening Sophie stood at the kitchen counter filling containers with leftover beans, cornbread, and the last piece of cheesecake so she could bring them to Tom's.

After Jon left earlier in the afternoon, she'd noticed she had texts from both Tom and Madeline, asking how everything had gone and wondering if they could stop by after work. Sophie had needed some time alone, so she texted them back:

Exhausted. Napping. Will bring supper later—don't cook.

Sophie carried the food out to her little car—it was too far for a bike ride—and arrived at Tom's house a few minutes later.

While Madeline fried potatoes and onions in a skillet, Sophie sat on a barstool and sliced strawberries. She loved the feel of her brother and sister-in-law's home. It was a modest size but open and inviting. As Tom and her father had built most of it themselves, it was tight and sturdy. The natural wood floors and rock fireplace were just an extension of the woods, which seemed an extension of Tom. Sophie felt safe there, and Madeline's simple approach to decorating, which reflected her approach to life, put Sophie at ease. It felt like a home.

They had just finished setting the table when Tom came in from the garden, where he was still coaxing a few things out of the tired plants before the first frost. River Bend was in the midst of what the old timers called an "Indian Summer"—a warm spell that usually came along in early October, just when the leaves were also starting to turn. He deposited two cucumbers and a red onion on the counter for Madeline to slice while he washed his hands in the sink. Then he poured a little cold vinegar over the slices in a bowl, shaking on some pepper, and they all sat down to eat.

"Well, tell us all about it," Tom said after they prayed. "And don't let me forget I've got a takeout order for tomorrow from the teachers at school." He was a middle school principal.

"I can't believe I can't come till Saturday!" Madeline interjected. She was a second grade teacher and had only thirty minutes for lunch.

"It was good," Sophie said. "We were so busy, it was really like a whirlwind for me. But it was fun and definitely challenging. If I can get more organized, I think I will enjoy it."

"Was all of your help good?" Tom asked.

"Well, yes—and no. Shannon was late, which stressed me a little bit. But of course when she got there, she was great. Everybody else showed up on time, except Andy, who didn't show up at all."

"Oh no," said Madeline. "Andy Mabry? That's not like him. I wonder what happened to him!"

"Poor kid—his grandma called me a couple of hours after closing to explain that he'd been in a car accident."

Madeline gasped and put her hand over her pregnant belly.

Sophie hurried on. "It wasn't anything major, though. More like a fender bender. But he will probably need to rest for a couple of days."

"What did you do about the dishes? Did you have enough?"

"That was unbelievable." Sophie paused. "Jon Anthony was there for lunch, and he came back and washed dishes for nearly two hours."

"Are you kidding me?" Tom looked at her, incredulous.

"No. I am not kidding. I saw him when he first got there, and then he came back to the kitchen when he was leaving to tell me good-bye. When he saw all of the dishes piled up, he just started washing. I don't know what we'd have done if he hadn't been there."

"Well, my word," said Madeline. "What a way to rekindle an old friendship."

"I know," agreed Sophie. "I hadn't seen him in years, but when he came in there rolling up his sleeves, it was just like it used to be. He really is a true friend. I don't deserve it."

"Jon's a good guy," said Tom. "He always was. I haven't seen him much since he moved back here though. I guess he's got a pretty busy schedule with all of his writing."

"Yeah. Apparently so. He wouldn't talk much about it, but I think he's pretty successful. He's going to New York in a couple weeks."

"Tom, you should have him speak at the school sometime," suggested Madeline. "He's a real author that you know—right in this town. That'd be a neat thing for the kids."

"That's a good idea. Are you going to see him again anytime soon, Sophie? Would you mind asking him about it?"

"I don't know when I'll see him…but I hope it's soon." Sophie smiled at the thought. She realized it was probably her first real smile in a long time.

Chapter Eight
....

Jon sat staring at his blank computer screen. Aslan groaned beside him as he rearranged his huge, furry form into a more comfortable position on the floor. Once settled, he looked like a giant white rug.

"My sentiments exactly, buddy," Jon grumbled. He was usually energized by the challenge of a new, blank screen, like an artist in front of a blank canvas. But today it was frustrating, even exhausting, just to look at it. After two cups of coffee he still could not clear his head enough to concentrate on writing. At least novel writing.

Jon decided to get out his journal instead. Taking the brown leather volume and a black ink pen out of his desk drawer, he moved from his seat at the computer to a cedar Adirondack chair on the deck. Aslan followed.

Turning to a new page, Jon wrote:

> *I am restless today. I'm sitting on my deck at the edge of a steep bluff, and it strikes me that it's a good picture of how my life feels right now. I'm on the verge of something that could be beautiful—or dangerous. Am I willing to plunge headlong over the edge?*
>
> *Sophie is here. If I am honest with myself, the knowledge she is near—and single—thrills me.*

Jon looked up from his writing and saw the river whirling below him. It was almost red today—colored by clay that had been stirred up from the bottom. Little eddies formed by undercurrents and big churning pools swirled quickly past, devouring logs and other debris. It was fast and furious—a hazardous day for fishing or any other activity.

> *Oh, Lord, help me. I am not wise enough to discern what's right. I can't trust my feelings—they are as tumultuous as the river below me. Unless You hold me back, they'll sweep me away. I'll be adrift, as I was before, when I thought she was lost to me forever.*

Again Jon's gaze traveled up from his journal and swept across the landscape. Above the river sat the eternal mountains, Jon's own home among them. They steadied him somehow…kept the river in its place.

> *No, I'll never be lost like that again—because I've found You, my Father. And in this above all I want to please You.*
> *I pray for Sophie. Lord, she looks tired. She seems so broken. I don't know what has brought her to this point, or even to this place, but You do. And only You can fix her. Bless her now, wherever she is and whatever she is doing. Let her draw near to You as a daughter. Let her see that You are working in her life and bringing about good. Give her the gift of a new beginning, a new life in You.*

Jon put down his pen in the middle of the open journal pages and closed the book loosely. He got up, stretched, and walked to the end of the deck, peering over the railing at the edge of the cliff that plunged only a few steps in front of him. Down below he could see the treetops, and beyond them, the river. He was glad for the strong railing.

There were two oak trees enclosed by his deck—he had cut holes around them rather than chop them down—and squirrels had scattered a few acorns at his feet. Jon picked one up and threw it as far as he could. He watched it arc and then heard a faint rustling as it fell through the trees and, presumably, to the ground. He went back to his seat, picked up the journal again, and added:

> *I trust You to show me what part, if any, I am to have in that new life. Don't let me take one step outside of Your will.*

Jon didn't write or even think the word "Amen." Over the last few years he had found himself very naturally in the practice of praying continually. Unlike some of his friends, who had specific "quiet times" set aside each day for prayer and meditation—"like keeping an appointment with God," one of his preacher friends had said—Jon just left the door open for whenever God chose to enter his thoughts. He figured the invitation went both ways. God was always there for him, and though he admired the discipline others seemed to have in their pursuit of holiness, that wasn't his style.

He reached down and patted Aslan on the head. The dog responded by laying his great white head across Jon's leg. When Jon stopped, he was mauled, gently, by Aslan's huge paw, prodding him to show more affection. After a thorough rub of his dog's head, back, and belly, and a subsequent lick on the face—Aslan's seal of approval—Jon went back in the house and washed his hands. Then he sat back down at the computer. He was ready to start writing.

Chapter Nine

. . . .

Sophie was getting into the swing of things, as Tom called it, and feeling a lot more comfortable with her abilities to manage the business. An old schoolmate-turned-CPA named Becky had set her up with the necessary paperwork and tax information she needed to run payroll and keep up her books. Madeline, who was good with numbers, and Tom, who was good with computers, helped her put it all into a system and walked through the process with her a few times till she got the hang of it.

During the week after the café's grand opening, she and Shannon established a good routine in the kitchen, working out the times it took for certain dishes and always finishing the set-up work before eleven o'clock. The servers were exceptionally good, and with Debbie as their natural leader, they managed the front quite wonderfully. After a rough start, Andy the dish washer had consistently shown up for work on time, and he worked hard. He was even growing on her. Now she was actually finding time to go out and visit with customers at their tables whenever a little lull came to her cooking duties in the kitchen.

It surprised Sophie to see who came in to eat each day. Other than the annoying encounter with Misti Clarkson, there had been very few difficulties or even less-than-pleasant experiences for her to face. Sometimes she could hardly believe there were so many residents of River Bend she'd never known. And the ones she did know were for the most part enthusiastic and very kind toward her, so much so that many of her initial inhibitions about coming home faded. She was actually enjoying herself.

In the past few days she'd seen her old second grade teacher, Eleanor Sigman, who had hugged Sophie and told the other ladies at her table how smart Sophie was and how much spice she had added to her elementary classroom. "Just like she's adding to River Bend now!" Mrs. Sigman had chuckled.

Harvey Weinberg, from the print shop, had also come in a few times, always bringing someone different with him—usually an old friend she remembered from years past in her father's church. It was fun to see them. "You are all grown up!" or "We're so glad you're home!" they would say.

Adelaide and Earl had come in for a late lunch twice, and Adelaide had complimented Sophie on her desserts both times, which she didn't take lightly. The older woman even asked her to collaborate on holiday baking, and they had already taken orders for seven cheesecakes, four pumpkin pies, and eight pecan pies for Thanksgiving.

Sophie's favorite new people so far were a couple of friends named Brandy and Paula, who met for lunch every day. They always had tea, one with lemon and one without, small grilled chicken salads, and loaded baked potatoes; no dessert.

Brandy Jones was a redhead in her midforties. From what Sophie could gather, she was one of those women who had never been just a girl, meaning when she was fourteen she looked—and acted—like a woman. She had a twenty-eight-year-old son who had never met his father and a fifth grader whose father had taken off with another woman while Brandy was in the hospital having a hysterectomy, leaving their son at a babysitter's. Brandy worked alongside her daddy in his trucking business and was currently in the process of being divorced from her husband of five years, a police deputy twelve years her junior. When Brandy ordered, she always wanted a straw with her drink, and she had Sophie reserve a special—to go—every day for her daddy.

Brandy's lunch partner was Paula Masters, who had big brown hair and ten piercings in each ear. The women had been friends ever since Paula began doing Brandy's nails at Patsy's Kut and Kurl a few years ago. Both women always had very colorful fingernails and toenails, and they were eager to show Sophie each time they changed to some new theme. Paula liked to get creative, and Brandy humored her. On the first day of fall, she was decked out in leaves—each nail a different color.

"Just wait till you see my snowmen," Paula told Sophie in anticipation. "I'll start doing those in January after all of my Christmas stuff."

Sophie was a little surprised by how much she liked Brandy and Paula. There were probably not two women in River Bend who were more outwardly different from her; they both wore more makeup in a day than Sophie wore in a month. But something on the inside connected them. Perhaps they were determined to see Sophie make her restaurant a go. Perhaps they saw, as women, underneath the surface of Sophie's skin to a heart that had been broken—and offered what they could do to fix it.

They came every day, rain or shine.

Sophie's other favorite was an ancient priest from the Catholic community nearby, who loved Sophie even more than he loved her omelets.

Father Hillary came in quietly every day at eleven o'clock. He sat by the window in the front room, sipped coffee, and read. He was small, with a wrinkly face and white hair worn wavy and combed back like Billy Graham's. Sophie met him when she went to his table to ask whether she could interest him in something more colorful than the plain omelets he'd been ordering every day for lunch. He'd told her that as long as she left out the meat, she could surprise him.

From that day on, Sophie had taken several liberties with the priest's breakfast. She made him Italian omelets with cheese and fresh basil and tomatoes, omelets with Parmesan and artichoke hearts, spicy omelets with peppers, onions, and Monterey Jack cheese, even omelets with mozzarella, onions, and little bits of pineapple. He seemed to delight in every one.

If Sophie wasn't too busy, she delivered the omelets herself in order to chat with Father Hillary for a few minutes. One day he surprised her by pointing out a movie advertisement in the paper he was reading.

"This is my favorite story," he said. "Have you seen it?" Sophie looked over his shoulder to find an ad for *Les Miserables*.

"No, I haven't seen the movie, but that is my all-time favorite musical. I saw it in London—the first real musical I'd ever seen. I was a student, and the only ticket I could afford was in the nose-bleed section behind a pole." She laughed at the memory, not mentioning that Stephen was with her. "I was captivated. I had those little binoculars, but I didn't really even need to see to understand the story. The music was so powerful I was just blown away." Stephen had fallen asleep halfway through it, jet-lagged, but she had hung on every word.

The priest smiled till his eyes disappeared.

"Me too," he said. "I've seen it many, many times. I wonder what the movie will be like without the music. But, of course, the book is very good without the music."

They both grinned.

A few days later, when she delivered Father Hillary's omelet, he held out a little bag, motioning for her to open it.

"What is this?" Sophie asked.

The priest just nodded and ate a bite of his omelet.

She opened the bag to find a collector's edition video recording of the musical *Les Miserables*. Sophie gasped and hugged him. "Thank you!" she exclaimed. She'd seen it for sale before and wanted to buy it but thought it was too expensive. "But I can't…it's too much."

Father Hillary shook his head.

"Well, then your breakfast is on me for the next month!" Sophie declared.

"Oh no, I cannot do that. I would have to stop coming in, which would make me very sad." He spoke honestly.

"You must let me do something—something to repay you," Sophie was pleading.

"It's a gift—just accept it, no strings attached." The priest was gentle but firm.

No strings attached. As the days passed, Father Hillary's words became a metaphor for what was happening emotionally with Sophie. The pain of her divorce—her shame and embarrassment—seemed to slowly slip away as she felt more accepted. The unconditional love of her people—her hometown people—was surprising to her. It helped her to heal.

And the more she healed, the more open she became to new possibilities, which somehow always led to thoughts of Jon.

Chapter Ten

. . . .

On Thursday morning, one week after his afternoon with Sophie at Harbor House Café, Jon sat at Adelaide's only round table by the window. Harvey was seated at another table with Earl and Bob, and they chatted with Jon about the cooler weather.

The door dinged, and in came the preachers. That's what everyone who ate breakfast at Adelaide's called the threesome of Danny Durham, David Fisher, and Jim Matthews. They'd been eating breakfast with Adelaide since shortly after all three moved into town several years ago.

As if by some collective pastor purging one year, the flocks of First Baptist and First Methodist found themselves without shepherds. After months of interviews, Danny was recommended by the Baptist search committee, and Jim was transferred in by the Methodists' bishop. David came that same year from a bigger place to start a nondenominational mission called The Bible Church—something that raised quite a stir among many of River Bend's older citizens. But the church and David had since been somewhat assimilated into the culture. He was the one who first got the preachers together. They'd decided to include Jon after observing that he attended all of their churches.

The preachers shook hands with the three older men and settled into "their" table by the window with Jon.

"What's happening, man?" David asked Jon.

Adelaide came with a pot of coffee and four cups. "Good morning, Brother Danny, Brother Jim, David, Jon. Good to see you all." She set it all down and then went back to the kitchen. In a few minutes she reappeared with chocolate syrup for Jon and a small pitcher of cream. Sugar was on the table.

Jim poured for everyone and they fixed up their coffees. Danny, who drank his black, laughed as he watched Jon pour the syrup into his for a makeshift mocha.

"When are you going to quit mixing up that women's stuff? You ought to try it black. Put a little hair on your chest."

Jon was nonplussed as he stirred his coffee. "I'll settle for having hair on my head," he told his friend, who was bald at forty-five but fought it by combing over large amounts of fringe.

Jim laughed. As a middle-aged bachelor, his hair was thinning too. "Are you ready for your trip to the big city next week?"

"I guess so," Jon answered. "It's all right to visit."

"Well, especially since you're getting that big award," David said. "That's cool, man."

"What award?" asked Danny.

Jon tried to stifle the blush creeping into his face. "Oh, it's an award for my book. A magazine up there prints this list of fiction writers, and somehow I got on it."

"It's *Time* magazine, and they said he was 'up-and-coming—a writer to watch,'" David quoted.

"That's great," Danny congratulated him. "Praise the Lord."

Jon smiled. "Yeah. It's a miracle."

"We won't see you for a while then," Jim said. "Think of us here at Adelaide's while you're wining and dining in New York next week."

"I'll be wining and dining Aslan for you." David laughed.

"Yeah, thanks for doing that. I'm glad it's only a week." Jon zeroed in on Danny and David. "Speaking of wining and dining, you all ought to take your wives to that new restaurant. Didn't you think it was good last week?"

"It's a nice place," Jim offered.

"Yeah, my wife would love it."

"I gotta know, though," David said. "What was up with you ditching us after lunch—is it true you went back and washed dishes?"

"Yeah, I did."

"What's the deal?"

"There's not any deal. Dr. Harper's daughter and I are old friends. Her dish washer didn't show up, so I just decided to help her out. That's all." Jon averted his gaze into his coffee cup.

"Hmm. You didn't say you knew her," David pressed.

"Why would I?"

"Why would you not?" Danny joined in on the questioning.

"Lay off, guys," Jim said, much to Jon's relief. "It sounds to me like Jon was just performing his Christian duty—helping someone in need."

"Someone who just happens to be female," Danny teased.

"And cute." David grinned. They were not ready to let the subject drop. Jon knew he was too good a target.

About that time, however, Adelaide descended on their table with breakfast. There were biscuits and gravy for Jon, a loaded omelet for David, and pancakes with maple syrup for the other preachers. The distribution of plates interrupted their thoughts enough that when she left, Jon was able to change the subject.

"What are you preaching about Sunday, Danny?" Jon asked, moving them into a conversation about their planned sermon topics, which led into a discussion of their varied preaching styles.

"Different strokes for different folks—different gifts for different needs," David finally said.

"But the same Lord," added Danny. "That's why we make a good team." He slapped Jim on the back as they started up to the register.

Adelaide met them there, rubbing her hands on her apron.

"Thanks, Ms. Adelaide." David smiled at her as he plunked down his money. "That sure was good."

"Yes, it was," said Danny. "I always say nobody can make breakfast like Sister Adelaide. People down at the church still tell stories about her firin' up her griddle for those community breakfasts. They say she could sure turn out the pancakes."

Adelaide smiled in spite of herself and handed Danny his change.

Jon laughed inwardly, sharing a private joke with himself as he remembered the typo that would have cost him dearly had it not been for Sophie. He handed Adelaide his money and told her to keep the change.

"A little tip for the chocolate," he said. "You take good care of us."

"We need to do something like that again," Jim suggested as he paid Adelaide. "Those breakfasts were a great outreach to the community. If we got it together, do you think you could help us, Adelaide?"

"Well, I suppose." Jon guessed she'd have a hard time refusing a preacher. "But I'm not as young as I used to be."

None of us are, thought Jon. And then it occurred to him that maybe, just maybe, for Sophie and him, that could be a good thing.

Chapter Eleven

....

The phone at Harbor House Café started ringing. Sophie was lying on the couch with her feet up, reading, Spot by her side, so she decided to let the machine get it. The café had been open for more than a week now; she had worked hard and was looking forward to a couple days of rest. The machine picked up.

"Sophie, hey. This is Jon—"

Spot's ears pointed, and Sophie lunged for the phone. "Hello?" she said, thinking she probably sounded too eager.

"You're there." He sounded relieved.

"Uh, yeah. Sorry. Just screening."

Jon laughed. "I can certainly relate. Hey, can you spare an hour tonight?" he asked her.

Sophie's heart flip-flopped. She had to remind herself that it was just Jon, her old friend. "Well, let's see. I've got this big deadline coming up with a major publishing house, and I need to pack for my next exotic trip...no, wait, that's you. The question is, can *you* spare an hour?" Sophie enjoyed teasing him. He was so refreshingly modest.

"Very funny. I'll come get you about six. How does that sound?"

"Gosh, I'll check my schedule. Let's see...I've got to make two cheesecakes by six. Yep, that's it, and after that I'm free." Sophie was starting to enjoy the position of humility that at first had tasted bitter to her but that had, with each swallow of pride, become a little sweeter and made her feel more and more free. "Do you want me to pack us some sandwiches? I know this great little café—"

"No. Thou shalt not cook. Except the cheesecakes of course."

"Well, I can at least drive myself. Why would you drive all the way into town to get me?" Sophie asked.

"I'd just like to. Besides, I want to take you somewhere. Humor me?"

Sophie's independent streak stalled her, but then she softened. What did she have to prove to Jon? "Okay, that's fine. And nice of you. I'll be ready around six."

Just don't be too nice, she thought.

* * * * *

At 6:00 sharp, Sophie spied Jon's Jeep pulling into the back parking lot of the Harbor House. She had been sitting on the porch waiting for him while Spot examined the yard, paying no heed to Jon or the Jeep. His manner suggested that it was completely Jon's responsibility to steer clear of him, which Jon did. Leaving the Jeep running, he jumped out and walked up to Sophie, smiling shyly.

The first thing she noticed was his footwear. They were brown leather cowboy boots, and though they were well worn, to Sophie's eyes they seemed totally new—foreign. The old Jon never wore cowboy boots. She liked them, and as her eyes moved upward, over his jeans, leather belt, and white T-shirt under a long-sleeved denim shirt, she realized again that she liked him. The old Jon she knew, who was so safe and simple and comfortable, and the new Jon who had grown and changed in her absence, who had developed tastes and ideas and a style she didn't yet know but longed to—this was a person she liked a lot. A combination that allured her. She looked up into his eyes, which were the same gentle penetrating eyes as always. If anything, they seemed a deeper brown.

She said, "Hey."

"Hey yourself." She saw the approval in his eyes as he looked at her. She'd dressed simply, choosing her favorite ripped jeans with a clean black T-shirt, her silver cross necklace, and a wide silver band on her right hand. She'd worn makeup, though in Sophie's case that amounted to a touch of lip gloss and a little mascara. She'd kept her shoulder-length hair straight.

Sophie grabbed her jacket as she stood up, then let Spot back into the house and locked the door behind him. Giving Jon a quizzical look for holding the door as she climbed into the Jeep, she reached out to shut it herself.

"Could you please let me be a gentleman?" he teased her.

"Tom is the only one I know who still insists on opening my doors, just like my dad used to…." Sophie tapered off.

"Well, that's one thing Tom and I have in common. I guess you'll just have to humor us."

Sophie relaxed again and sat back, laughing. "Okay, I can do that."

They drove through the Dairy and got their old favorite drinks, and then Jon headed in the opposite direction, out of town.

"Where are we going?" asked Sophie.

"It's a surprise," he told her mischievously.

They drove about five miles before she figured it out. "St. Catherine's!" she exclaimed. "Are we going to St. Catherine's?"

Jon just grinned.

They passed into the next little hamlet, a Catholic community just outside of River Bend that was famous for its beautiful church and vineyards. A sign beside the road read WELCOME TO ARKANSAS' WINE COUNTRY.

Jon turned left onto the road that wound up St. Catherine's Mountain, stopping at a small restaurant situated at the foot of the mountain and styled like a Swiss chalet. He jumped out but left the Jeep running.

"I'll just be a minute."

When he returned, he had two French onion soups, a baguette, and a piece of strawberry pie.

"That smells delicious!" Sophie said, delighting in the idea of someone else's cooking for a change.

They climbed the rest of the mountain up to St. Catherine's Church, loftily perched at its summit, and pulled over to the edge of the parking lot, which was bordered by big, mossy boulders. Jon took the top off the Jeep and they sat in the fresh evening air, looking out at the magnificent vista. From St. Catherine's they could see the whole village below and all the way to River Bend. They looked down over the tops of trees that blazed with amazing fall colors. Far and away on the horizon were more mountains, but for miles and miles between were rolling hills, fields that were mostly golden now. Winding through it all was the river.

* * * * *

"Do you remember the last time we came up here?" Jon asked Sophie. He stared at her, thinking that her hair looked like spun gold against the black of her shirt.

"I was just thinking of that. It was after high school graduation."

"Yeah, we decided not to go to the big party and had a little party of our own up here with St. Catherine." Jon laughed lightly at the memory.

"It was actually a beautiful evening—till the cops showed up." Sophie reminisced. "They couldn't believe we were really drinking plain cokes and just talking. That Buford Bailey had the nerve to make me walk a straight line!"

"I know...and your dad the preacher. That was the worst part. Telling your parents and Margaret that we got a police warning and were kicked off St. Catherine's Mountain. It's hilarious now."

"It was pretty funny then, actually, and so typical of the police around here. Bothering with us when they probably could have busted the rest of the class at that party! I hear they're a little more sophisticated now that Buford is gone." Sophie shook her head, and Jon noticed that the setting sun highlighted it for a moment.

"We've had some good times, haven't we?" he asked her, not really looking for an answer.

But she answered anyway. "Yes, we have. Many of my best times have been spent with you."

Jon looked out at the view, soaking in her words. "Want some soup?" he asked finally, unpacking the sack. "I got extra cheese."

"Oh, that sounds so good." Sophie took her Styrofoam bowl from him and opened the lid. Steam rose as she stirred it, and the Swiss cheese at the bottom strung out endlessly, wrapping itself around her plastic soup spoon.

Jon broke a piece of the baguette off and gave it to her to dip. "Do you still like the heel?" he asked, remembering one of her many quirks.

She smiled. "You bet—it's the best part." She dipped the end of her bread down into the soup, twirling it round and round in the gooey cheese before taking a bite. "Thank you so much for bringing me here—and for dinner."

He looked up at her with a string of cheesy soup on its way to his mouth. "Thanks for coming. It's a treat for me too. I don't get out that much unless it's with Margaret or my preacher friends." Jon smiled sheepishly as he took a bite. It tasted wonderful—the caramelized onions and tangy cheese forming a perfect union.

"Well, at least you're getting out at all! I've seen hardly anything but my bed and the inside of my kitchen!"

They both laughed at the challenge of trying to have a conversation while sipping and stringing the delicious brown goo.

"So you should be leaving for your trip tomorrow." Sophie blushed at admitting she remembered. "Are you excited?"

"It should be fun," Jon said. "Do you like New York City?"

He noticed her stiffen and wondered if she'd been there with Stephen. But she simply replied, "In moderation."

"Me too. I always say it's a good place to visit, but I'd go crazy trying to live in a big city. Even with all of its culture and energy. Whenever I'm there for very long I start to crave the quiet. There's just no place like home."

"Dorothy herself never said it better," Sophie teased him, then she added, "but I think I agree."

"I have a great song I want to play for you." Jon took out his iPhone. Scanning through his playlist, he found Ray Lamontagne's "New York City's Killing Me" and turned it up. He and Sophie sat in the waning sunlight, listening. Jon fancied that they were both also silently agreeing with the singer about the need to leave the city for the country.

When the song was over, Sophie sighed. Jon worried for a moment that he might have triggered some memory that made her sad. But then she put down her soup bowl and looked squarely at him. "Jon, I'm so proud of you. It's amazing what you've accomplished...how you've grown...the dreams that are coming true for you. Congratulations." She reached over and squeezed his hand for just a moment.

He relished the feeling before she picked up her soup bowl again.

"Thanks. But you know I'm the same person I've always been," he told her, serious.

"And I think that's the best part of it all."

At that moment Jon's heart was full. He tried to contain it, telling himself not to assume anything, not to rush. But Sophie's sweetness, her innocence, her beauty, and her nearness were nearly overwhelming. He wanted the evening to last forever.

They looked out into the fading landscape again. The hills were turning to blues and grays under the fading light, and the river looked a shiny black, like patent leather. The sky above the fields had a soft lavender glow, which melted into pink and then a burnished amber.

"Look at the bridge!" Sophie said with wonder.

The bridge over the river in town had lit up. Way down below them, it looked like a tiny jewel glittering on the darkening horizon.

Labeled "the most beautiful bridge in the South" by a magazine—
Jon couldn't remember which one—it was lovely with its grand silver
arch stretching the width of the river. Under it, the Arkansas River
flowed into its biggest curve, making the bridge the official symbol for
the town of River Bend.

Sophie drew her jacket around her and settled back in her seat. She
looked peaceful. As they shared the strawberry pie in the dusk, she told
Jon about her week at the café and the gift from Father Hillary. "No
strings attached! That's my new mantra."

Jon breathed his own silent prayer of thanksgiving to God for the
healing he could see taking place in her. It was an answer to his own
prayers for her—and, dare he admit it?—for them.

"Sophie, can I get your cell phone number?" He planned to at least
text her while he was away.

She picked up his phone and entered her number into his contacts,
as familiar as she'd always been. Jon relished the old, easy feeling of
her company.

"I hate to go, but I think we should," he said finally as the lights
in the parking lot came on, their sensors indicating it was dark. He
turned on the Jeep so he could see to put its cover back on.

"This was really fun—a great way to end the day," Sophie told him
when he got in the driver's seat. "Thank you."

* * * * *

When they got back to the Harbor House, Sophie remembered to wait
while he opened her door, and then she slid down beside him. He shut
it behind her, and they walked closely together to the door. Neither one
hurried. Here and there they brushed against one another—his denim
shirt against her jacket, boot against boot. She was conscious of every
touch and wondered if Jon felt it so keenly.

The moon was high in the sky, and it gave little light. It was just a tiny, silver detail on a vast black canvas—as if it were drawn with a single, narrow stroke of an artist's brush. But its presence made all of the difference.

They stood looking at each other under the porch light as though waiting for something, not really wanting to say good-bye. She wondered if Jon considered kissing her, and she wondered how she'd respond if he did.

He reached out and squeezed her hand. She loved the feel of it, even for just that moment.

"I'm so glad you're here," he told her, eyes shining.

"Me too."

They stared into each other's eyes for a long moment before she went in and closed the door.

Sophie was inside before she realized Spot hadn't been at the door to greet them. That was most unusual, and she felt a little fear creep into her heart. Quietly making her way to her room, she switched on the light, and there he was, curled in a crescent on her pillow. Sophie sighed with relief. He lifted his sleepy head and seemed to smile at her. She didn't make him get up to go out.

As Sophie got undressed for bed, she took off her ring and cross, looping them together and laying both in the plate on her dresser. She caught a glimpse of herself in the mirror, and the soft light was kind to her face, she thought. But even without it, there was new life there—new color. Her eyes seemed, even to her, not so hollow and sad. She thought of Jon, their friendship, his kindness, and something else—the thrill of holding his hand—and a smile broke out across her face. The smile erupted and she found herself laughing as she looked at herself in the mirror. Crazy as it seemed, it felt good, and she didn't try to suppress it.

Spot lifted his head again, ears up, and turned it back and forth, as though trying to figure out what on earth was happening. She walked over to him and rubbed his ears, and he licked her face.

Climbing into bed and under the covers with Spot, Sophie did something she hadn't done in a long time. She opened her Bible, and not knowing really where to look, she turned to a random place. As she read the words she allowed herself to be loved by her childhood Savior, her old friend, Jesus. And she could almost hear His voice as He whispered to her from Song of Solomon:

> *Arise, my darling, my beautiful one,*
> *And come with me.*
> *See! The winter is past;*
> *The rains are over and gone.*
> *Flowers appear on the earth;*
> *the season of singing has come,*
> *the cooing of doves*
> *is heard in our land.*
> *The fig tree forms its early fruit;*
> *the blossoming vines spread their fragrance,*
> *Arise, come, my darling;*
> *my beautiful one, come with me.*

Chapter Twelve

....

"Hey, Andy!" Sophie yelled as he entered the back door. She was so glad that things were working out with him after their rocky start, when he'd had his wreck.

Andy put his keys in the bin, wrote down the time on his card, and placed it back into the basket. "Hey, Miss Sophie. How's it going?"

"I told you to quit calling me 'Miss.' Do you want to make me feel old? For the hundredth time—it's 'Sophie.' And that's an order!" She raised the butcher knife she was using and waved it at him.

"Okay, okay, Sophie. Easy with the knife." He grabbed the red apron from its hook and started putting it on. "What's cookin' today?"

"We've got shrimp skewers on the grill for a special, baked sweet potato, and sautéed fall veggies. Everything else is the usual."

"Dessert?" Andy, as Adelaide's grandson, had a certified sweet tooth.

"The normal stuff.... Oh yeah, I made some of my grandma's chewy molasses cookies today."

"Try not to sell out of those." He smiled and plunged his hands into the hot, soapy water.

Sophie had to admit, Andy was a hard worker. There wasn't any need for Jon to come back to the kitchen and rescue her...which was probably a good thing since he was in New York. He'd texted her once, but that was all. She wondered how he was doing and when he'd come back to the café again.

They worked steadily through lunch. Sophie was filling her last order before she could go check on Paula and Brandy, when Debbie came in with a new order and a funny look on her face.

"What is it?" Sophie asked her.

"Well, it's a retired major in the army, that's what it is—and here's his order."

Sophie looked at Debbie's careful handwriting describing an intricate Build-Your-Own sandwich.

"Okay, well, this shouldn't be a problem. Thanks, Debbie."

"Be sure you get it right," Debbie warned, which was odd for her. "I've been at his table for ten minutes explaining where we get our meats, and that yes, the Swiss is big-eye, and the onions red, and that you won't toast the bread too crisply." She rolled her eyes.

Sophie laughed. "Yes, sir!" She saluted.

Debbie returned her salute, then turned on her heel and headed back out the kitchen door.

* * * * *

After the doors were closed, Sophie invited whoever could to join her at the big round table in the front room for leftovers. As it turned out, everyone was busy—which never happened when she offered free food—except for Andy.

He got the last shrimp skewer and a big bowl of banana ice cream and sat down across from Sophie, who was eating a plate of sautéed veggies and a baked potato.

"Man, it was pretty busy today," he commented.

"Yep—a good one," she said. "Busy days pay the bills."

"This is a pretty cool place to eat, especially when it's free." Andy grinned at her, pulling a shrimp off the skewer and popping it into his mouth.

"Watch it." Sophie grinned back.

They were both hungry and tired, so they ate a few bites in comfortable silence. It felt good to slow down after being in constant motion.

After a few moments he asked her, "Was that guy really in the army?"

"What guy?" Sophie couldn't remember.

"Whoever Debbie was talking about—the one who was so fussy about his sandwich."

"Oh, him. Debbie did say he was retired from the army, didn't she? I went out to meet him, and he introduced himself as Major Louis."

Andy stared out the window for a moment. "I don't like army people," he said, changing the mood.

"Oh, why not?" Sophie asked, surprised by his comment.

Andy squirmed in his seat. "My brother was in the army, and he died. I hate the war."

She prodded gently. "What happened?"

"Matt was killed by some crazy suicide bomber. He was a medic— he didn't even carry a gun." Andy suddenly sounded far away.

"I'm so sorry, Andy. That's so awful." Sophie reached across the table to touch his hand.

"It ruined my whole family...my whole life." Andy shoved his bowl away from him.

Sophie put down her fork and moved closer to him. "Can I help?" she asked.

"Thanks, but there's nothing you can do...nothing anyone can do. He's dead."

"I know, but you're alive." She wanted to hug him—he seemed like such a child—but she held back.

Andy looked up at her. "Sometimes I don't know *why* I am. Like that car wreck—why did I survive when Matt died?"

Sophie understood. She measured her words.

"Those are questions that have no answers. My own dad died in a car wreck when I was halfway around the world. I never got to tell him good-bye, or how much I loved him.... Believe me, Andy, I know all about those questions. But at some point we have to let them rest. We have to accept what has happened before there can ever be any peace.".

Andy looked back down. "My mom hasn't accepted it. I heard her crying this morning. She didn't know I heard her, but she was crying in her bedroom when I walked by the door. And my dad…all he does anymore is work. I know he does it just so he doesn't have to think about Matt."

"Andy, do you ever pray?" Sophie surprised herself by asking this.

"Oh, sort of. I mean, I believe in God, but it's hard to really talk to Him."

"Would you pray with me now?"

"I guess—you're saying it, right?"

She bowed her head. "Lord, I don't know what to say. It's hard for me to talk to You sometimes too. Especially about my dad. I miss him, Lord, just like Andy misses Matt. We don't understand why they had to die. Sometimes it seems our lives will never make sense…that we will never be whole again.

"But my daddy taught me, Lord, to always take my problems to You. I'm not good at that, but I want to be better. I want to know You, and trust You more. Please help me, and help Andy to trust You with the things we can't understand. We receive Your peace into our hearts now. And we ask You to lead us through our grief and our loss. In Jesus's name."

As Sophie prayed, she had the sense that even the words she was saying were not her own, but that rather she was guided by some deep inner voice. Someone who spoke for her. Someone who knew her better than she knew herself.

"Thanks," Andy said, and Sophie thought he meant it. "I guess I better get going." He picked up his dishes and carried them into the kitchen, washing them off in the sink.

Sophie watched him go and sat watching even when he was out of sight. She stayed at the table awhile as though in a daydream—almost uncertain whether their conversation and prayer had really taken place. But it wasn't a dream. The peace in her heart, which she had received in faith, was real. She hoped Andy had received it too.

Chapter Thirteen

....

The café was empty, and the kitchen help and servers had just gone. Sophie, still in her red apron, was erasing the special from the chalkboard on the porch when she heard a car pull up in front of the Harbor House. She turned and was happily surprised to see Jon's Jeep, with the cover off and the back full of pumpkins.

"You're home!" she called as he got out.

He was wearing work clothes—old jeans, lace-up boots, and a faded green shirt. Bounding up onto the porch, Jon hugged her, and Sophie thought she smelled the sweetness of hay. Without thinking, she pecked him on both cheeks, like Italians do. It was only when he colored that Sophie realized what she'd done. She'd kissed Jon! *Oh. My.* Regaining her composure, she reached up and pulled a piece of hay out of his hair then examined it in her fingers. That way she didn't have to look into his eyes.

"Sorry for my appearance." Jon brushed his hands on his jeans. "I've been out at the Mabrys' farm hauling hay. David, a preacher friend of mine, is having a hay ride out there tomorrow night for his youth group, and he needed some help getting it ready."

Sophie was impressed, with his appearance as well as what he'd been doing.

"Well, I'm sorry for mine too, I guess." She grinned as she looked down at her food-splattered apron, worn camouflage capris, and ancient Doc Martens. Slipping the apron over her head to reveal a brown T-shirt, the rest of her hair came out of her clip, so she twisted it up and stuck the clip back in. "There," she said, still a bit self-conscious.

"Has it been a good day?"

"It has—a little on the slower side, but that's okay once in a while. It's so beautiful, though, I've been itching to be outside instead of stuck back in the kitchen." She wadded the apron in her hands. "How was your trip?"

"It was good, thanks for asking. But I didn't come here to talk about that." He grinned. "I had a wild idea while I was over at the Mabrys'. Interested in joining me for something?"

"What is it? If it's wild, you know I'm probably interested." Sophie smiled impishly.

Jon laughed. "Well, it's not really that wild…. Just short notice, I guess."

By now Sophie felt nearly *wild* with anticipation.

"I was wondering…would you want to come home with me? You haven't seen my place, and Mr. Mabry gave me all of these pumpkins. I know October is almost over, but I thought we might carve some of them, and you could put them around your porch—I mean, if you wanted to." Jon looked like he was about five years old, and it was adorable.

"I'd love to!" Sophie lit up. "That sounds fun! Let me just change— and tend to Spot." She turned to go in.

"Don't change!" he called after her.

Ten minutes later, Sophie came back down. She hadn't changed clothes, as instructed, but she had washed her hands and face and sprayed on a little perfume, which at least made her feel fresher.

Jon walked her to her side of the Jeep even though there was no door to open and gave her a hand as she climbed in. Then he swung up into his seat.

"We're off!" He chuckled, and then as he pulled out of the drive, he asked, "Can I get you a drink at the Dairy?"

"I'll buy this time," Sophie asserted, pulling three dollars out of her pocket. "With the proceeds of my only tip!"

"Your only tip? Were the customers stingy today?" Jon looked at her, wondering.

"Nope, I only served one person. The major."

"I see. Well, knowing the major, it's a pretty good tip, isn't it?" Jon asked her.

"You bet it is," Sophie answered.

"I need one Dr Pepper and one Diet Coke with extra vanilla," Jon ordered when they got to the window at the Dairy. He handed the clerk Sophie's money.

"How many times do you think we've done that?" she asked him as they pulled back out onto the road.

"Aw, about a thousand." Jon smiled at her and lifted his Styrofoam glass to hers.

"Cheers!" they said together.

"Cheered" is just what Sophie felt as she rode through town with Jon. They turned down River Street, and she gasped at the maples in Brenda Moffatt's yard, with their black trunks and flaming red leaves, and the huge orange and yellow mums on Mr. Appleby's porch. As they crossed the river bridge to the south, the air had just that hint of cold in it—a crispness—and she relished it. It smelled like autumn. She loved the changing seasons, and fall in River Bend was her favorite.

Jon motioned to the Mabrys on the right after the bridge. She knew their place already, but he pointed out the pumpkin patch there in the rich soil of the river bottom. It was fun and festive-looking, bursting with orange. A school bus was parked nearby, and climbing into it were what looked to be first graders, each holding a small pumpkin.

"They must be heading back to school," he said. "Remember those days?"

They reminisced about their own field trips to Mabrys' Pumpkin Patch in elementary school and agreed it was a wonderful tradition.

"I hope the Mabrys can carry it on through the years," Sophie said. "But Andy Mabry doesn't strike me as the farming type."

"How is Andy doing?" Jon was genuinely concerned.

"He got in some trouble," Sophie answered. "Nothing real horrible, but enough to get his family's attention, I think, and that's a good thing. What bothers me, though, is his response to it."

"What do you mean?"

She recounted the conversation she'd had with Andy earlier that day, when they took a break out back during a lull in business. His mother had called Sophie the night before to tell her Andy was not to leave work with anyone but a family member. Apparently Andy had gotten caught smoking cigarettes in the parking lot before school, and the principal had found a bottle of whiskey in his car.

Tenderly but firmly, Sophie had warned him against messing up his life with bad choices. She'd been down that road and knew enough to tell him not to go there.

Andy had fidgeted but hadn't met her gaze. He had told her that he appreciated her concern but that he didn't regret anything because in a way it "set him apart."

She had known just what he meant, but unfortunately their break had been over too quickly. Sophie had gone away from that conversation uneasy, and as they sat in the car now, she related it to Jon.

"Of all people, I understand the need to be sort of 'set apart'— the longing for it. But I also know from experience that just being different—setting yourself apart—is not inherently good. I accomplished that with my bad choices, but to what end, Jon? Disaster. I so don't want that for Andy."

His eyes were compassionate. "You're the perfect person to help him, if he'll be helped."

They had talked all the way to Jon's driveway and were now on the dirt road that rambled through his property. It was bordered by trees of all kinds, gorgeous wildflowers, ferns, bushy plants like wild sumac, and muscadine grape vines. Here and there they saw rabbits hopping, and doves, and the burst of royal blue color that indicated an indigo bunting.

"This is pretty—and pretty wild," Sophie observed. "How did you end up out here?"

Jon just smiled as he guided the Jeep up the steep hill.

When he stopped the Jeep in front of the cabin, Sophie instantly said, "Jon, I love it!"

He helped her out just as Aslan bounded up to greet them, bathing Jon in slobbery kisses and attempting to lavish Sophie with the same preferential treatment had Jon not held him back.

"This is Aslan." Jon introduced his dog affectionately.

Sophie, awed by his size and fur and friendliness, fell instantly in love.

"How long have you had him?" she asked, rubbing Aslan's mane of white hair.

"Since I built this house. He just appeared one day while I was working, acting this same way, as though we were long lost friends. I looked for his owner, even put out ads for someone to call, but got no response. After about two weeks I decided perhaps we were long lost friends. And he's been with me ever since." Jon slapped Aslan on the back.

They climbed up the stairs to his front door, and Sophie was busy taking in details—cedar boards, natural stone, an inviting porch swing—when Jon stopped her.

"I want to answer your question," he told her.

"What question?"

"About how I ended up here," he said. "I need you to put this on."

He pulled a red bandanna out of his jeans pocket and folded it neatly to wrap around her head.

"What?" Sophie was suspicious.

"Trust me."

He placed the bandanna over her eyes and tied it gently behind her head. She took out her hair clip to accommodate him, trusting him but wondering what in the world he had in mind. He took her by the hand as he opened the door and led her through his house. She heard him open a second set of doors.

"Are we outside again?" Sophie turned her head side to side, smelling cedar in the fresh, country air.

Placing her hands on the railing, Jon gently took off the blindfold.

Sophie caught her breath. The afternoon sun glinted on the water beneath them like diamonds in her eyes. She watched the river rolling toward them from the east and winding away toward the west and felt its eternal pulse beating in her veins. Across the water from where she stood was a palette of such rich color she could scarcely take it in— rolling hills with flames of red and antique gold, amber, yellow, fuchsia, purple, and orange all melting into each other, blended together like threads of some magnificent, divine tapestry. Blue skies above. And Jon beside her, sharing it all.

Sophie felt like she was standing on the threshold of heaven. "Jon…I don't know what to say. This is the most beautiful place I've ever been."

"Me too. That's how I ended up here. After I saw it, I didn't want to leave." He smiled humbly. "Why don't you stay here while I go get the pumpkins?" Jon said after a moment, and then he left Sophie standing in awe of the view.

He made several trips from the Jeep to the edge of the deck, depositing pumpkins, before he emerged from his house with sharp knives and a few other tools.

Sophie still leaned over the railing. "I can't believe it," she said softly. "You can just stand here and feel the peace. It washes over you."

"I'm so glad you like it," Jon said, joining her.

"That is an understatement!"

They walked over to the table Jon had set up for the carving.

"We could sit here, if you want. Why don't you sit on that side so you can have the view?" he offered.

"Why don't you sit beside me so we can both enjoy it?"

They worked away steadily for two hours, till their hands were sore from carving through the tough meat of the pumpkins. They'd compiled quite an array of faces and designs, which were lined up, like orange soldiers, across the table.

"Have you ever roasted the seeds?" she asked Jon.

"No, what about you?"

"I haven't, but my mother used to. They're delicious. Want to try it?" Sophie laid down her knife and started sorting the seeds from the slimy pile of pulp they'd acquired.

Jon went into the house and came back with a bowl, which they filled with seeds. Then they both went into the kitchen where Sophie washed and salted them. Then she spread them out on a cookie sheet and placed it in the oven.

"Do you want to look around while we're waiting?" Jon asked her.

"Sure." She loved how his reserve—the privacy he was known for around River Bend—seemed not to apply to her. The old trust he'd always had, the openness, was a gift he freely held out for her to take. *Even though I don't deserve it,* she thought.

And then her inner voice whispered, *That's what makes it grace.*

They walked through the house, with Jon explaining a few things here and there, mostly answering her questions.

Sophie stopped in the center of the great room to admire the exposed cedar trusses in the cathedral ceiling above her. "This is amazing, Jon," she said, looking up.

"Thanks—it's because of David. He's an artist, can do anything with his hands. I just mostly did the grunt work and left the details to him."

They walked over to the rock fireplace at the far end of the room away from the kitchen, where Sophie admired the mantel. Sitting in its center was an ornate iron gate, and on one end was a primitive-looking platter on an iron stand, with a matching water jug beside it.

"How interesting," Sophie said as she looked at them.

"That gate is from Egypt, and I picked up the platter and jug in Kenya. These animals and things are from Kenya and Tanzania," Jon said, pointing to the other end of the mantel.

Sophie turned and picked up one of the carvings—a wooden lion—to admire its artistry. It was fearsome and majestic, with a full mane and mouth open to roar, exposing powerful wooden teeth. *Like the real Aslan,* Sophie thought, and remembered her favorite line from *The Lion, the Witch and the Wardrobe*, where Mr. Beaver is describing Aslan to the Pevensie children: "'Course he isn't safe. But he's good. He's the king, I tell you."

She smiled as she carefully put the lion back in his position. Grouped around him stood a tall giraffe, an elephant, and a zebra. A scowling water buffalo, with its curled horns, looked especially mean.

"He is the one most feared by the natives," Jon told her, holding it out for her to examine. "I would have thought it would be the lions, which steal their cows, but apparently the water buffalo is the most aggressive toward the people who live in the bush."

"How weird," Sophie commented, running her fingers over the smooth back of the buffalo. "They don't seem much more than cows."

"Had I better check those seeds?" Jon remembered, and walked toward the kitchen.

"Yeah, why don't you give them a stir," Sophie answered, placing the water buffalo back in his spot on the mantel and moving over to the wall opposite the bluff windows, which was full of photographs. Sophie felt like she was at a National Geographic exhibit.

"Jon, did you take these?"

"Uh, yeah, just a minute." She heard the oven door slam closed.

When he walked back across the room to her, she looked at him with her mouth open.

"You took these?"

"Mm-hmm. I couldn't believe how well they turned out," Jon said modestly.

In an assortment of sizes, the photographs hung straight and neat in a square pattern. They were all black and white—sepia, actually—and were framed in dark brown wood with ivory matting. Sophie was astounded, again, by the depth and scope of Jon's experiences since they'd parted ways. He seemed so sophisticated now, so alluring. And yet he was also still her same Jon.

"Margaret framed them all and hung them as a surprise when I moved in," Jon explained. "'Housewarming'—she called it."

Sophie's eyes lingered on each picture, some of places she'd been, and others she hadn't. There was the Sphinx, and next to it, St. Peter's Basilica in Rome, and under it, an enlarged one of a child with her hands raised, singing. It was the only photograph of a person on the wall.

"What is this one?" Sophie pointed to it.

"That's my favorite," Jon said. "In Uganda, I visited an orphanage on a Sunday when they were having their church service. It was hot. There was a dirt floor and no music other than their voices. Most of them were in rags. But I'll never forget what those children taught me about worship, just by being among them. They were reaching out for life. It was quite a powerful experience."

Sophie stared at the photo for several minutes, introspective. *Reaching out for life. That's me,* she thought—*I'm as poor as that girl. Lord, help me reach out for the life You give.*

As Jon walked back over to take the roasted seeds out of the oven, Sophie scanned the rest of the wall.

"This is so cool!" she exclaimed. "I've been here, to the Leaning Tower, and isn't the David statue incredible?"

Jon nodded in agreement. "I'd say it has to be one of the most perfect man-made objects in the world."

There were photos of more famous things, like the Parthenon, the Eiffel Tower, and Big Ben, and then there were mountains—presumably the Alps—a waterfall, and a Norman tower Sophie didn't recognize.

"The waterfall is Thomson's Falls in Kenya," Jon clarified. "I hiked down to the foot of it to take that picture. And that tower is where the poet Yeats lived and did much of his writing. It's from the thirteenth century."

"'Things fall apart; the centre cannot hold....'" Sophie quoted Yeats's famous poem. "My mother and Granny are over in Ireland right now. I bet they saw this when they went to Yeats's country."

"You know why I had to go there?" Jon queried her. "I had to see the Lake Isle of Innisfree. Turns out it is just this tiny, unimpressive little island in the middle of a lake—it looks like some of the brushy sandbars we have here in the river. But that poem has some of my favorite lines in all of literature."

"Which ones?" Sophie asked. "Oh—oh—I bet I know: 'I will arise and go now, for always night and day I hear lake water lapping with low sounds by the shore; While I stand on the roadway, or on the pavements gray, I hear it in the deep heart's core.'"

"How did you know?" Jon's eyes were twinkling.

"They're some of my favorites too. I feel that way about home—the river. It's who I am. I guess that's why I had to come back after being gone so long. It was always in my 'deep heart's core.'"

"You're just as big a nerd as I am!" Jon declared, gently thumping her on the arm.

"Well, then, we're in good company!"

* * * * *

They made their way back to the kitchen, where Jon heated some apple cider and Sophie poured the warm seeds into a bowl. The sight of her doing something so simple there in his kitchen sent an electric current through his veins.

"Want to go back out on the deck?"

"That would be great," said Sophie, and she opened the French door for him to go through with the mugs of cider.

He set them down on the little table between his two Adirondack chairs and motioned for her to sit while he went back inside to get a soft chenille afghan for Sophie. The evening air was getting chilly.

"I guess we're going to need two bowls for these seeds," she said reluctantly.

Instead, Jon moved his chair right beside hers and set his cider down on the deck beside his chair, leaving hers on the table where she could easily reach.

They sat crunching seeds and listening to the evening. Crickets chirped, leaves rustled, a squirrel played along the railing of the deck farther down. A chipmunk came up from one of the holes cut for the oak trees, gathering seeds that had fallen from one of the feeders.

Sophie gasped, pointing to it, and Jon was delighted.

At another feeder, there were gold finches with their dazzling yellow plumage, Carolina chickadees, and a male cardinal.

"No wonder you never want to leave here," Sophie whispered to Jon, so as not to disturb the animals.

Jon smiled at her and struggled to remain focused on the scenery. She was almost too near. His eyes lingered over her profile as she watched the birds—the high forehead, the long eyelashes, the slightly upturned nose, and the full lips. He could smell the light freshness of her perfume and feel the warmth of her hand as it met his in the bowl of pumpkin seeds.

It was so easy, now that she had been here and shared his home—and had such an overwhelming response to it—for Jon to want more. He wanted to touch her, to kiss her, to keep her here always. To sit in these chairs with her and watch the seasons change. But Jon stopped himself.

In silent prayer Jon willed himself to want one thing—the will of God—above everything else. He mustn't rush things. He must be patient. He knew she needed time. And he knew if anything was ever to happen between him and Sophie, it would be in God's time, His way.

Jon rose and walked over to the railing.

"Look, Sophie, there's a barge!"

She put down the bowl of seeds, and wrapping the afghan around herself like a shawl, came up beside him to see.

They counted, "One, two, three, four, five…" all the way to ten. The tugboat was pushing ten barges joined together and moving down the river.

Just then, as if on cue, a train whistled and drew their attention to the tiny tracks on the other side of the river.

"This place is an endless feast!" Sophie declared. "I'm glad you brought me here to see it."

"I'm glad you came." Jon looked at her tenderly. "But as much as I hate to, I think I should get you home." *Before I lose it,* he mentally added.

* * * * *

They drove back to the Harbor House with the cover on the Jeep since the temperature had changed. Jon started unloading the pumpkins, carrying them to the front, while Sophie went to let Spot out the back.

Spot was dancing his greeting when Sophie opened the door, and while she sat down on the back stoop to pet him, he immediately sniffed her from head to toe, discerning the new scent of Aslan on his master. She rubbed him all over and kissed his nose.

Jon finished with the pumpkins and came around back to wait with her while Spot ran around the yard doing his business. They sat comfortably together on the stoop.

"What have you got going this week?" she asked him.

"Writing," he said, stretching his legs out in front of him and crossing his boots. "What about you? Is it a busy week?"

"I never know. I just kind of have to go with the flow." Sophie smiled at him and kicked her boots back and forth like a little kid.

"Maybe we could get together again sometime soon…"

"I'd like that." She actually loved the idea but appreciated the fact that Jon was not pushy.

Spot returned to the porch, and Jon stood, offering Sophie his hand to help her up. He squeezed her hand for just a moment, looking down at their hands, and said good-bye.

Sophie turned to go in and waved to Jon, who started his Jeep as she shut the door behind her.

Spot's toenails clicked on the floor in a happy little gait, making their way into the kitchen where she washed her hands and threw on a clean apron. He lay down on the rug and watched her.

As Sophie prepared her cheesecakes, her mind kept wandering over the particulars of the afternoon with Jon. Like a scientist, she examined it—taking pleasure in each remembrance, from the magnitude of the view from the bluff, to the minutia of the cinnamon stick in her cider. She liked Jon; that was sure. He intrigued her as much as he comforted her with his old, familiar kindness. But did he like her for anything more than a friend? Did she really want him to?

She'd never dated anyone who hadn't tried to kiss her by the second date. Certainly not Stephen, who kissed her the day they met. Sophie rolled her eyes at the memory.

Maybe these weren't dates she and Jon were having. After all, they were the same types of things they'd done as friends. Going up to St. Catherine's, getting cokes at the Dairy, even stuff like carving pumpkins. Still, something was different. Surely it wasn't all her imagination? Or was it different only for her?

Sophie worked herself into such a dither over these questions that she put Amaretto in the turtle cheesecake and topped the plain cheesecake with the chocolate and caramel intended for the turtle.

Oh brother, she thought, covering them and placing them in the refrigerator. *I hope no one notices.*

That night before bed, Sophie took Spot out in the backyard and opened her Bible under the porch light. She flipped to the second chapter of 2 Timothy and read about being sanctified for "noble purposes, made holy, useful to the Master." She could remember her dad saying sanctified means "set apart."

As Sophie read and then prayed, her thoughts turned to Andy. He reminded her of what she was like as a teenager, at least in his search to find his place. She thanked the Lord that she was finally learning what it meant to be "set apart"—that it has a higher purpose than just being different. She didn't have to be with someone like Stephen to have a meaningful life. In fact, sanctification for her was beginning to look more like the quiet beauty of Jon's place.

Chapter Fourteen

·················

Jon knew Sophie was busy.

The Chamber of Commerce, which had claimed him as a reluctant member, was having its November luncheon in the café and, by the looks of things, had requested some special extras. René and Rhonda were working the full banquet tables that had been set up in the parlor, which had been set apart for private parties. He noticed Shannon and Sophie both running back and forth to help Debbie with the regular dining room, which was overflowing with people. At least it was too windy for many people to sit on the porch.

Jon waited till he saw Sophie start back to the kitchen from the front room and then slipped out of his seat.

"Sophie?" He touched her arm softly.

"Jon!" She was flustered and a little harried-looking, but her face lit up in a smile when she saw him.

"I won't keep you long. I just wanted to ask you—are you free tonight?"

"What's today? Saturday? Yes. I think I'll crash and burn." She reached out quickly and grabbed a lemon from a tea glass that Debbie was carrying by.

"Mrs. Koch is allergic to citrus!" Sophie whispered.

Debbie smiled her thanks.

"Oh, well, never mind. You probably need a rest."

Sophie asked him, "What is it?"

"The River Valley Theatre guy just told me the University of the Ozarks is putting on *A Christmas Carol* tonight. I know Christmas is still a ways away…but I thought I might go." Jon looked at his boots.

"I'd love to go with you." Sophie pepped up. "What time is it?"

"Well, the play's at seven, but if you want to do dinner beforehand, we'd need to leave about four thirty or five o'clock to get there. Could you do that?"

"How about we skip dinner and maybe do something afterward, like dessert? I don't think I can be ready till a little before six." Sophie looked toward the kitchen nervously.

"That's fine. I'll be here to pick you up then."

* * * * *

The café was a disaster when lunch was over that day. Sophie and the others had to fold up the banquet tables and carry them out to the storage building, then set the parlor to rights. There was a mountain of linens to be washed, Andy was working overtime on the dishes, and all of the usual Saturday deep cleaning still had to be done. It was nearly four o'clock when the last worker cleared out, and Sophie lay across her bed to rest her aching back.

She didn't linger there long, however; the claw-footed tub that sat in the corner of her suite beckoned her. She filled it up with bubbles and water as hot as she could stand, got in and soaked for a full hour, in and out of sleep.

When she glanced up at the clock and saw that it was five, she jumped out and dried off with a towel before drenching her skin in lavender-scented lotion. In her terry-cloth robe, she dried her hair, curled it into soft waves, and put on her makeup. This time, since she was going to a play, she went a little heavier than her usual mascara-and-lip-gloss-only routine. Then she slid on her dress, which was plum-colored with three-quarter sleeves and simple lines, and tall boots. Her hair went up, with a few curls cascading down, and she wore no jewelry.

She was slipping lip gloss and some money into her hand bag when she heard a knock and then Spot barking.

Spot was jumping up and down at the door, and when she opened it, he ran out on the porch, sniffing Jon's legs for signs of Aslan. Jon bent down to pet him, then scooped him up.

Jon came in holding a bemused Spot and smiled when he looked at her. He seemed suddenly shy. "You look pretty," he said.

"So do you—handsome that is." Jon was wearing dark blue jeans, a white shirt, and a black sport coat. He had on black boots that Sophie had never seen. "Although, I'm afraid you're getting Spot hairs on your jacket."

"Oh well, no outfit is complete without a little dog hair, isn't that right?" He grinned.

Sophie grinned back. "That's right."

They let Spot out for a spin around the backyard, deposited him inside the door, and walked around the sidewalk to the front where the Jeep was parked. Sophie submitted to taking Jon's arm as they walked; the sidewalk was uneven and a little precarious to maneuver in her heeled boots.

She was a little surprised to find that Jon's arm underneath the sport coat was as hard as a rock. The feel of it—of his strength—in her hand gave Sophie a new kind of thrill. It was not only the joy of physical attraction, though that was certainly there. There was also something deeper. Like the help and comfort that came from walking next to Jon along the sidewalk, Sophie had the sense that walking through life with him— or someone like him—was what the Bible meant by having a helper.

She was disappointed to see the sidewalk end.

As Jon helped Sophie up into the Jeep, someone honked obnoxiously from the road in front of the Harbor House. They both turned to see Misti Clarkson driving slowly past with her old high school friend Jade Thomas beside her, both of them gawking from the height of Misti's imposing SUV.

A girls' night out, Sophie assumed. The overdone clothes and hair and abundance of makeup were obvious even from a distance. She smiled and waved politely.

Jon lifted his hand in a token salute as he shut Sophie's door and then walked to his side. He glanced over at Sophie, rolling his eyes.

* * * * *

The drive went by quickly for Jon. They talked about their favorite Dickens characters—hers was Miss Havisham—as well as their plans for Thanksgiving. Sophie had lots of baking to do for others, but then he found out that she would be alone over the holiday, as Tom and Madeline were going to Madeline's parents' house. Jon made a mental note to do something about that.

The fact was that Jon would like to spend every holiday with Sophie. And every day in between. Her presence made his Jeep smell faintly of lavender, which he found intoxicating. His skin prickled every time he glanced at her in her plum-colored dress. He longed to touch the tendril of hair that dangled beside her ear, to bury his face in the softness of her neck.... Jon shook his head as if to focus his muddled brain as he pulled into a parking spot.

The campus of the university was quaint. The main part of it was situated on a hillside in the old section of Oliver, a town about forty miles to the east of River Bend. It was a Presbyterian school and had a gorgeous stone chapel as its centerpiece. Large oaks marked the lawn and gave the setting a timeless feel. The performing arts center, which was relatively new, was down the hill.

When they entered the lobby of the performing arts center, Jon paid for their tickets while Sophie went off to find a bathroom. She came back out to find him talking to a distinguished-looking man.

"This is Dr. Sikes, head of the English department," Jon introduced her. "And this is Sophia Harper."

"It's nice to meet you." Dr. Sikes shook her hand warmly. He smiled at Jon as if impressed.

"You too," Sophie said, returning his firm grip.

They exchanged a bit of friendly small talk before Dr. Sikes said he had to go find his seat. "I hope you enjoy the show," he said as he moved on.

Sophie and Jon walked to their seats in the theater, and several people turned to look at them as they passed.

"I forget that you are a celebrity," she ribbed him when they were seated.

"I imagine they're all looking at you."

* * * * *

After the play—which was excellent—Jon and Sophie sat over peppermint mochas and a shared piece of chocolate pie at a nearby coffee shop. The place was warm and festive, with holly garland strung around every possible surface, and a Christmas tree already up in the corner. It had big Charlie Brown lights blinking in all colors. The windows were frosted with spray snow, and there were candles on every table. But in spite of the atmosphere, Sophie felt pensive, and she could tell she shocked Jon by comparing herself to Scrooge.

"That's crazy!" Jon laughed but stopped when he saw she was serious.

"Not really." Sophie's gaze was unwavering.

"How?"

She twirled the little straw around in the whipped cream on top of her mocha and then licked it off.

"Well, I've been very selfish, chasing after my own happiness, missing out on what's truly important. And while I was doing this, my dad died. I didn't get the chance to make it right, as Scrooge finally did."

"There are obvious disparities," Jon observed.

"Okay, so I wasn't a heartless workaholic hoarding my fortune at the expense of everyone in my life, but I still abandoned the people I love to live some pipe dream life." She shook her head.

"What if you'd chosen to be a missionary? Or your husband had been wonderful, but his job took you to a different state? What then? You had no control over your dad's death, Sophie." His eyes were kind.

"I know, Jon—and I'm starting to come to terms with that—but I will always regret that I married Stephen and that I was far away 'searching for myself' when the accident happened. I'd feel different if it had been like you said—if I had been following a noble calling. But too much of my life has been about me. So selfish. Why didn't I see through Stephen in the first place? And why didn't I just come home as soon as I got divorced?" Sophie bit her lip. "I had to do things my way," she spoke from a deep place of regret. "I was such a prideful person—and I kept clinging to my pride until my dad died. Then I hit rock bottom."

Jon reached across the table and took her hand.

A tear slid down her cheek as she felt the tenderness in his gesture and heard the compassion in his voice.

"It's not selfish to have dreams," he said.

"But mine took me so far away from everything that really mattered. I see that now." Sophie pulled her hand away and wiped her face with a napkin.

"Your best dreams—of home, family, love—have brought you back. You're here now, and the Lord is doing a new thing." Jon's eyes were full of promise.

Sophie's heart caught in her chest. Did he mean between the two of them? She looked long into his eyes, absorbing the hope she saw there. They stared at each other as though sealing a silent agreement, and then she smiled.

The grace of God, came the thought again. Sophie put down her napkin, and they left the table.

* * * * *

Their ride home was very subdued and quiet compared to their usual banter. Jon was lost in his thoughts as he drove, praying and considering where his relationship with Sophie was going. He had the sense that something had changed tonight in one magic moment, like the initial crack in a baby robin's egg or the first hint of butterfly emerging from a cocoon. It frightened even as it exhilarated him.

He went back over everything they had said, laying it bare before himself and God. Had he spoken amiss? Assumed anything? Set up expectations? Rushed? He had prayed not to take one step outside of the divine will—but his emotions were getting harder and harder to control.

Sophie, in the seat next to him, seemed strangely at peace. In an odd way, he thought, the play itself did her good as it helped her confront some ugly truths. Leave it to Dickens. Their conversation—the working out of her conflicting feelings, and his bold suggestion—seemed to move her along toward resolution. He knew she couldn't yet, but maybe someday she might actually be able to let go of the guilt and pain she held so tightly. Jon sensed that Sophie was loosening up—and perhaps the pain itself, and all of the regret, were loosening their grip on her.

There was no sound but the hum of the motor. As Jon looked over at Sophie beside him in the Jeep, he realized she was asleep. Her head was bent at an uncomfortable-looking angle, so he reached over with one hand still on the wheel and leaned her seat back just a notch. Then he gently touched her face, turning it slightly, setting the position of her neck at ease.

He exhaled and looked back at the road.

I love her, Lord.

And then the word came, silent, lucid: "I know. I do too. Trust Me."

Chapter Fifteen

. . . .

"Hey S and S!" Andy greeted Sophie and Shannon as he hurried in the back door of the Harbor House.

"Hey, kiddo," Shannon replied.

"Hey A—although maybe I should call you B-minus today, since you're late!" Sophie chided him, looking up from the dish of lasagna she'd just taken out of the oven for the special.

"I'm really sorry, Sophie," he said as he threw on his apron and got right to work on the dishes. "I was trying to get away from Mrs. Ruston. We read this excerpt from that book *Life Without Father* today in her AP English class, and she was bragging about how the author had been her student. Then after class she pulled me aside to say how she thought I had potential like that guy, and she wanted me to make her proud."

Sophie grinned while she listened to him. "Good old Mrs. Ruston. I didn't know she was still teaching."

"I mean she's nice and all, but good grief." Andy scrubbed at a mortar and pestle. "What did you make in here?"

"Pesto," Sophie answered.

"What's pesto?'

"It's a green sauce you make with basil. It's in the lasagna." She pointed to the pasta, sticking a knife into the middle of it to discern whether it was done.

"I hope I get some of that," Andy said, smelling the aroma.

"I'll get you out a little bite, at least, when it's done."

When Sophie had finished all of her preparation, and before the orders started pouring in, she asked Andy to come to the back with her for a second. "I have something for you," she told him, pulling a brown package out of her desk drawer.

Andy looked relieved—did the poor kid think he'd be in trouble?—and happily surprised. "Is this an early Christmas gift or something?"

"Go ahead and open it now."

He untied the string around the package and found a dark brown leather book inside. It was a journal, and the ivory pages had gilded edges. Andy opened it and found the inscription on the inside cover:

> *To Andy Mabry. May writing be an outlet and a refuge*
> *for you as it is for me.*
> *Jon Anthony*
> *Romans 8:28*

"That's the *Life Without Father* guy! Cool!" Andy exclaimed, and then he looked perplexed. "But why'd he give this to me?"

Sophie smiled at him. "Well, he's a friend of mine, and I told him about that awesome essay you wrote. The one you showed me, that Mrs. Ruston wants to put in the paper—"

"She did put it in the paper," Andy interrupted her. "I got bonus points for letting her put it in there this week."

"Great! That's great. I wanted Jon to read it, so I'll show it to him." Sophie made a mental note to mention it. "Well, anyway, he just wanted to encourage you—you know, writer to writer. He thinks journaling is really important."

"That is so awesome. Tell him I said thanks."

"I will," Sophie promised. "Now get back to work!"

* * * * *

Father Hillary was at his table by the window when Sophie took his omelet—a pesto creation—out to him.

"That looks delicious. And how are you this fine morning?" he asked, when she set his plate down.

"I am very well," Sophie said, meaning it.

"You seem to have an extra spring in your step," he observed. "Anything I should know?" His blue eyes sparkled like brand-new buttons on his wizened face.

"You should know that you make a difference—by your presence, your prayers, your practice of sharing God's grace with others."

His face burst into a smile. "Why, I wasn't expecting that!" He stared in disbelief.

"It's the truth," declared Sophie, and she bent down to give him a hug. "And that omelet is on me today—no strings attached!"

She skipped off to the kitchen before he could say another word.

Later that afternoon, Sophie deposited yellow roses at both place settings on the same table. Just in case, she also made a little sign that said RESERVED.

Brandy Jones popped her head in the kitchen moments later, when Sophie was back at the stove, and asked, "Who stole our table?"

Sophie smiled at her, flipping a skillet of pasta and vegetables, and said, "It's reserved for you."

"Oh." Brandy cocked her head to the side. "Okay."

It was a little while before Sophie could make it out to their table, and when she did, they were finished eating.

"What's all this about?" Paula inquired, twisting the stem of her rose.

"It's about friendship," Sophie answered simply. "Just to say thank you for being my friends."

"Are you closing?" Brandy smelled her rose and eyed Sophie suspiciously.

"No! Heavens no!" Sophie laughed at them. "I just wanted to do something nice for you guys. To say I love you."

"Well, we love you too, sweetheart." Paula reached out to hug her.

"That's so nice," Brandy said.

The major was in fine form when Sophie stopped at his table for a visit a half hour later.

"Who made this sandwich?" he demanded, pointing to his half-empty plate.

"Shannon. Why—is something wrong?" Sophie had a sinking feeling.

"I knew it wasn't you, since you didn't bring it out here." His voice was gruff.

"Well, I've been really busy. But if there's something wrong, we can fix it—"

"There's nothing wrong," he interrupted. "If anything it's better. A little less mayonnaise than you've been putting on there. And she cuts it in half. Tell her to make it this way from now on."

Sophie let out her breath. "Yes, sir!" She saluted.

"But you can keep bringing it out. If you have time." And without breaking his face, the major smiled.

Chapter Sixteen

. . . .

It had been a good week, but Jon was glad it had gone by fast, because he had a date with Sophie for Thanksgiving.

Margaret was helping Jim Matthews with the Methodist Community Dinner, and Jon had been planning to help out as well. However, as soon as Sophie told him she didn't have plans, Jon changed his. He didn't want to ask her to help him cook and serve food, since it was something she did every day, and Margaret and Jim both assured him it was okay. They had plenty of volunteers.

Jon and Sophie hadn't seen each other since the play. He had texted her a few times, and she had written back, usually late at night. She'd been extremely busy. She and Adelaide Mabry had been working around the clock doing other people's holiday baking.

Sophie wrote in one text that they enjoyed sharing stories about Andy, about how well he was doing in school. It seemed the journal writing had been cathartic for the boy. He'd even written a great story about his brother, Matt. In another text Sophie said they had created a new recipe for pumpkin cheesecake using her granny's molasses cookies in the crust.

Even though the distance of the past week felt healthy and safe and mature, it also stunk. Jon missed Sophie. His heart skipped a beat when he pulled up and saw her; she was waiting on the stoop watching Spot.

"Hey," she said, smiling, when he got out of the Jeep.

He walked toward her. "Hey." It seemed neither one knew what else to say.

Sophie looked stunning to Jon. She also had on jeans and a soft pink sweater. He noticed her nails were painted the same pink. She wore very little makeup as usual, which he loved.

Her hair was the fanciest thing about her appearance. It was an explosion of springy, satiny curls all over her head. Jon wanted to reach out and play with it. *Fantastic,* he thought but didn't say.

Their awkwardness at first was always so curious to him, but also wonderful somehow. There was mystery in this new place, even with all the depth of knowing they shared underneath it—especially with that depth.

* * * * *

Spot, ambling over to the Jeep, made a quick inspection of Jon's tires, leaving his mark on all four.

Sophie was a little embarrassed but mostly amused. "I really don't know why Spot does that, but I imagine it has something to do with alerting Aslan to his existence and exerting his own dominance." Her bulldog was not near as short on ego as he was on size.

Jon laughed. "Well, it's good he's getting his bluff in early on Aslan. Although I don't know if it would help him much if they ever conflicted over the tires. Aslan's pretty tame, but he's still the size of a lion."

The thought of the dogs meeting was funny to Sophie, who imagined what her fourteen-pound dog might think if he ever faced Jon's mammoth beast.

As they drove away, Sophie looked out the window and felt herself loosening up and relaxing. The late sunshine glimmered on the river as they crossed the bridge, coloring the water a soft amber hue. The sight of it, along with the fresh earthy smell of Jon's Jeep and his hands on the steering wheel, warmed her, in spite of the fact that it was nearing wintertime. She put her head out the window and tasted the air. The breeze coming off the river tasted like a ride on her dad's boat, cutting a clean line through the water and sending up mist in her face. It reminded her of carefree days—her family, picnics, and river catfish waiting to be caught.

Jon was relaxing too—she could feel the awkwardness leaving and the old familiar friendship taking its place. They had done stuff like this a million times. Driving through town and over the bridge and past the fields and houses and cows. It was in this place where everything started with them. It was home—a common ground. Sophie had the river in her blood, just like Jon did, and the mountains and the trees. No matter where their different roads had taken them, they'd both gone out from the same place, and now, it seemed, they were returning there together. But she still mustn't assume anything.

When they pulled up to Jon's house, Aslan bounded over to the Jeep to meet them. Sophie got out before Jon could get around to her door and was rewarded by a big bath of slobber on her jeans, compliments of Aslan, who was very happy to have her as company. He almost knocked the cheesecake out of her hands with his giant paw, but she petted him on his great white head.

Jon said, "Stay right there a minute," and ran up the steps and into the house for something. He came back with a big wicker basket and a quilt. "Okay," he said, "I think we're all set."

She raised a playful eyebrow, and he just smiled. Then he led her around the edge of his cabin and away from it just a little distance. They walked out to a point, where a huge rock jutted over the bluff. To the right was more bluff, and then the cabin and deck. To the left, downward from where they stood, was a rolling hill and woods.

"This is where the bluff begins," Jon told her. "When I was deciding whether to buy this place, I came and sat on this rock and prayed. Looking out at the river I felt sure in my heart.... I felt like I was home."

Sophie soaked in the beauty of the scene and the moment. She understood how Jon could sit there looking out and know it was where he belonged. It was perfect for a writer—a thinker—a spiritual man. It was perfect for Jon.

He spread out the quilt and invited her to sit with him.

The sun was just beginning to set, and it turned the water golden. The atmosphere was a mix of lavender, pink, and indigo, those colors all blending and converging toward a huge orange ball that didn't want to give up the sky just yet—the sun.

It reminded Sophie of the Cinque Terre. She told Jon this, and he listened as she described how she'd hiked and picnicked along the trail called Via dell'Amore high in the cliffs above the Mediterranean.

"That sounds pretty romantic, Sophie," he said. "Almost like it couldn't be a real place."

"Well, it is very romantic—or could be—although it wasn't for me at the time I was there. I was alone, unless you count the little twins who scampered and played along it with me."

Jon reached over casually and picked a wildflower, the very last of the season, handing it to Sophie. "Happy Thanksgiving, Sophie. I thank God for you."

Sophie twirled the stem in her fingers, drinking in his words. "And I thank Him for you, Jon."

Then he took two little candles out of the basket and lit them. Next he took out two stemmed glasses and a bottle of chilled wine.

"What else do you have in that basket?"

He unwrapped a loaf of homemade bread in foil and set out a dish of soft butter. Then he opened a little round crate of Camembert and set it on a plate. He drizzled something over the cheese that looked brown and gooey, like caramel, and sprinkled it with pecans. Then there were more cheeses, cubed, and some crackers in the shape of butterflies. A bowl of fruit completed their picnic.

"Bon appétit!" He smiled at her proudly.

It was certainly a nontraditional Thanksgiving dinner, but she loved it. After serving Thanksgiving specials all month, she was sick and tired of turkey and mashed potatoes. Had Jon known? At any rate, nontraditional hit the spot.

They sat side-by-side and feasted as the sun set and the moon rose. It was about a three-quarter size, and in the clear sky it shone like a white flame. Cedars, their eternal roots clinging to the rocks along the bluff, were suddenly illumined by the moonlight and cast stark but lovely shadows on the ground. In contrast, their neighbors, the great oaks with their finger-like branches adorned with shapely leaves, formed delicate filigree patterns against the lighted sky. Sophie thought they looked like elegant old ladies in black lace dresses. They watched her, nodding here and there in the breeze, as she sampled Jon's gourmet offering.

"When did you learn how to cook?" she asked him, spreading butter on the heel of the homemade bread.

"Oh, I don't know—just along the way. I've picked up a lot of ideas working in restaurants."

"Did you make this bread?" Sophie loved the sugary, tart taste and wondered what was in it.

"Yeah. Now that's an original concoction. It's a version of sourdough I made up after visiting San Francisco."

She smiled. An open window into his life and who he had become. She liked peeking in those windows.

"Well, what about this?" Sophie spread some of the soft caramelized cheese on a cracker and popped it into her mouth. It tasted wonderful— creamy, sour, sweet, buttery—embellished with toasted pecans.

"I had it at a dinner party once. It's easy, but nothing I'd have expected—or thought of myself. Do you like it?" Jon asked.

"Mm-hmm…" Sophie grinned between gooey bites. Her fingers were sticky with caramel and nuts, and she licked them, just a little, trying to keep from making a mess.

They laughed.

"I'm glad you like it. It's a little bit intimidating cooking for a chef like yourself." He was humble, tender.

"Phooey," Sophie said, blushing. "This is a little bit out of the Harbor House Café range, I think."

They were quiet. A comfortable quiet, as they listened to mourning doves cooing softly. Jon told her he rarely heard them in the evenings, and she loved their sound. One called on one side of the woods, and another answered across the way. It was a peaceful, soothing song. It spoke of no desperation or frantic searching, just the comfort of the other's presence. As if one dove was assuring the other, "I am here."

Jon stretched his boots out in front of him and leaned back, supporting himself with his hands. Sophie leaned back too, and her hand touched his by accident. But she did not move it. When he covered her hand with his, she scooted a little closer to him and they sat there— silent—and watched the moonlight on the river. It spilled out in front of them like liquid fire. The water seemed to quiver underneath it, as if it could not bear the burden of such unspeakable beauty. Silver melted into white gold into platinum. The elements all brooded there together on the water. Then the brooding turned to play and the play into dancing, as if there was some glorious symphony only they could hear.

Sophie had the sense that she was in a dream. Jon's big, strong hand covered hers completely. It was warm. She could feel the roughness in it—the wood chopped and carried for the fire, the rocks gathered and placed along the sidewalk and retaining wall. She felt the energy in his hand—the digging and planting bulbs, the stirring of dough for bread, the typing and creating of words. She loved the feeling of his hand on hers. She could see, but not hear, the rise and fall of his chest as he breathed.

For the first time in a long time, Sophie didn't question anything. She let the moment of her life be. She allowed herself to feel happy and safe and still—to believe in miracles. She didn't want to say anything because if she did, the stillness might vanish. And it was in that stillness she felt herself being healed.

The candles dwindled down to nothing, and Jon moved to blow

them out. He tossed the remains of the picnic into the basket, smoothing out the quilt, and then he sat down by Sophie's feet, facing her. She could not imagine what he was doing, but she didn't care. For once Sophie didn't want to be in control.

Jon held her gaze a moment and then went to work undoing her shoes. He slipped them off, one by one, and carefully removed her socks. Taking each foot in his hands, one at a time, he began to massage her feet. He started by stroking lightly, up and down all over, top and bottom. Then he kneaded her foot like bread. He rubbed each toe between his thumb and fingers, and pulled them all gently. Next he took her heel in his hands and caressed it firmly. With his thumb he drew a line from her heel through her arch and up through the sole of her foot and out her toes.

Sophie felt the tension leaving her body. She'd never complained to Jon about her feet, but he must have known how they hurt. Even in good shoes, it was hard to stand for so many hours in the kitchen.

"Wow—thank you," she said when he had finished and replaced her socks.

He smiled at her and stood up to stretch. He walked out a little closer to the bluff and looked out over the water.

Sophie rose from her position on the quilt and moved to join him. When she was close beside him, she reached out and put her arm around his waist, her heart thumping in her chest. Jon turned to her and stared into her eyes. Then he lifted his hands to cup her face and held it there, like a piece of fine china.

She blinked at him and tilted her head a little to one side.

And then he bent and kissed her, slowly, softly, deftly.

Chapter Seventeen

. . . .

Sophie didn't explain what she was doing to anyone but Tom. Shannon and the rest of the crew at Harbor House Café knew only that there was "an emergency with an old friend." Rather than closing, she had trusted them to manage things without her—and without a daily special—for Friday and Saturday. She was closed Sunday and Monday and would surely be back before Tuesday. With the help of Adelaide, who was going to furnish desserts, and Andy's mom, who would help out in the kitchen, Sophie felt good about the business at least while she was gone.

That was really the only thing she felt good about as she drove southeast on I-90. The rest of her feelings were as convoluted as the network of knots that attached themselves between her shoulder blades. Realizing she was tense, Sophie willed herself to relax. She eased up her grip on the steering wheel. She moved her shoulders up and down and slowly tilted her head to each side to try to break up some of the tight muscle cobwebs that had formed. She tried to think clearly and get prepared for what—and who—she was driving toward.

She replayed the phone conversation from the night before in her head.

"Sophia?" The voice on the phone made Sophie break out in a cold sweat.

"This is Sophie."

"This is Stephen."

Silence.

"How are you?" Stephen asked her, obviously nervous.

"Why are you calling?"

"Look, I'm really sorry to bother you. Really. It's just…"

More silence. She wasn't going to give him an inch.

"My dad asked me to call you."

"Your dad?"

"He's dying."

Sophie felt like someone had hit her in the stomach.

"He has cancer—it's very advanced—and he's at home. Hospice is there, trying to control the pain. The doctors give him days."

"I'm so desperately sorry. What can I do?"

"He wants you to come."

Stephen's parents were divorced. His mother, whom Sophie had only seen a few times, lived in Florida. His father, Frank, lived in the town a hundred miles from River Bend, where she, Stephen, and Jon had gone to college. Stephen had grown up there and, as a teenager, had chosen to stay with his dad when his parents divorced. He was already starting to play music with some of his friends, who later formed the band they became in college. Dr. Frank, as everyone called him, was a chemistry professor at the other college in town. He worked with old lab equipment in cramped classrooms that were bursting at the seams with med-school hopefuls—and he made magic. Even Sophie, who hated math and only tolerated science, liked to hear him talk about chemistry. He made it come alive.

Frank had loved Sophie enough to warn her about Stephen.

"Stephen's my son and I love him, but I don't think he's ready for you, girl," he had told her one evening. She had brought over groceries to make lasagna for him and Stephen and was enjoying a little time alone with him while Stephen finished a rehearsal. As she unpacked the bags onto the counter, he helped her.

"What do you mean?" Sophie had been shocked.

She remembered his response to this day. "Sophie, I want you for my daughter-in-law, but I don't want you to get hurt. I learned a lesson about marriage too late for me but not too late for you. I know you love him, and I know he loves you—as much as he can. But I did not do a good job of showing him what it means to be a husband. I have begun to see that I made so many mistakes. I was so selfish. I didn't really know how to love my wife."

"Don't worry, Dr. Frank," she'd said. "Everything will be okay. You'll see."

It was a moment of truth, Sophie thought as she drove down the road. A red flag. *And I ignored it.*

She hadn't seen Frank since she and Stephen moved to California. They'd e-mailed frequently and talked on the phone some, but after the final disaster occurred and she left Stephen, their contact was abruptly cut off. Severing ties with Stephen, to her, had unfortunately meant severing ties with Frank.

When she thought of Frank, it was as an oasis in the desert that was her marriage. And now he was dying and wanted her to come. How could she ever say no?

As she pulled onto the exit ramp, Sophie breathed a prayer. "Lord, please fill me with Your Spirit to minister Your grace and peace. Make me strong and let this trip be an expression of my faith—and may everything I do be done through Your love."

Chapter Eighteen

. . . .

Margaret's truck had to go into the shop, so Jon met her there and gave her a ride home.

She searched his eyes as he held open the Jeep door for her. "So, how was your holiday with Sophie?"

"It was nice. Very nice." He shut the door and smiled to himself as he walked around to his side. "How was yours with Jim?"

"Nice." Margaret raised her eyebrows as if to say that two could play his game.

Jon chuckled. "Well, that's nice."

She punched him gently in the ribs.

"What are you going to do today?" he asked her as they pulled into her driveway.

"Nothing much. Jim is supposed to come by." Jon thought he noticed the hint of a smile at the edges of Margaret's lips.

"Another date?" Jon looked over at her, grinning.

She cleared her throat, ignoring his question. "We're going to clean up the community center and then distribute leftovers. We've also got to talk about the Christmas party he's asked me to help plan. It's a ministry thing." Margaret got out of the car and out of the conversation. "Do you want any of the leftovers?"

"No thanks, I'm not hungry. I'm going to try to go home and do some writing."

"Okay. Well, thanks for coming to get me. I'll talk to you later."

Margaret leaned into the car to kiss his cheek and then trotted up to her door.

Jim Matthews, Jon thought. *Wonders never cease.*

Jon surprised himself on his way through town by pulling into the parking lot of Harbor House Café after leaving Margaret's. It was one thirty in the afternoon, and he was hungry.

Liar, his inner voice said. *You just told Margaret you weren't hungry when she offered leftovers.*

Okay, he admitted to himself with a grin, *so I'm not hungry for food.* He went in and hung around near the counter in case Sophie came out to talk to her guests. By this time, she had told him, she was usually about done in the kitchen. At least enough to walk around and visit.

"Did you have a to-go order?" René asked him

"Uh, no," he told her. He felt stupid and conspicuous.

"Oh, okay. Well, would you like a table, or do you want to place an order to go?"

Jon fidgeted, trying to decide what to do. If that kitchen door would just swing open and he could see Sophie and she could see him… He felt a hand slide through his arm from behind him. It was Misti Clarkson's.

"He's with us!" she told René, who eyed her warily as she pulled Jon in the direction of the parlor.

"Hi, Misti," Jon said, subtly uncoiling her from his arm.

"Oh, Jon, won't you join us? We're just having a little book club meeting, and it would be amazing to have a real author there!" Misti was smiling.

Jon looked toward the parlor, where a newly single Jade Thomas was smoothing her hair. A few other women, mostly former members of the infamous "Nails" group, were sitting around their table with notebooks and pens. The Nails was the name he and Sophie, in high school, had surreptitiously given to the group of girls led by Misti and Jade, who were obsessed with the fad of long, fake fingernails. Most of them had their nails done once a week at Patsy's, and they competed within the group for the longest and brightest ones. A nail broken on a locker might signal a wail that would be heard all through the halls of their high school. Sophie had told him stories of dashing into the girls' restroom between classes and finding the group in a nail mending conference. They had enjoyed many a laugh with each other in school at the unknown expense of the Nails group.

"Well," Jon said, "I was actually here to meet Sophie." Misti frowned, and he truthfully enjoyed the feeling of taking her down a notch or two.

"I'm sure she'll be out in a minute. Why don't you keep us company in the meantime?"

Misti dragged him to the table, glowing like she'd captured a trophy. "Look who's here, guys! Our class's famous author—and most eligible bachelor!"

The women giggled. Jade batted her eyes at him and made room beside her. Misti practically shoved him into the chair between them.

Jon was mortified. He couldn't wait for Sophie to come out so he could escape.

René came over to the table and asked what he wanted to eat.

"Well, what's easy? I know Sophie must be about finished in the kitchen. I don't want to order anything big."

You're also not hungry, remember? the voice reminded him.

"Oh, Sophie's not here," René explained. "She's out of town for a few days. But Shannon's back there and can make you a sandwich."

There was silence all around.

"Okay," Jon's mouth said as his heart sank.

"What kind of sandwich would you like?" René asked gaily.

"Uh, turkey," he answered. The voice chuckled. *You are what you eat.*

"Oh, you know what?" declared Misti, rolling her eyes as if she was just recalling something. "I remember now. Someone said something about Sophie having an emergency. Come to think of it"—she goggled her eyes at Jon—"it was something about an old friend. But all of her old friends are here, aren't they? I can't imagine who it would be!"

The Nail group all looked at each other as if on cue, acknowledging the great mystery of where Sophie was.

Jon felt sick. He didn't comment.

When René returned with his sandwich, he started planning his escape. He would eat it and leave.

Just then one of the nicer Nails spoke up. "Jon, I really liked your book. It's great."

He looked up from his sandwich and met her eyes. They looked sincere. "Thanks, Jenny," he said. "It's nice that you've read it."

"Read it? Of course we've *all* read it!" Misti interjected.

Jon didn't know what to say—or believe.

"I've got my copy right here," said Jade, and pulled the book out of her enormous purse. "Would you sign it for me, Jon?"

"Uh, well, sure." Jon sheepishly signed his name.

"Thank you!" she exclaimed, holding the open book to her chest.

"Oh, wait, let me get a picture," Misti called, digging through her beaded bag. "I just happen to have my camera."

Jon was half-flattered and half-frightened. Fear took over, however, when Jade reached up and kissed him on the cheek just as Misti snapped the picture.

"I really must be going." He rose from the table, leaving his sandwich half-eaten on his plate, and left the restaurant.

* * * * *

Misti knew Sophie wasn't there. That's precisely why she had planned the meeting for that day. Jon had seen it all in the look on her face when she'd said significantly, "I can't imagine who it would be!"

And neither could any of the other Nail group members.

But Jon could. In fact, as he sat on his deck with Aslan, his imagination was running away with him as fast as the river.

I knew it was too good to be true. She won't be here long. She's gone back to Stephen. He's charmed her back somehow. The snake! Why is this happening? I'm such a fool! She's played me like a piano. She's always played me. Why did I dare to believe I was anything to her?

But even as he felt angry with Sophie, cursing and questioning her character, the contrast between her and the other women that day held itself up in his mind. She was deep and they were shallow. She was real and they were counterfeits. She was who and what he wanted—and if he couldn't have her, he would rather be alone. No amount of flattery or batting eyelashes would change that. They were repulsive to him. He repulsed himself that he even sat down with the Nails—and worse, allowed himself to be flattered by them. Who cared what they thought of his book, or of him? He only cared what Sophie thought—and apparently it wasn't much. She was the real thing, but he would never be enough for her.

He stood up and walked over to one of his oak trees. He picked some green acorns from a branch and began to chuck them over the railing towards the water. Jon hated himself in that moment for being a romantic. For being idealistic. Even for being an optimist. He felt bitter and cynical and dark. The memory of Sophie in her wedding dress floating down the aisle to Stephen brought bile to his throat. *I can't live through this again*, he thought. *If it happens, I'm not going to be here to watch.*

He looked at the river below him, endlessly flowing on, not minding his mood. The bluff in that moment seemed an abyss—like the one he was mentally plunging into. He closed his eyes and prayed.

Lord, You are in control. Nothing takes You by surprise. As crazy as things look right now to my eyes, Your eyes see the beginning from the end. You promise good for me and I can trust Your goodness. I choose to trust You now with my feelings for Sophie, my plans for the future, my whole heart and life. I relinquish my rights, my anger, my pride. I receive Your grace. Give me the peace I need to walk in faith.

Chapter Nineteen

. . . .

Sophie was thankful when the front door was opened by a hospice nurse and not Stephen. She led Sophie through the foyer and into the den, where a hospital bed was set up by the sliding glass doors that faced the backyard. The house itself looked pleasant, but the smell was dreadful. It smelled like death.

"He wanted to be able to see his birds," the nurse said. Her dark caramel-colored face had the soft and comforting look of a leather easy chair. She left Sophie alone beside the bed.

Sophie stood there and stared at its emaciated occupant. His head faced the glass doors, where he presumably had been looking before he dozed off. There was no hair where the rich, dark locks had once been, and no shadow of hair to come. The olive complexion that used to match Stephen's was a ghostly pale white—almost blue—like the flame on a Bunsen burner, except cold. Before she took his hand, she felt the chill of the harsh and barren land that his body had become. Being in the valley of death made her shiver.

Frank opened his eyes and turned them to her when he felt her hand. She could tell the instant his eyes recognized her, before any words came out of his mouth. He was studying her and taking his time. It was as if he was recording every feature of her presence in some secret place inside himself.

Sophie didn't know how long she stood there with tears sliding down her cheeks before she said, "Dr. Frank."

"Dr. Sophie," he whispered.

She was afraid for a moment that he was confused—that he had lost her just that quickly.

But then he continued. "Now—this is—some good medicine." He smiled at her.

Sophie laughed and choked a little through her tears.

"How you been?" he asked in that frail, raspy voice.

"Okay. Good." She nodded.

He looked interested.

"I moved home recently to be with my family. I've started a business...a café. It's going pretty well."

"It's good you're home...," he said. "But that sounds like hard work."

It sounded like it was hard work for him to talk. "You're right. It is. Thanks for giving me the day off." She smiled.

He smiled back. "Thanks—for coming." As Frank said this, he dozed back off to sleep.

The nurse came in with a chair for Sophie, so she sank back into it and kept holding onto Frank's hand.

* * * * *

"Miss..." Someone was gently shaking her awake.

Dusk had fallen, Sophie noted, as her eyes opened to slowly focus on the hospice nurse.

"I'm sorry to bother you, but I need to get him ready for the night."

Sophie gently pried her hand away from Frank's as he was waking up. She told him she'd be back when they were finished and slipped out of the room. As Sophie headed through the foyer, thinking of what to do next, she ran right into Stephen. He had come in so quietly that she hadn't heard the front door open. She jumped back, shocked, a little horrified, a little afraid, when she realized it was him.

"Excuse me," she said. "I guess I wasn't paying attention." She felt like she might crumble to pieces with the exhaustion of the day, and now this encounter.

"It's okay, Sophia. I didn't know you were here. Thank you for coming." Stephen's voice was soft.

"I was just, uh, going to my car. I came straight here when I got into town. I need to get a hotel room."

"You don't have to do that. You can stay here." Stephen sounded sincere.

"No," Sophie said emphatically, then backed up a little, reminding herself this wasn't about them. "I couldn't do that. But I don't really know what to do. I didn't know what I would find when I came. I don't want to be in the way, but I don't want to leave him either—if he wants me to stay." She was thinking aloud.

"There's no one else he wants here. The nurse leaves at six and comes back in the morning, early. I've been sleeping on the couch. You can have the guest room or my room—you can have any room if you want to stay here."

"Well, I guess," Sophie conceded. What if Frank cried out... or passed away in the middle of the night? She wanted to be there. "I'll go get my stuff."

Stephen followed her to her car and reached benignly for her bag. She fought an impulse to argue with him about it. Had they met on any other terms, it would have been totally unacceptable for her to stay there and a violation for him to carry her bag. But they would not be meeting except for these terms, she reminded herself. And the magnitude of Frank's situation superseded anything there was between her and Stephen. It was as if suddenly the other people they were and the lives they'd lived did not exist. They were reduced to simply the two human beings connected with Frank. And that connection—that mutual love—was all that could possibly matter in this moment. It was actually freeing.

Following her up the stairs, Stephen set her bag down in the guest room, which she had chosen. He stood in the doorway as she looked around. It was just as she remembered. The antique cherry bed with a peach coverlet and light green accent pillows were the same, and so were the dressing table and mirror and the photo of Frank's parents.

When her eyes fell on Stephen, standing there in the doorway, he was not as she remembered. His shoulders, narrower than before, slumped, and he had dark circles under his green eyes, which were dull with grief. His hair was cut short, which looked so odd to her, and he had a funny bit of fuzz under his bottom lip—undoubtedly a type of fashion statement. It was starting to blend, however, with the rest of the beard he had not shaved in days. His eggshell-colored linen shirt was wrinkled and untucked from faded jeans. The only thing she recognized were his boots—clunky army boots she'd bought for him in Capitola by the Sea. The memory didn't faze her.

"Would you like some coffee?" Stephen asked her.

"Yeah," Sophie answered. "I'll be down there in just a minute."

When she got to the kitchen, Stephen was pouring cups of coffee for the two of them. Sophie sat down at the table and rubbed her temples, trying to clear her head. She noticed that he put the right amount of cream and sugar in hers without asking. Then, handing her the coffee, Stephen sat down at the table and stared at his cup.

They sipped their coffee and talked quietly for a few minutes about Frank. Stephen briefed her on the condition, how it had developed, and how the doctor was surprised he had lasted this long. "I think he was waiting for you," Stephen said thoughtfully.

Sophie shrugged. "It's an honor that he wanted to see me. Thank you for calling."

Stephen seemed to come alive for a moment and looked into Sophie's eyes. His gaze was so intense it almost frightened her; the atmosphere till now had been so subdued.

"I am so sorry, Sophie." He spoke the words deliberately.

She was the first to look away. As Sophie stared into space, her thoughts went swimming in a deep river, but she was not drowning. She felt buoyed up—surrounded by peace. She closed her eyes, floating, and could see moonlight quivering on the water. She was out on that bluff with Jon, watching the water carry away the past and all of the pain with Stephen. It was like casting bread on the waters. As she let it all go, the river moved her into new life, new vistas, new courage. Even new feelings toward Jon. Refreshing little breezes blew, creating tiny waves that undulated over the surface of the water with no beginning, no end.

It was all grace. Grace upon grace upon grace, Sophie thought; and then she whispered to Stephen, "I forgive you."

* * * * *

When the hospice nurse came in to say she was leaving for the night, Stephen and Sophie walked together into the front room.

"What's this?" Frank asked them, searching their eyes. "You mean you two are both here at the same time? I must be really sick." He attempted a smile.

Stephen bent over one side of the bed and looked his dad in the eyes. "I apologized, and Sophie has forgiven me, Dad. There is peace between us."

Peace—his dying gift to them, and theirs to him.

"Thank You, Lord," Frank breathed as a tear slid down his cheek.

Sophie came up close beside him then on the other side of the bed and took hold of his hand. She started to sing, and Stephen joined her.

> *Amazing grace! How sweet the sound*
> *That saved a wretch like me!*
> *I once was lost, but now am found;*
> *Was blind, but now I see.*

Frank mouthed the words and sang softly, looking past Stephen and Sophie, as though to someplace—Someone—beyond them, and yet there with them.

> *Through many dangers, toils, and snares,*
> *I have already come;*
> *'Tis grace hath brought me safe thus far,*
> *And grace will lead me home.*

They were silent as the song ended, and Sophie held the moment in her heart.

Then she bent over and kissed Frank's face, lingering awhile with her warm cheek against his, and whispering, "Thank you for loving me. I will always love you."

She drew her face away, and their eyes locked for just a moment more. Then squeezing his hand, she said, "I'll see you in the morning."

He nodded, blinking slowly.

She smiled at Stephen and walked up to her room. As she lay in bed that night, she could hear Stephen softly talking with his dad, perhaps reading, and then singing. There was faint guitar music—he was playing—and then silence. She fell into a light sleep.

Late in the night, she heard a knock on her door and flew out of bed to open it. "He's gone," Stephen said, in tears.

She hugged him for a moment then stepped away, leading them back down the stairs and into the great room. There was dim light, but she could see Frank's body, motionless and gray, in the hospital bed.

That body looks as cold and empty as the tomb on Easter morning, thought Sophie. And even though she felt sad and strange, her heart rejoiced for Frank. He wasn't in that body anymore—he was free.

* * * * *

Sophie had stayed till after the funeral Monday afternoon. She was able to help Stephen with the details of receiving people and food and tending to the loose ends of the service. Thankfully, Frank had planned it well in advance. It was short, simple, and classy—very fitting for such a man's life.

As she pulled out of the driveway, she left Stephen standing on the porch looking after her. He seemed so alone that Sophie felt sorry for him. But she also felt tremendous peace and a sense of closure between them. She was glad she had been there and honored to have shared the experience with Frank—but now that he was gone, nothing in her wanted to stay with Stephen. Her life was somewhere else. With someone else.

As she exited onto the highway toward River Bend, Sophie mentally began tossing out all other thoughts like one tosses old clothes out of a closet. The only thought she kept was of Jon, and their kiss. Sophie luxuriated in that thought, trying it on again and again, and speeding up her car toward home. She was finally and completely free to love him.

Chapter Twenty

....

The Harbor House was empty when Sophie arrived that evening; it was a Monday. Spot greeted her at the door as she opened it, jumping up and down, his nub of a tail wagging wildly. She'd gotten a text from Tom, explaining that he'd brought Spot over in case she was too tired to come out and get him, and to call them. Shannon, God bless her, had come in and made the cheesecakes for tomorrow so that Sophie didn't really have to do anything to get prepared.

Checking her phone for the umpteenth time, Sophie saw that she had several texts and a couple voice messages, but as she ran through them quickly, she found nothing from Jon. Disappointing. Sophie picked up the mail from the table and, with Spot in tow, went to her room and spread herself across the bed to sort through it.

After reading a postcard from her mother from the Ring of Kerry in Ireland, she whisked through several bills and some junk and decided to read the paper. Like everyone else in town, she subscribed to Harvey's paper, *The River Bend Record*, which was delivered while she was gone. Sophie gasped when she saw the headline on the Community page: LOCAL WRITER JON ANTHONY SPEAKS AT BOOK CLUB MEETING.

Underneath that caption was a picture of Jon surrounded by a group of women. The Nails group! They were in the parlor of Sophie's café. Jon was sitting close beside Jade Thomas, who was holding a copy of *Life Without Father* to her bosom—her long nails curling around it like a buzzard's talons—and kissing Jon on the cheek!

Sophie groaned as she stared at it. She could hardly believe her eyes.

Jon and the Nails? Jon and Jade? In her restaurant? On the front page of the newspaper? Sophie was dumbfounded. It was too much. *No!* She threw the paper across the room, scaring Spot to death. He hid himself under one of her throw pillows, peering out at her guardedly. She cozied up to him and apologized, petting his ears. Then she got off the bed and picked up the paper, smoothing it out, and studied the picture some more.

Feeling emotionally exhausted and disgusted with the picture, the people of River Bend, and the drama that seemed to never end in her life, Sophie decided to call Tom. She could talk to him no matter what state she was in, and she knew he was waiting to hear she was home. She sank back into the pillows beside Spot at the head of her bed and hit Tom's contact name on her phone.

"Hello?"

Her brother's voice was good to hear.

"Hey, it's me. I'm back."

"Sophie! Welcome home."

"Thanks for bringing Spot—and for taking care of him, of course."

"Well, he ate us out of house and home, but other than that he was no trouble." Tom laughed lightheartedly.

Sophie laughed too. Spot didn't eat much at all—and especially not if she left him with someone else. Such an outrage would usually put him on a hunger strike. She patted his silky ears, smoothing them between her fingers.

"So," Tom said, "how are you?"

"Oh, okay. I'm really tired, you know."

"Spending a few days with death will do that," Tom reflected.

"Yes. But it was good overall. Good to be there, good to know Dr. Frank's not suffering now, even good with Stephen."

Spot groaned and rolled over.

"Good with Stephen? Really? I can't wait to hear about that."

"Good in the sense of closure," Sophie explained. "But I will tell you all the details later." Sitting up straight, she went on. "Hey, Tom?"

"Yeah?"

"Did you see the paper this week?"

"Yeah, I think so." He seemed unimpressed.

"Did you see the picture on the Community page?"

"I don't remember anything. Why? What was it? Something interesting?"

"Well, I don't know if I'd call it interesting," Sophie said sarcastically, "but Jon Anthony's on there surrounded by a bunch of adoring women."

Tom laughed out loud. "Oh yeah! I remember that. Raised quite a stir around town for a day or two. I ribbed Jon about it today, actually."

"Today? You saw Jon Anthony today?" Sophie's heart began to beat faster.

"Yeah, remember? He came to speak to my school. Did a good job too. It was a really neat deal."

Sophie took a moment to digest that. Then she said, "Well, what did he say?"

"Oh, he just talked about becoming a writer, really. Sort of the story of how he got into it, and then he described to the kids what he does. You know, how he works at home and stuff, and how he gets ideas. It was really interesting to a lot of them, I think. Especially Mrs. Ruston's class, since they read his book. They asked a lot of questions."

"I don't mean what did he talk about!" Sophie was exasperated with Tom's story. "I mean, what did he say to you? About the picture?"

"Sophie Harper? Are you actually jealous of the Nails group?" He sounded incredulous.

"No." Sophie tried to lighten her tone. "I just wanted to know, that's all. I thought it was a little odd."

"What's the deal with you and your old buddy Jon anyway?" Tom was enjoying himself now. "You haven't told me much about that lately."

"Nothing to tell."

"Well, wasn't there some date—a Thanksgiving picnic, I think, before you left?" He was prying at her shell.

"It was a picnic. I wouldn't call it a date."

"Hmm…okay." Tom was smiling, waiting. She knew his brother instinct told him he had her.

Sophie waited for a moment before she finally gave in. "So will you please tell me what he said about that picture?"

"Not much. I think he was embarrassed about it."

What could he say? Sophie thought to herself, still steaming at the thought of Jade Thomas's lips anywhere near Jon's general vicinity.

"But he did ask about you." Tom was tapping at the crack in her shell. But the clam wasn't budging. At least for a few seconds. "And?"

"Oh, he just asked how you were doing, where you had been."

"And what did you tell him?" Sophie quizzed her brother for possible errors.

"Just that you had gone to see an old friend who was sick and then ended up staying for the funeral."

"Did you say who it was?"

"I really wanted to, but I didn't. I knew if I said Stephen I would need to explain, or else it might lead him to conclusions, and I knew you didn't want me explaining. So I left it."

"That's good." Sophie approved.

"Funny how your calling to report in with me has changed to my reporting to you," Tom teased her. "How long has that been going on, I wonder?"

"Since I was born first," Sophie concluded.

"That's the sad truth," Tom acknowledged with good humor. "Oh, Soph, before I forget. Are you going to the community Christmas party next week? Jim Matthews asked me to read the Nativity story."

"Yeah." Sophie wasn't really looking forward to it though. After the newspaper fiasco, she felt a little bit like last year's fruitcake. "I was planning to go. I'm donating several batches of Granny's cookies."

"Ooh, yum. Okay then. See you there, if not before."

Chapter Twenty-One

....

Harbor House Café was bustling the next day. Father Hillary was back, plus Paula and Brandy and the other regulars, and Sophie felt like she was at a family reunion. She was also very glad to see Shannon, Andy, and the rest of her staff and get back into a groove with them. But lunch was so busy she hardly had time to catch up with anyone before it was quitting time.

At two o'clock Misti Clarkson poked her head in Sophie's kitchen. "Sophie! I'm so glad I caught you."

"Oh, hi, Misti. How are you?"

"I've been better. I wanted to complain to you about our service today. It was very slow."

Sophie cringed inwardly. "I'm sorry to hear that, Misti. We've been extra busy. Can I offer you a free piece of cheesecake to take home?"

"Well, I guess so." Misti snorted.

When Sophie handed it to her, she took it and turned on her heel, offering a weak "thanks" as she headed out the door.

René edged up to Sophie surreptitiously. "Her service was not slow!" she whispered. "I just don't have time to stand around and gossip the way she wants to. I know we're supposed to be nice to everyone, but I just can't stand that woman!"

Sophie laughed. "We go way back. She's not that bad, as long as you can take her in small doses." She looked at the empty doorway with relief.

René squinted at her.

"Okay, really small doses," Sophie admitted.

"Well, I've had my fill for a lifetime," René declared, writing her time down on her card. She returned it to its place, a basket Sophie kept on her desk in the back room, and turned again to Sophie. "It seems like every time she comes here, she sits in my station."

"I haven't seen her here that many times," Sophie said, "but maybe I'm luckier being in the kitchen." She got out a fresh white cloth and some spray cleaner.

René sat down at the bar, which divided the kitchen and back room. "She was here every day when you were gone. One day your friend, that Jon Anthony, was here too. He came in by himself, sort of looking around, so I asked him if he wanted to place a to-go order. I think he was looking for you, actually—I noticed he kept looking toward the kitchen. Then that woman just appeared out of nowhere and practically dragged him to her table!"

Sophie tried not to act too interested. She wiped the prep table ferociously.

René went on. "You probably haven't seen it yet, but she took a picture of him and the women at her table—her 'book club' she said—but I didn't hear them talk about a book one single time while I was serving them. It was just men and clothes and gossip. Anyway, right when she snapped it, one of them reached up and kissed him! Another one works at the *Record*, and can you believe she put it in the paper! It was like they had it all planned. I feel so sorry for that man."

"Why do you feel sorry for him?" Sophie asked. She stopped wiping. "It sounds to me like he played right into it. And he's really not stupid."

"Well, I think he was just trying to be nice, and then they embarrassed him. I'm sure he had no idea they were going to put his picture in the paper."

"No, probably not," Sophie said. *I'm sure he had no idea he would be caught,* she thought irritably.

Chapter Twenty-Two
....

The afternoon sun pouring through his windows seemed cold. Even though it was now December, Jon didn't feel the least bit festive. He wondered about Sophie as he dressed. She was back now, he knew; had been for more than a week. Would she be at the Christmas party? She had agreed to donate cookies when Margaret asked her, but that was before she left town.

He'd seen her car parked at the rear of the café whenever he'd driven by. *Why hasn't she called?* he thought as he pulled a white V-neck undershirt over his head. His starched white oxford shirt crackled as he buttoned it up, bottom to top, and then tucked it in. The waist of his khakis was loose.

He went for his brown leather belt and took it from a hook in his closet. There on the shelf above the hook was the butterfly quilt his grandma made, and it reminded him of the picnic he'd had with Sophie not two weeks ago. It almost seemed unreal now, that they'd been so close. He ran his hand over the quilt and sighed. Had it been real? Had he really held her in his arms—kissed her?

As Jon slid the belt though his belt loops, he went over the last week in his mind. Each loop was like a rung in the mental hand bridge he was maneuvering. After the perfection of Thanksgiving, he'd gone over to Sophie's place to see her. He slid his belt through the first loop. She wasn't there; the waitress said she had gone to see an old friend. Another loop. The information he'd gotten seemed sketchy even when he asked Tom about it. Why hadn't Tom said who the old friend was?

Next loop. Jon had a strong feeling it was her ex-husband. And while he'd tried to figure out what to do, he'd also been dealing with the embarrassment those women had inflicted on him when they'd put his picture in the paper. Another loop. He'd decided to give Sophie space. He knew that in the past her dad had never let her call boys— but he wasn't a boy. And she wasn't a little girl anymore. He'd been trusting that she'd call him by now, but she hadn't. Final loop. As he buckled the belt, he had a sinking feeling. He really didn't feel like going to the party.

He went out to his deck and sat there in the cold, listening to the river and thinking. After a while, his head dropped into his hands.

Lord, I'm sorry. In my jealousy I've made this about me, when Sophie was burying a friend. Whoever it was, and wherever she's been, she deserves better than this from me. Forgive me for being so prideful and stupid.

* * * * *

"You should go see him, talk to him," Brandy had told Sophie at lunch today.

Sophie thought about Brandy as she put on her makeup. They were fundamentally different people, but Sophie loved Brandy and had learned from her. But Brandy wasn't always right.

I won't do it, Sophie said to herself as she got ready for the Christmas party Jim Matthews and Margaret had planned. She brushed blush on her cheekbones. Sure, she'd made a mess of things with her first marriage and had come back home with nothing. But she was doing what she could. She bathed her long eyelashes in mascara. She had started a successful business and was contributing to the life of the community. She was also growing and changing as a person. She dabbed on some gloss, popped her lips, and took inventory of herself in the full-length mirror. Hair up but loose, gold earrings dangling. Wine-colored sweater, dark-gray skirt with a big slit, gold cuff bracelet, tall boots. *Acceptable*, she thought.

She kissed Spot good-bye, leaving a lipstick stain on his forehead, and got into her car. Feeling a little weak, she started it. *Unacceptable*, she thought about the weakness. *I've faced a lot worse things than this.* She pulled out onto the Main Street and headed in the direction of the community center.

When she came to the stoplight it was red, and by the time it turned green, Sophie had changed her course. She decided to go to Jon's first. If he was home, she was going to see him and get the picture thing settled once and for all.

* * * * *

The cabin looked lonely sitting in the dusk with no lights. Aslan was on the porch, watching her with big, brown eyes. He bounded down the stairs to greet her when she got out of her car. His fur was thick and soft like a sheep's wool in her hand, and she managed to stay clear of his slobber. Sophie knocked, but Jon wasn't there.

As she guided her car back down his driveway, she tried to keep her heart from racing. *This is so stupid*, she thought.

Since Sophie no longer cared what her hair looked like, she rolled down her window to feel the cold. Smells of cedar and wood smoke wafted through her car, and the sun warmed her face as she left Jon's property and headed toward the river bridge and town. On the bridge, Sophie drove as slowly as she could still safely go and leaned her head out the window to watch the sun play on the water. A Jeep pulled up beside her from the other direction, blocking her view. Her heart stopped, then her car, when she realized it was Jon. Their eyes locked for just a moment and then he was out of the Jeep and kneeling beside her window.

"I just came from your place," he told her, breathless. "I had to see you."

"I just came from yours, and I have the dog hairs to prove it." Sophie smiled just a little, showing him the white Aslan fur on her skirt and sleeves.

"Sophie, I've been thinking about our picnic. About you, and me, us..."

"I've been thinking about you too—our kiss, as well as the kiss you shared with Jade Thomas in front of the whole world." She narrowed her eyes at him, boring a hole through his heart.

"I am so sorry. That was stupid..." A car was coming up behind Jon's Jeep on the bridge, but he didn't seem to care. "I should have called you...."

Sophie interrupted him. "Are you hungry?"

Jon brightened. "Starving."

"I've got pumpkin cheesecake for you." She held his gaze just a moment, blue eyes blazing, while the other car honked.

"That sounds great," Jon said, and for a moment he looked down at her lips. Then he seemed to get an idea. "Follow me back to the cabin?" He jumped back in his Jeep, and she turned around at the end of the bridge and followed him home.

* * * * *

They took their seats on the deck, as they had the first night Jon brought Sophie to his house. He was the first to speak.

"Sophie, I am sorry about that picture." He ran his fingers through his hair. "I know what it looks like, but it wasn't that—they asked me to speak to their book club and totally staged that picture. I have no idea why, except to stir up trouble." He sighed. "Jade and Misti, you know how they are."

"Yes, I do. But I think it was pretty gullible of you to get into that situation." Sophie's nostrils flared. He could sense her anger, and it was legitimate, if a little bit funny to him.

"Point well made." He risked a grin.

"And you've given me the silent treatment. After kissing me, no less."

"I am so sorry." Jon became serious again. "I was wrong. The truth is that I was jealous. I thought you might be with your ex-husband, thought he might beg you back.... I thought too much about all of it and let my mind run wild without talking to you. I was prideful. It was stupid. Please forgive me."

"I *was* with Stephen."

Jon's heart sank in his chest.

"But we were putting his father to rest. And while my marriage was awful, my father-in-law was wonderful. I needed to be there."

Jon wondered if she noticed his sigh of relief.

"The cool thing is"—Sophie's voice softened—"I was able to also put my marriage to rest. Once and for all." She reached out and touched Jon's hair at the temple. "I feel so free now. No strings attached." She smiled and stroked his cheek.

Her touch was soothing and electric at the same time. Jon leaned over, cupping her face, and kissed her. She leaned in and kissed him back, more passionately than before.

Chapter Twenty-Three

....

"Do you still love Christmas?" Jon asked later as they sat on his deck, snuggling under a blanket to keep out the cold.

His question seemed so random to Sophie, and she laughed. "What?"

"Do you still love Christmas? You used to get really geeked about decorating and everything. Made me get a tree for my dorm room. Remember?"

"I could never forget that."

"Well? Do you still get into all of that?"

Sophie thought about it, and she realized that over the past few years she'd not cared near as much about Christmas, with her marriage falling apart and then her father's death. With a deep sense of joy, the present came back to her, and the thought of her new life warmed her.

"I could get into it again," she said, smiling.

"Let's go get a Christmas tree!" Jon rose from his chair and held out his hand to her.

"Really? You're serious?"

"Yes! My place is full of them."

Jon grabbed his handsaw, a hammer and nails, and a couple of boards from the garage and hopped into the Jeep with Sophie. He drove them down the driveway and then veered off across the pasture, slowing down so as not to jar them too much. They entered a woodsy area that opened up into a cedar grove. Jon got out, and as always, walked around to open her door.

"Pick any you want!"

They walked around. He watched her as she sized up each tree.

She stopped in front of one that was about nine feet tall. "This one seems the right height, and I love all of its berries."

Jon sawed it down for her and loaded it into the back of the Jeep, tying it in. The top hung out the back over the seat, but they didn't have far to go.

Back at the Harbor House, Jon worked on making a stand out of the boards while Sophie fixed them hot chocolate. She emerged from the kitchen with two steaming mugs topped with whipped cream and cinnamon and found him stringing lights on the tree. He had placed it in the center of the picture window that looked out from the dining room. It was perfect.

"I'll go get the ornaments!" Sophie set down the mugs on a table and ran to hunt for the box. She remembered seeing it when she unpacked, and she found it stashed underneath the staircase in a small storage area.

As she unwrapped each ornament, she told Jon the stories behind them, and he listened attentively. Most of them were heirlooms, which her parents divided between Sophie and Tom when they each married. They sparkled and shone as she hung them on the branches of the cedar.

Sophie smiled as she fingered a few of them. There was the gingerbread girl her mother had made out of felt and sequins when she was ten. Tom had the gingerbread boy on his and Madeline's tree. And Raggedy Ann—he had Raggedy Andy—and the funny soldier whose legs danced and kicked when you pulled his string. Each held a special memory, and Sophie swallowed a lump in her throat as she imagined her father's voice reading the Christmas story from the Bible. It had been a family tradition of theirs every Christmas Eve.

Her favorite ornament was a red glass ball that had been in their family since the forties. Sophie purposely hung it front and center, and now it sparkled in the lights. The ball had belonged to her grandmother,

Ruby, and had been a gift from Sophie's grandpa, Cliff, before they married. She plucked off the metal topper to reveal the ball's hollow center, and Jon thought it wildly romantic that Cliff had declared his love to Ruby with a note hidden in that secret compartment.

"That story needs to be in a book someday," Jon said, turning the ornament over in his hand to examine it before he handed it to Sophie to place on the tree.

* * * * *

"Thank you, Jon, for the tree, and for this whole evening." Sophie stood by the door of the back stoop.

"Thank you for forgiving me for being a jerk."

"Um, I've known jerks, and you're not one." Her eyes twinkled. "I'm glad we talked finally."

"Me too."

He trailed his fingers down her arm, ending with her hand, and raised it to his lips. "Good night, my friend."

"Friend?" A playful smile crossed her face.

"Well, whatever you are."

Chapter Twenty-Four
....

Harbor House Café was closed for Christmas Eve, but Sophie worked as hard as ever in the kitchen that day. She'd only recently finished the last batch of molasses cookies and gotten herself cleaned up. She glanced down at her watch, surveying the dining room, and smoothed her champagne-colored dress. Then she adjusted her string of pearls. Everyone who mattered most to her in the world would come together tonight around her table. She wanted everything to be perfect.

The table, covered in Italian lace she'd brought back from her travels, was set with China and silver. The lights of the chandelier above it were turned down low. It was laden with all of her family's favorite foods—candied sweet potatoes, homemade yeast rolls dripping with butter, warm wilted greens, cranberry salad, and Silver Queen corn she'd frozen from Tom's garden. The turkey waited in the warm oven for Tom to carve, and their mother was bringing the dressing.

The nine-foot cedar, which she and Jon picked out of his woods, stood proudly in front of her picture window adjacent to the table. Its scent filled the room, and it glowed with all colors of lights and assorted ornaments. Sophie sighed with contentment, remembering the night that she and Jon decorated the tree.

The door jingled and Sophie's mother came in with Granny, who hugged Sophie and greeted her in a funny Irish brogue. "Merry Christmas, me darling!" She kissed Sophie on both cheeks.

Sophie was so happy to have them home. She took their coats, hanging them on the hooks inside the door. They were soon followed by Tom, who ushered in Madeline and a very tiny baby Stone, who was covered in wrappings. Sophie took him immediately and began peeling them back.

"Here's my baby—on his very first outing! You're at Aunt Sophie's house!" She kissed his little face and nuzzled his cheek.

"He recognizes your voice, that's for sure." Madeline handed Tom her coat. "Look at how he turns his eyes toward the sound!"

Tom and their mom went to the kitchen while the others moved into the parlor. Granny, Madeline, and Sophie were admiring the tree when the door jingled again. Sophie answered it with baby Stone in her arms.

"Ho ho ho!" Jon stepped in. There were snowflakes in his dark hair.

"Hey!" Sophie laughed, hugging the baby to her and reaching up to dust them with one hand.

"Here's the little man I've been hearing about!" Jon closed the door behind him and bent down to see the baby. "Wow." Looking up at Sophie, he said "wow" again, and then he kissed her.

The evening was everything Sophie had hoped it would be. Everyone loved the food, and Jon fit with her family as he always had, ever since second grade. He asked Granny all about Ireland, talked easily with her mother, and was obviously smitten with baby Stone, which pleased Madeline immensely. It was nice—and important, Sophie thought— to see Tom enjoy the presence of another man in her life.

After Tom read the Christmas story from the Bible, they prayed together. Granny and baby Stone were obviously tired from the festivities, and while Madeline and Mom were reluctant to leave dirty dishes, Jon assured them he would help.

"I've heard he's actually good at dishes," Tom said good-naturedly as he gathered their things.

* * * * *

The kitchen clean, Sophie suggested she and Jon sit upstairs in her comfortable little den, but he wanted to go back to the parlor.

"Let's go sit by the tree just a minute," he said. "After all, it's Christmas Eve."

They pulled up dining chairs and gazed together at the tree. Sophie turned on some quiet holiday music. The picture window was frosted and served as the perfect frame for their masterpiece.

"Tell me again about this ornament." Jon pointed to the red ball, and Sophie plucked it from the tree.

"It's cool, isn't it?" Sophie cupped it in her hands. "Like our family, it has been through a lot, but it's never been broken. I hope I never break it!" She reached up to place it back on the tree.

Jon stopped her. "Where's the note?"

"What note? You mean the one that my grandpa put inside it?"

"Yes. The one declaring his love."

"I don't know what happened to it. I'm sure Granny has it somewhere."

"Could it still be in there?" Jon's eyes glittered.

"Surely not. I mean, no. Don't you remember when I took the topper off a few weeks ago and showed you the inside?"

He nodded.

Sophie held the ornament up to the light. "That's weird, though. Look! There does seem to be something inside it." She took off the topper, just as she had before, but this time there was a note inside. Her heart skipped a beat.

She turned the ball upside-down, and a tiny scroll fell into her palm. She handed the ornament to Jon and unfolded the scroll.

> *Dear Sophie,*
> *I've loved you since the second grade. And I always will.*
> *Jon*

Sophie gasped.

Jon looked at her, eyes shining.

She pulled him into her arms and kissed him, knowing she was home.

Sophie's Pumpkin Cheesecake with Molasses Cookie Crust

....

1-1/2 cups Ruby's Chewy Molasses Cookies*, crushed
   (see page 160 for recipe)
3/4 cup ground pecans
3 tablespoons brown sugar
6 tablespoons unsalted butter, melted
24 ounces cream cheese, softened
1 cup brown sugar
1-1/2 cups pumpkin
1/2 cup heavy cream
1/3 cup maple syrup
1 tablespoon vanilla
3/4 teaspoon cinnamon
1/2 teaspoon allspice
4 eggs
Candied pecans and whipped cream, to serve

Preheat oven to 325 degrees. Grease and flour a 9-inch springform pan. Combine first four ingredients with a fork. Press onto bottom and two inches up the sides of the pan to form a crust. Beat cream cheese and brown sugar till light and fluffy, then stir in pumpkin, heavy cream, maple syrup, vanilla, cinnamon, and allspice. Beat in eggs one at a time, mixing until smooth. Pour batter into crust and bake in a water bath for 90 minutes or until center is set. Allow to cool for 30 minutes, then refrigerate overnight. Garnish the top of the cake with whole candied pecans. Serve with whipped cream.

Can use crushed gingersnaps in place of molasses cookies.

About the Author

....

Gwen Ford Faulkenberry lives and writes in the Ozark Mountains of Arkansas. She is married to Stone, and they have four children—Grace, Harper, Adelaide, and Stella. In addition to mothering and writing, Gwen teaches English at Arkansas Tech University—Ozark Campus. She is the author of *Love Finds You in Branson, Missouri, Love Finds You in Romeo, Colorado,* and three devotional books—*A Beautiful Life, A Beautiful Day,* and *Jesus, Be Near Me.* Look her up on Facebook; she would love to hear from you.

Want a peek into local American life—past and present?
The *Love Finds You*™ series published by Summerside Press
features real towns and combines travel, romance,
and faith in one irresistible package!

The novels in the series—uniquely titled after American towns with romantic or intriguing names—inspire romance and fun. Each fictional story draws on the compelling history or the unique character of a real place. Stories center on romances kindled in small towns, old loves lost and found again on the high plains, and new loves discovered at exciting vacation getaways. Summerside Press plans to publish at least one novel set in each of the fifty states. Be sure to catch them all!

Now Available

Love Finds You in Miracle, Kentucky
by Andrea Boeshaar
ISBN: 978-1-934770-37-5

*Love Finds You in
Snowball, Arkansas*
by Sandra D. Bricker
ISBN: 978-1-934770-45-0

Love Finds You in Romeo, Colorado
by Gwen Ford Faulkenberry
ISBN: 978-1-934770-46-7

*Love Finds You in
Valentine, Nebraska*
by Irene Brand
ISBN: 978-1-934770-38-2

Love Finds You in Humble, Texas
by Anita Higman
ISBN: 978-1-934770-61-0

*Love Finds You in
Last Chance, California*
by Miralee Ferrell
ISBN: 978-1-934770-39-9

*Love Finds You in
Maiden, North Carolina*
by Tamela Hancock Murray
ISBN: 978-1-934770-65-8

*Love Finds You in
Paradise, Pennsylvania*
by Loree Lough
ISBN: 978-1-934770-66-5

*Love Finds You in
Treasure Island, Florida*
by Debby Mayne
ISBN: 978-1-934770-80-1

Love Finds You in Liberty, Indiana
by Melanie Dobson
ISBN: 978-1-934770-74-0

Love Finds You in Revenge, Ohio
by Lisa Harris
ISBN: 978-1-934770-81-8

Love Finds You in Poetry, Texas
by Janice Hanna
ISBN: 978-1-935416-16-6

Love Finds You in Sisters, Oregon
by Melody Carlson
ISBN: 978-1-935416-18-0

Love Finds You in Charm, Ohio
by Annalisa Daughety
ISBN: 978-1-935416-17-3

*Love Finds You in
Bethlehem, New Hampshire*
by Lauralee Bliss
ISBN: 978-1-935416-20-3

*Love Finds You in North
Pole, Alaska*
by Loree Lough
ISBN: 978-1-935416-19-7

Love Finds You in Holiday, Florida
by Sandra D. Bricker
ISBN: 978-1-935416-25-8

*Love Finds You in
Lonesome Prairie, Montana*
by Tricia Goyer and Ocieanna Fleiss
ISBN: 978-1-935416-29-6

*Love Finds You in Bridal
Veil, Oregon*
by Miralee Ferrell
ISBN: 978-1-935416-63-0

*Love Finds You in Hershey,
Pennsylvania*
by Cerella D. Sechrist
ISBN: 978-1-935416-64-7

Love Finds You in Homestead, Iowa
by Melanie Dobson
ISBN: 978-1-935416-66-1

Love Finds You in Pendleton, Oregon
by Melody Carlson
ISBN: 978-1-935416-84-5

*Love Finds You in Golden,
New Mexico*
by Lena Nelson Dooley
ISBN: 978-1-935416-74-6

Love Finds You in Lahaina, Hawaii
by Bodie Thoene
ISBN: 978-1-935416-78-4

*Love Finds You in Victory
Heights, Washington*
by Tricia Goyer and Ocieanna Fleiss
ISBN: 978-1-60936-000-9

Love Finds You in Calico, California
by Elizabeth Ludwig
ISBN: 978-1-60936-001-6

Love Finds You in Sugarcreek, Ohio
by Serena B. Miller
ISBN: 978-1-60936-002-3

*Love Finds You in
Deadwood, South Dakota*
by Tracey Cross
ISBN: 978-1-60936-003-0

Love Finds You in Silver City, Idaho
by Janelle Mowery
ISBN: 978-1-60936-005-4

*Love Finds You in Carmel-
by-the-Sea, California*
by Sandra D. Bricker
ISBN: 978-1-60936-027-6

Love Finds You Under the Mistletoe
by Irene Brand and Anita Higman
ISBN: 978-1-60936-004-7

Love Finds You in Hope, Kansas
by Pamela Griffin
ISBN: 978-1-60936-007-8

Love Finds You in Sun Valley, Idaho
by Angela Ruth
ISBN: 978-1-60936-008-5

*Love Finds You in
Camelot, Tennessee*
by Janice Hanna
ISBN: 978-1-935416-65-4

*Love Finds You in
Tombstone, Arizona*
by Miralee Ferrell
ISBN: 978-1-60936-104-4

*Love Finds You in
Martha's Vineyard, Massachusetts*
by Melody Carlson
ISBN: 978-1-60936-110-5

Love Finds You in
Prince Edward Island, Canada
by Susan Page Davis
ISBN: 978-1-60936-109-9

Love Finds You in Groom, Texas
by Janice Hanna
ISBN: 978-1-60936-006-1

Love Finds You in Amana, Iowa
by Melanie Dobson
ISBN: 978-1-60936-135-8

Love Finds You in
Lancaster County, Pennsylvania
by Annalisa Daughety
ISBN: 97-8-160936-212-6

Love Finds You in Branson, Missouri
by Gwen Ford Faulkenberry
ISBN: 978-1-60936-191-4

Love Finds You in
Sundance, Wyoming
by Miralee Ferrell
ISBN: 978-1-60936-277-5

Love Finds You on
Christmas Morning
by Debby Mayne and Trish Perry
ISBN: 978-1-60936-193-8

Love Finds You in Sunset
Beach, Hawaii
by Robin Jones Gunn
ISBN: 978-1-60936-028-3

Love Finds You in
Nazareth, Pennsylvania
by Melanie Dobson
ISBN: 97-8-160936-194-5

Love Finds You in
Annapolis, Maryland
by Roseanna M. White
ISBN: 978-1-60936-313-0

Love Finds You in
Folly Beach, South Carolina
by Loree Lough
ISBN: 97-8-160936-214-0

Love Finds You in
New Orleans, Louisiana
by Christa Allan
ISBN: 978-1-60936-591-2

Love Finds You in
Wildrose, North Dakota
by Tracey Bateman
ISBN: 978-1-60936-592-9

Love Finds You in Daisy, Oklahoma
by Janice Hanna
ISBN: 978-1-60936-593-6

Love Finds You in Sunflower, Kansas
by Pamela Tracy
ISBN: 978-1-60936-594-3

Love Finds You in
Mackinac Island, Michigan
by Pamela Tracy
ISBN: 978-1-60936-594-3

COMING SOON

Love Finds You in
Glacier Bay, Alaska
by Tricia Goyer and Ocieanna Fleiss
ISBN: 978-1-60936-569-1

Love Finds You in
Lake Geneva, Wisconsin
by Pamela S. Meyers
ISBN: 978-1-60936-769-5